ADVANCE PRAISE FOR
THE CIRCLE OF A PROMISE!

D1469158

THE PROMISE

"That was quite a feat of horsemanship," Stephen repeated dryly. "I suppose you're going to tell me next that you can defeat me at swordplay as well."

Mara blushed. "I doubt I could best you," she replied honestly. "But I might just hold my own against you." Stephen felt his jaw drop. Although, he realized, he shouldn't be at all surprised by now. This was a woman of many wonders.

"What's wrong?" Mara asked, suddenly apprehensive.

"Nothing." Her betrothed shook his head. "I must say, however, that I am glad you are to be my wife, if only so I will never have to face so formidable a foe as you in battle."

Mara laughed. "Quite so, my lord. You will never have to face me over the point of a sword. But know that, should you ever need it, my sword will be at your back."

He didn't know why, but a sudden chill ran down Stephen's spine and something cold clutched his heart. To lighten the darkness that threatened to settle on his soul, he forced a laugh to his lips, pulled his sword from its sheath, and tossed it hilt first to his lady.

Mara caught the weapon easily, as if it had no weight at all, and balanced it in her hand. "My arm for you, Lord Baron. And my life."

She had meant the comment, and the moment, to be lighthearted, and was dismayed by the expression on Stephen's face. She lowered the sword, and he took it from her.

"No," Stephen murmured as he re-sheathed his weapon. "Rather, my life for yours, Lady. Always and forever, my life for yours."

Other *Love Spell* books by Helen A. Rosburg:

CALL OF THE TRUMPET

The CIRCLE of a PROMISE

HELEN A. ROSBURG

LOVE SPELL

NEW YORK CITY

To my husband, James A. Rosburg,
whom I will love in all my lifetimes to come.
And to my children: Erik, Will, Ali, and Freya.

LOVE SPELL®

June 2003

Published by

Dorchester Publishing Co., Inc.
276 Fifth Avenue
New York, NY 10001

ISBN 0-505-52545-3

The name "Love Spell" and its logo are trademarks of Dorchester Publishing Co., Inc.

Printed in the United States of America.

Visit us on the web at www.dorchesterpub.com.

ACKNOWLEDGMENTS

I would like to acknowledge the invaluable assistance of Christina Johnson in the creation of this manuscript. She is also pretty darn good at cracking a whip.

Additionally, I would like to thank my wonderful editor, Chris Keeslar. It's so nice to be home again.

The Circle of a Promise

Chapter One

The morning mists had long since blown away. The sun was high and hot. The stench from the battlefield was nearly overpowering.

Stephen's knights, victorious, drifted back toward him. They shuffled slowly, battle weary and bloodied, cleaning the blades of their weapons as they went. Occasionally a man stopped to pat the neck of a faithful mount, or to lean, exhausted, against a massive shoulder. Many of the horses themselves bore ghastly wounds. Others lay dead on the ground amidst the bodies of the fallen soldiers. The earth was red with blood. Stephen ignored it all.

His eyes searched desperately for one face. Sunlight glinting from bright armor made him squint. He turned and looked in the other direction. Saw her.

The form was unmistakable. Even among men she was tall. Their gazes met.

Mara smiled. She pulled the mail hood from her head and shook loose her magnificent hair. It tumbled in waves across her shoulders and down her back, and Stephen knew there was not a more beautiful, desirable woman in the world. He started toward her.

There was blood on her hauberk, but he knew instinctively it was not hers. Thank God. Thank God. She had made it through the battle unscathed. He could tell by the way she moved, walked slowly toward him. The tip of her sword dragged on the ground. Hero, her enormous warhorse, plodded along behind her, head low. He, too, appeared uninjured.

Stephen let his blade fall to the ground. He opened his arms to receive her, and Mara stepped into his embrace.

There were no words; they were too exhausted. Yet none were needed. The pair was husband and wife, companions of heart and soul, lovers. They were also victors. At long, long last, the terrible struggle was over. Many deaths were avenged. They were finally free to be together without fear. It was over.

For a long moment they simply leaned against one another, arms loosely clasped. Then Mara looked up at him. Her eyes were the color of a deep, deep lake. The lake beside which she and Stephen had first made love.

He did not see—*no one* saw—the hidden archer: one of the earl's men, hidden in the tree at the edge of the glade.

Stephen smiled into Mara's eyes. The blood, death, and destruction all around them disappeared. Trey, their deerhound, whined and pushed at their legs, but they barely noticed. They could not tear their gazes from each other.

It was thus that Stephen saw the life go out of his wife's eyes when the arrow struck. She was gone from him almost instantly. Mara slumped, was caught up in her husband's arms for the last time.

Steve Bellingham woke up screaming.
The clock radio read 2:00 A.M.

Chapter Two

"No."

The word, spoken so firmly, echoed in the relative silence of the great hall. Mara shook her head slowly, deliberately, from side to side. "No," she repeated.

Ranulf, the barrel-chested, red-bearded Lord of Ullswater, quailed beneath his daughter's stubborn gaze. He turned to his wife for support.

Lady Beatrice sighed and clasped her pale, slender hands in her lap. Despite the furs draped over the wooden chair, a familiar pain in her lower back had returned to plague her. She shifted slightly and returned her daughter's wide, blue, unblinking gaze.

"You heard your father, my dear," she said in her soft voice. "And you will respect him."

Mara's head continued to shake.

"It is long past time, in fact, that you wed," Beatrice continued, unruffled. "You knew it was inevitable. You knew the time would eventually come. And it has."

"No," Mara said. But the conviction was gone from her

3

denial. Her eyes grew wider as she gazed at her mother.

"I know how skillful you are at putting unpleasant subjects from your mind, Mara. Now, however, you are going to have to face this."

"Mother—" Mara began.

It was Beatrice's turn to shake her head. "No, Mara, hear me out. Your father and I are not getting any younger, and neither are you. We have no sons. You will need both a protector and a provider. These lands will need an overseer. A husband there must be, and a husband you shall have."

Mara remained motionless. Silent. Every word her mother had spoken was true. Marriage was an inescapable fact of life; she could avoid it no longer. Still, it was a bitter and difficult remedy to swallow. Almost without realizing it, Mara shook her head one last time.

"Obstinacy will do you no good, daughter." Beatrice leaned a bit closer to the fire that roared in the hearth. "A marriage will be accomplished. It will be accomplished, moreover, in as short a time as possible."

The woman ignored the hiss of her daughter's indrawn breath and glanced at her husband. "It has become imperative, in fact, that this alliance be made with the greatest haste."

Something unpleasant stirred in the pit of Mara's stomach. "Am I to be informed of the reason for this . . . haste? What is it, Mother? What trouble befalls us?"

Husband and wife exchanged another quick glance. This time it was Beatrice who implored Ranulf with her gaze. The man's normally ruddy cheeks flushed a deeper shade of red, and he took a long, deep breath.

"It's . . . *Baldwin!*" The name was spat like something foul tasting. Ranulf's thick, rusty brows drew together, storm clouds massing over the mountains and canyons of his weathered face. "He's asked for your hand. Again."

As if to underscore his statement, Mara's father's

meaty fist slammed down, hard, on the table. The table shuddered, and a pewter cup overturned.

Beatrice flinched, and Mara wrapped her arms across her chest. Her blood turned to ice. *Baldwin.*

"I . . . I thought the earl understood that I . . . that *you*"—Mara looked pointedly at her father—"would never consent to give him my hand."

Ranulf grunted something unintelligible. "I thought so as well," he added after a moment. As he gazed into the liquid blue of his daughter's eyes, he saw that her memory had returned along with his to that fateful day nearly six months earlier.

Mara had been practicing her swordsmanship in the castle yard with one of his skilled but aging retainers. Despite the man's years, Douglas's arm was yet strong, and he had forced Mara back a few steps. She parried defensively for several breathless seconds before finding her balance and coming back at him with the speed for which she had become renowned. A grim smile touched the knight's thin mouth, and he lifted his left hand in a gesture of surrender.

"Well done, my lady," he panted. "The swiftness of your stroke makes up for what you lack in strength. You have learned your lessons well."

Mara bowed her head modestly in acknowledgment of the compliment. But before she could speak, a shout went up from the guard in the gate tower.

"Fetch my lord Ranulf," the man cried. "The Earl of Cumbria comes with a great force!"

Mara could not forget the icy hand of fear that had clamped her heart. Earl Baldwin was one of the most powerful men in the land. His wealth was vast, his strength of arms impressive. Her father's forces, on the other hand, consisted of a few men like Douglas. And Baldwin coveted her father's lands—rich, fertile acres that bordered his own. If he had come to take them by force, he would be met with precious little resistance.

5

Baldwin had not, however, come to take what he coveted at the point of a sword. His plan had been far worse.

"When you last met, Father," Mara said at length, breaking the tense silence, "you told the earl in no uncertain terms that he would never have either me or Ullswater. Does he think you soft or of wavering mind?"

"He knows exactly what everyone else knows," Ranulf said in a subdued voice. "That my knights age as I do. That I have no son to attract and lead a larger, stronger force. It would be easy for Baldwin to take what he wants, and only the king's peace protects us from his aggression." Ranulf sighed. "But it does not lessen his greed for what is mine."

"Yet you humiliated him when he came to ask for my hand!" Mara protested. "You did not even open your gates to him."

Ranulf did not miss his wife's quick glance in his direction. "Yes," he admitted slowly. "And the action was perhaps impulsive and ill-considered."

Lady Beatrice spoke up. "There has always been bad blood between the earl and your father." She knew how difficult it was for her husband to compromise his pride and confess his mistakes. "They are as different in temperament and outlook as night and day. Baldwin well knew what his reception might be when he came to your father's hall. He hoped his show of arms would serve to intimidate. It did not."

"And, as you know," Ranulf continued, "I told him so. It did not improve his temper. He is as poisonous and dangerous as a viper, and it is never wise to kick at a coiled snake."

A blade of fear seemed to stab directly into Mara's heart. Her body went rigid. "You . . . you're not telling me that you've changed your mind, are you? That you've decided to give me to—"

"No! No, of course not."

Beatrice rose stiffly and laid a pale, elegant hand on

her husband's muscular forearm. She smiled gently at her daughter. "There's no need to look so stricken, my dear," she said quietly. "Or you, my husband. As long as there is breath in our bodies, Mara, Baldwin shall never have his will. You must know that we would never, for any reason, force you to marry a man like that."

"Or," Ranulf added, "be forced ourselves to give you to him. No. That will not happen. Never!"

For a second time Ranulf's broad, scarred hand crashed down on the nearby wooden table. The pewter cup, already on its side, rolled off the edge and clanged loudly on the stone-flagged floor. No one paid it the slightest heed.

Mara gazed levelly at her father, then her mother. The room was still. "But you have someone else in mind," she said at length. "Don't you?"

Beatrice did not respond at once. She regarded her daughter thoughtfully. Then: "Yes, Mara, we do. We have the kind of man, the kind of marriage we always hoped we would be able to secure for you."

"Aye," Ranulf said, picking up the thread. "He is a strong man, powerful in his own right. Baldwin will not be pleased with our decision when he learns of it."

The Lord of Ullswater glanced at his wife. Her expression remained serene, so he continued. "In spite of Henry's laws, and the peace now in the land, there may be repercussions when we're gone, Mara. I doubt Baldwin would move against me now, but . . . someone may one day have to fight to protect these lands, Mara. Henry's reach may not always extend this far. The king is just and his power great, but it is not infinite. And I have given Baldwin even greater reason than its riches to want to see Ullswater either under his banner or destroyed. Do you understand? You *must have a husband.* Soon."

Yes, Mara did understand. All too well. Life as she knew it had just come to an end. Not only was the specter of marriage now a grim reality, so was war with Cumbria. Bloodshed. Her parents' eventual demise. It was all too much at once.

Mara pressed her hands, so cold, to her cheeks. She closed her eyes.

"Mara—"

"Don't say any more, Mother. Please. I don't want to hear it. I don't even want to think about a time when you and Father won't be with me, much less think of a husband, a—"

"Amarantha!"

Mara fell silent immediately, clamping her jaw shut as if she had been slapped.

Her mother's eyes glittered darkly. "The time has come not only to face facts, Mara, but life," she said sternly. "You've been spoiled, shamefully so, by both your father and me. You've been allowed to run wild, without a care in the world. But that must end. Now."

Mara clasped her hands tightly beneath her chin. She opened her eyes, but her gaze remained downcast.

"I'm sorry, daughter. Truly, I am." The hard edge of Lady Beatrice's tone had softened. "I regret if my words are harsh, but I have no choice. *We* have no choice. I must impress upon you how important this matter is. You need a husband, and your father believes he has found the right man—someone he has met only briefly but knows well by reputation. A just and honorable man. Letters have been exchanged, and the matter has been agreed upon. The union is advantageous to all concerned. Your betrothed has agreed, in fact, to come at once to meet with us."

Mara felt as thinly stretched as a tanner's hide. Though she often argued companionably with her father, she had never once talked back to her frail and lovely mother. Now she found herself suddenly unable to control the bitter words that tumbled from her tongue.

" 'Letters have been exchanged'? 'The matter has been

agreed upon'? Is that what I am, Mother? A 'matter'? Is that all I am in the end—a deal to be negotiated? Doesn't anyone care what *I* think? What *I* want?"

Ranulf's reaction was instant.

"Never let me hear you speak that way to your mother again." His tone was dark. "We are only doing what is best for you, and when you've had time to think about it, I know you will agree."

"Never!" Mara snarled. Her eyes were clouded with the intensity of her emotion. Her pale, straight hair tumbled about her shoulders and across her heaving breast. "Tie me up and drag me to the altar if you wish, but that's the only way—the *only* way—you'll be able to get rid of me by marrying me off to some . . . some *stranger!*"

The stricken look in her parents' eyes was more than she could bear. She had hurt them, purposely, and Mara instantly regretted it. But she couldn't apologize without also giving in, and that she could not do. Not now, not yet. Not with her own pain, her own fear, so fresh and aching in her breast. The threat of Baldwin did not even touch her. As a sob choked in her throat, Mara spun on her booted heel and fled her parents' apartments.

Lady Beatrice sank back into her fur-draped chair and sagged as if with defeat. Ranulf came immediately to her side and gently took her hands in his.

"Don't worry, my dearest wife," he said with gruff tenderness. "You know her nature. Mara will come to her senses eventually."

"Oh, I know. I know she will." Beatrice turned her eyes to her husband and smiled. "Mara is a good girl, a sensible woman. She will see the wisdom of our decision." The woman paused, her smile fading. "But will she find happiness, Ranulf? Will she be blessed as I have been blessed? Will she bear a child, children perhaps, with love and joy as I have? Or will it be in loneliness and pain? Are we truly doing the right thing, Ranulf? Are we?"

He gave no answer. There was no honest one to give. Sharing the only response and solace that he could, Ranulf cupped his wife's pale and lovely face in his great, gnarled hands. With infinite gentleness, he pressed his lips to hers.

"I know not," he murmured against her fragrant flesh. "I know only that our daughter must marry. She must."

His wife nodded. Indeed, none of them had a choice. Baldwin must never be allowed to have Mara.

Chapter Three

Stephen sat up and swung his legs over the side of the bed. He buried his face in his hands, but only briefly. He wanted away. Away from the dream. Away from the place of its origin. He pulled on his robe even as he left his bedroom.

"Steve, are you all right?" Amanda emerged from her room, pulling the door closed behind her.

"Go back to bed, Mandy. I'm sorry I woke you. Again." He turned and started down the stairs.

"Mom?"

Stephen groaned. His sister hurried down the corridor and pulled her son into her arms.

"It's all right, baby," she soothed. "Uncle Steve just had a bad dream."

Stephen didn't wait to hear any more. He took the stairs two at a time.

The overheads in the kitchen came on with the flick of a switch, and he blinked in their sudden glare. He opened the refrigerator door. It wasn't that there was anything in there that he wanted; looking was simply habit. And the cold air felt good. The sweat had not yet dried from his face.

"Stephen?"

Stephen sighed and closed the refrigerator door. "I'm sorry, Amanda," he said without turning. He heard the scrape of a kitchen chair being pulled away from the table.

"It was that dream again, wasn't it?" his sister inquired, a little too casually.

"What difference does it make?" he replied tiredly.

"Sit down, Stevie. Please. Talk to me."

What difference *did* it make? None. Nothing made any difference anymore. Stephen joined his older sister at the kitchen table.

"Come on, Steve, tell me. Was it the dream?" Amanda persisted.

Stephen nodded. The pain of it rose up in him: a sudden, terrible rush. Tears sprang to his eyes, and he ground his fists into them.

"Steve. . . ." Amanda tried to capture one of his hands, but he pulled away from her.

"Eight years," he said bitterly. "Eight years, the same dream. Seven years of psychotherapy. And what do I have to show for it?"

"Stephen!"

"No. Don't touch me! I don't want your sympathy." He rose from his chair so quickly and violently it toppled over backward. He ignored it.

"It's bad enough you have to put me up," he went on, "give me a place to sleep, and feed me."

"Steve! John and I don't—"

"I can't hold a job anymore. Antidepressants don't work. I can hardly even manage to be an uncle to your kid, for God's sake!"

"Stephen, stop it!" Amanda stood and threw her arms around her brother in an attempt to stop his pacing. He shook her off and walked away, arms clasped tightly across his chest.

"Now they're telling me they want to *institutionalize* me? Try a new kind of drug therapy?"

"It was just a suggestion, Steve, honey. It's strictly voluntary. Dr. Krieger is just trying to—"

"Just trying to *what*?" Stephen whirled on his sister, hands pressed to his temples. "Trying to generate a little more money from the insurance company? For God's sake, Amanda. It's been seven years and I'm not better—I'm *worse!* I'm not working. I'm hardly sleeping. All I'm doing is leeching, sucking off you and John. Scaring Tim. What kind of a life is that?"

"Steve, sit down and listen to me. Please," Amanda begged. "Please!"

Stephen stopped his pacing, but his fists remained balled at his sides. He kept his back turned to his sister. "I'm sorry, Mandy. I'm so sorry. I'll never be able to thank you for all you've done for me. But I'm not going to let you do any more. I'm going to take Krieger's advice and . . . and go to the hospital."

"Steve—"

"Let me finish, Mandy. I want you and John and Tim to go on with your lives. You and John go ahead and have that other kid you've been talking about. Make the guest room into a nursery. You've carried this burden—*my* burden—long enough. I'm outta here."

"I hope you're outta speeches as well," Amanda said tartly. "Now sit down, damn it, and listen. It's the least you can do for me, Stephen."

The tone of his sister's voice managed to pierce the armor of his misery. Stephen turned.

"Sit," she repeated.

Slowly, reluctantly, he righted his chair and sat down. He kept his eyes on his tightly clasped hands.

"I'm actually kind of glad this happened tonight,"

Amanda admitted. "It gives me a chance to bring up something I've had on my mind."

Stephen glanced briefly at his sister from the corner of his eye. She took it as encouragement and drew a deep breath.

"I've been talking to someone, Steve. About . . . about your dream. And about your steadily worsening depression."

"Another shrink?" he asked sarcastically.

She ignored his tone. "No. I think it's become obvious that psychiatry isn't working. I . . . I'd like you to try . . . well, something else."

She had his attention at last. Stephen looked her squarely in the eye. "What something else?"

Amanda took another long, deep breath and straightened her spine. She returned her brother's gaze. "I've been talking to a woman who does past life regressions, Stephen."

"Oh, Mandy."

"No—listen, Steve. I really think she might be able to help you. She's been telling me about cases similar to yours—people with psychological problems, even physical problems, that couldn't be helped by traditional therapies. But, when they were regressed, they found something in a past life that was keeping them from going forward in their present one."

"Mandy, come on. You know I don't even believe in re—"

"There was this woman, for instance," she continued as if he hadn't spoken. "She developed bursitis in her shoulder. That's a pretty common problem, and pretty easily taken care of. But no matter what her doctor did, this woman couldn't get any relief. She finally took the advice of a friend and was regressed."

He couldn't help it; his curiosity was piqued. "And?"

"And she went back to a life when she was a man—a Greek charioteer. She relived a time when she was in

14

battle. There was an accident and he—she—was thrown from her chariot. She sustained a broken shoulder, and a piece of bone was driven through her lung and killed her. The accident was untimely—in other words, it wasn't her time yet to die in that lifetime. Her soul never reconciled to that early death, and she was unable to move on. Hence, the incurable chronic bursitis."

"So?"

"So, once she relived that experience through regression, she was finally able to come to peace with her accidental death. The bursitis never recurred."

Stephen stared at his sister for a long moment. He was tired, exhausted both mentally and physically. For eight years—ever since his twenty-second birthday—his life had been going steadily downhill. He had become more and more depressed, less and less able to function and lead a useful, productive life. Even the doctors had given up on him. The only thing that lay in his future was the prospect of hospitalization and drugs. Why not try this "something else," wacky as it sounded? Why not?

"You say you . . . you know this woman? You've talked to her?"

Amanda nodded.

"You're sure she's not just some . . . charlatan?"

His sister sighed. "I'm not sure of anything, Steve. I only know I *don't* want you to go into that hospital. Obviously, the doctors don't really know what they're doing in your case, or how to make you better, and I. . . ." Tears sprang to her eyes, and Amanda clamped a hand over her mouth as she hiccoughed on a sob.

Stephen took his sister's other hand and held it gently between his own. The only real thing left in his life, the only true emotion, was the love he felt for his sister and her family. He had nothing else at all. Nothing.

"I'll go, Mandy," he said softly. "I'll call your friend tomorrow. OK?"

Chapter Four

Even had she not been the daughter of the lord of the manor, Mara would have commanded the total respect of every servant within the castle walls. She had inherited not only her father's full height, but nearly the breadth of his shoulders. Her waist-length hair was as pale as the frosts that rimed the winter hillsides and, although she normally wore it plaited, today it was unbound and whipped about her shoulders in the cold spring wind. Her stride was long and purposeful, and her blue eyes glinted with fire. She was a Valkyrie, a vengeful goddess, and those who worked in the stables sprang into action when they saw her hurry down the steps from the great hall with her deerhound at her heels.

The dappled palfrey was her favored mount. The sturdy gray mare was saddled and waiting by the time she had crossed the yard to the low wooden outbuilding. Mara mumbled a hasty thanks, ignored the hand prepared to aid her, and swung into the saddle. Eyes were averted as she pulled her skirt down over a muscular but well-toned thigh and slim, booted calf. She gathered her reins, fitted her feet to the stirrups, and put her heels to the palfrey's flanks. The mare started off at once.

Though the reign of his predecessor had been fraught with civil wars, Henry III enjoyed a serene rule. The barons had no quarrel with him. Thus, Ullswater too was at peace—secure except for its recent tension with the Earl of Cumbria. The gate was open and the bridge across its dry moat lowered.

The guard in the watchtower hailed her, but Mara rode past without comment. She kept the mare to a collected canter until they were beyond the castle walls, then gave her mount its head. Her hound loped at her side, pink tongue lolling, but Mara didn't slow. Her father disapproved of unchaperoned rides and would send a loyal retainer after her as soon as the gate guard reported her departure. She wanted to get as much of a head start as possible.

The gray mare was heavily built and sturdy, rather than swift. Nevertheless the miles fell away. Soon her father's castle, built on a hilly slope near the great, dark Ullsmere, lake without depth, lay far behind, and still the mare galloped on. Mara's heart hammered along with each pounding hoofbeat.

Marriage. It would be the end of the world as she had known it. Mara had no illusions; no husband would ever be as accommodating as her father had been. There would be no more wild gallops through the countryside, no more hawking or hunting. Her husband would not care that she could accurately throw a dagger or competently aim a crossbow. He would have no pride in the fact she could effectively wield a broadsword. No. None of those things would impress a man. A *husband*.

Nostrils flared and neck lathered, the mare slowed to a trot. Mara did not urge her back into a gallop. The horse's flagging steps were in perfect rhythm to her own faltering heart and hopes.

Beatrice, her mother, was as fragile as she was beautiful, intelligent, and devoted. Two sons had been stillborn before Mara, and there had been none after. Doting on their daughter, Ranulf had encouraged—and Beatrice had allowed—Mara's training in what otherwise were masculine pursuits. She had not, however, neglected her daughter's education in the feminine arts.

Mara sighed and allowed her mare to fall into a plodding walk. She was, she mused unhappily, amply prepared to run a manor. She was familiar with the spices that turned an ordinary table into a grand one; she knew how to store and use medicinal herbs, how to dry certain flowers with which to sweeten dank rooms; and she could even ply a needle with a certain degree of competence, if not artistry.

Yet to spend the rest of her life engaged in these mundane pursuits? Never again to feel the wind of freedom in her face, or experience the thrill of a hunt? The thought was intolerable. Not to mention thoughts of the man himself. Her life, her future, would now belong to someone else. A stranger. An intimate stranger.

The palfrey halted when she felt Mara stiffen unnaturally in the saddle. Mara didn't notice. Her hound sat down nearby and gazed up at her, panting, his tongue lolling. He cocked his head and uttered a thin whine.

The sound intruded on Mara's reverie, and she turned her attention to the huge, shaggy dog. A bitter smile touched her mouth. "Would to God I had been born like you, old friend," she murmured dryly. "A *male*."

But she had not. She had been born the weaker sex and so must have a man to protect and provide for her. Mara snorted. It didn't matter she was likely more capable than most men. As her mother had said: a husband there must be, so a husband she would have. And if her immediate betrothal would save her from the clutches of the unspeakably cruel and avaricious Earl Baldwin, she supposed it was at least one small thing for which to be grateful.

She had to admit her parents were right: Only marriage to another would save her. Of that there was no doubt. If she remained unmarried and refused to wed Baldwin, the earl would simply petition the king for her hand. And although Henry was just, he was also a man. He would neither understand nor countenance Mara's refusal. He would grant Baldwin's request.

Mara shuddered. Death would be preferable to life with the Earl of Cumbria.

Absorbed in her thoughts, Mara was unaware of how far she had ridden, or in what precise direction. She did not notice that she had come to the southernmost border of her father's lands, to the point where they joined with Baldwin's. She likewise did not notice the small band of riders that crested a distant, brown hill and halted, their attention turned in her direction. She noticed only that the day seemed to have grown considerably colder. She pulled her cloak more tightly about her shoulders, and shivered.

Hawk-nosed and thin to the point of emaciation, Earl Baldwin knew he did not make a good first impression. All his wealth, all his power, could not compensate for his lack of physical attractiveness. He was aware, moreover, that his predilection for wearing black caused many people to liken his appearance to that of a crow. But these days that was only whispered behind his back. The penalty for such an insult, should it be overheard, was a just and fitting one, rendered swiftly. Death.

Baldwin smiled to himself. His brother had learned that lesson: not to cross him. Howard, the elder, the chosen, the handsome, the shining one. Howard, who had been petted and fawned over by their mother. Howard, who had become their father's constant companion, accompanying the old earl everywhere as he learned what he must to assume his birthright upon his father's death. Howard, who had unfortunately chosen to eat those delicate mushroom pasties prepared for the boys' noonday meal, the pasties Baldwin himself had so wisely declined to touch. . . .

Naturally, the cook had been blamed. An accident, surely, choosing the wrong, the most poisonous mushrooms from the forest's bounty. But such an accident could not afford to be repeated with just one precious little heir remaining. The cook had been summarily hanged.

No one had ever suspected. Not really. Just Baldwin's mother, who had never liked him very much to begin with. And then he had grown tired of her long, wary looks, the expressions of disgust and revulsion that occasionally passed over her fine, pale features. When she'd finally died, after a long, wasting illness, no one had suspected the honey mead that she took each night to help her sleep. She had never been the same, anyway, since her eldest son's death.

Baldwin's smile of satisfaction deepened. He smoothed back his long, glossy black hair. Unfortunately, although certainly his finest feature, those locks did not, he knew, enhance his unusually pallid complexion or pale, slightly protuberant blue eyes.

Still, those were things that would be overlooked by his future bride. If she knew what was good for her.

Baldwin licked his thin, colorless lips and cast his gaze down in dreamy contemplation of the bony hand that gripped the reins. The hand that would soon stroke that firm, white flesh, that extraordinary hair of Ranulf's brat. Baldwin's smile gathered into a chuckle.

Yes, indeed, the incredible Amarantha would soon be his. This time, he had an offer her father could not refuse. *This* time, if an alliance with the Earl of Cumbria was not enough for the old fool, Baldwin would offer more. Surely hunting rights in Cumbria's vast and bountiful forests, and the gift of several hundred acres of land along Ranulf's borders, prime grazing land, should be. He could afford to be generous, as generous and magnanimous as he wished. He would get it all back soon enough when the miserable old fool died and his daughter inherited.

Armarantha.

The mere thought of her thickened the blood in his veins. Mara. Haughty, arrogant, magnificent Mara. A woman so extraordinary Baldwin was willing to forget, temporarily at least, the humiliation of his last attempt to press his suit.

"My Lord . . . Excuse me, Earl Baldwin. Look there, just ahead, at the foot of the hill."

Irritated by the distraction, Baldwin waved his man away as if shooing a fly. But his thoughts had been interrupted. Rewarding the offending knight with a scowl, he gazed in the direction the man indicated. . . .

And saw *her*. Like a dream come to life, there she was. Unmistakable, larger than life. Amarantha. Ranulf's daughter. She sat her mount rigidly erect, chin high. Her nearly white hair was unbound and caressed her shoulders like a rare silken cape. There was no one else like her, and soon, very soon, she would be his.

The four knights who accompanied their earl watched a smile briefly light their lord's usually bleak countenance and knew they were in for a bit of sport. Not a man among them blamed the earl for his all too obvious desire, and not one of them wouldn't have given much, if not all, he owned to be in the earl's position.

"There she is, lads," Earl Baldwin called. "My bride-to-be. My beauty. What say we give her a warm welcome and escort her home?" Then, wanting no reply—expecting none—Baldwin cruelly spurred his mount into a dash down the hill.

*   *   *

21

Trey's growl was low, ominous. Mara knew immediately the sound meant someone approached. She looked up, and movement on the distant hill caught her attention. She saw the riders headed in her direction.

She was relatively safe, even unaccompanied, on her father's lands. However, it was never wise for a woman to be caught out alone by a group of men; and Mara experienced a prick of apprehension because, in her haste to leave the castle, she had come away unarmed. Then she caught a good look at the lead rider, black cape flapping like a raven's wings, and the prick of apprehension turned to a thrill of fear that chased up her spine.

She might, she thought quickly, wheel her mare and make a run for it. But the animal was already winded from before. They wouldn't make a hundred yards before being caught. Besides, it was against Mara's nature to turn tail and flee. Especially from a worm like Earl Baldwin.

She cursed herself for her thoughtlessness in leaving without so much as the dagger she habitually carried in the silver girdle at her waist. But for Trey, she was helpless and soon to be alone with the most treacherous and loathsome man in all of England.

Mara held her mare steady and turned to face the oncoming riders. Squaring her shoulders, she let the faintest of smiles lift the corners of her mouth. Her enemy would never know she felt so much as an instant of apprehension.

The girl's expression of disdain instantly destroyed Baldwin's good humor and set him to fuming. But he would soon wipe that smile from her face. He would crush her lips with his and take what belonged to him. In fact, if he did not, wisely, fear the king's justice and Ranulf's righteous retribution, he would have done it right there and then.

Controlling himself with visible effort, Baldwin point-

edly avoided a greeting and motioned his men to surround horse, hound, and rider.

Mara did not acknowledge the movement of the men
to encircle her by so much as the blink of an eye. If
Baldwin sought to discomfit her, he was going to be sadly
disappointed. Trey growled, but Mara silenced him with
a wave of her hand. She gazed levelly at her would-be
tormentor.

"So, Earl Baldwin," she said at length. "What is this, a
hunting party? It must be. I've heard this is how you
bring down both hart and hind, and particularly the doe:
Have your men surround her, cut her off. Cut her down.
How clever, Baldwin. How courageous."

The earl's knights had the grace to look abashed. Baldwin felt only rage. He knew an unattractive flush rose to
his face, and he fixed his glare on the woman who had
lit the fires there.

"I would mind my tongue if I were you, woman," he
hissed through gritted teeth. "My memory is long. And
the time till I take you to wife is short."

Mara snorted. "Wife? I'd rather be dead, Your Grace.
Painfully."

The Earl of Cumbria had never been noted for either
patience or restraint. What little he had possessed now
deserted him completely. With a hard spur to his horse's
flank, he lunged the animal forward and slapped Mara
across the face.

The blow took her by surprise. The anger that swiftly
followed, however, was not hot and heedless as Baldwin's
had been. It was steel-edged, cold, and calculated. Ignoring entirely the men who surrounded her, Mara
made a grab for the shortsword the earl wore at his side.
Her motion was as quick as the strike of a snake, and
Baldwin soon found himself vainly reaching for his
weapon already firm in Mara's grip.

The metallic hiss of steel whispered in the sudden silence as his men drew their own swords. Mara pivoted

23

her mare, blade raised menacingly, threatening each and every man; then she returned her hard, dark stare to the earl.

It was the moment Tully had waited for most of his young life. As the newest knight in Baldwin's retinue, he saw an opportunity for rapid advancement. He felt his blood surge as he gazed at the woman's unarmed back.

Mara's warning came from the expression in Earl Baldwin's light eyes. They widened slightly; then the fear in them was gone like fog before a wind. Years of training took over at once.

Having recently worked with the heavy and unwieldy broadsword, Mara found its smaller cousin amazingly light, well balanced, and graceful in her hand. She swung it upward in a near-perfect parry even as she pulled her horse sharply to the left. Steel clanged against steel.

The quickness of the woman's defense took Tully completely by surprise. The young knight's grip on his weapon was momentarily loosened. Mara's next stroke, driving across from the downward parry, sent the blade spinning from his hand. Just as rapidly, the girl's mare completed its spin, and Mara was once again face-to-face with the earl. She pressed her sword to the hollow of Baldwin's throat.

The earl's natural pallor deepened. His knights exchanged glances, and Mara spoke to them without taking her eyes from their leader.

"If another of you moves, I'll put this point home." Mara smiled. "Do all your men love you as much as that impetuous young knight, Baldwin? Do you trust them? Or do you think another of them will attempt to disarm me and soon find himself looking for another lord to serve so well?"

"Witch!" the earl spat. "You'll pay for this. By God, I swear it!"

"The only payment you'll get, Baldwin, is further humiliation should you ever think to come near me again.

And don't bother to waste your time importuning my father—if that is, indeed, what you had in mind. His answer will always be the same, Baldwin: There is no bride for you at Ullswater Castle."

The woman's gall was insupportable, the embarrassment unendurable. In spite of the sword pressed to his throat, Baldwin was no longer able to contain his fury.

"You forget who you are. Who *I* am," he rasped, jaw clenched to avoid excessive movement. "I am the Earl of Cumbria. And you *will* do as I say."

Mara laughed. "*Will* I?" she mocked. Her taunting smile disappeared abruptly. "I will do only as my husband says, the man my father has chosen for me to wed. A *real* man."

Mara was acutely aware her danger had increased. An expression of implacable hatred slowly replaced the outrage on Baldwin's sallow features. She was not, therefore, disappointed to hear the sound of rapidly approaching hoofbeats—her father's men, searching for her. They had to be. Their timing couldn't have been more perfect.

"It's your lucky day, Baldwin," she sneered, unable to resist a final taunt. "I've decided not to kill you." Before he could react, she flipped his broadsword into the air. It rose, then plummeted to earth and impaled itself in the dry ground mere inches from the earl's mount. Well trained, the animal did not flinch. The earl's indrawn hiss, however, was audible.

Mara's icy smile never faltered.

Purple veins corded in the earl's neck. He tried to speak, but rage and humiliation had paralyzed his tongue. Lacking orders from their lord, Baldwin's men drew aside as Mara rode between them. Without a backward glance, she signaled her father's oncoming riders to come no farther, but to turn and ride back the way they had come. Spurring her horse, hound at her side, she joined the men at a gallop.

Baldwin choked, gathered what spittle his suddenly dry

mouth was able to summon, and spat. To think he had actually wanted that witch as a wife! Mad. He must have been mad to think the woman good enough to wed! What had possessed him? She was nothing more than an ignorant and foul-mouthed shrew, a whore of a peasant who did not even deserve the merciful death she would soon receive.

Rages had come upon him like this before. He seldom remembered the actions he took once the red veil descended upon him; he simply responded to the heat in his blood. His roweled spurs bit cruelly into his stallion's sides, and the beast leapt into a gallop. His knights, albeit reluctantly, followed him as he sprang in pursuit of the woman and her small retinue.

It was Trey who, once again, warned Mara. The hound had been loping at her side when he abruptly veered away, then stopped. This sharp, angry bark halted all three of the Ullswater riders.

"We are pursued, my lady," one of Mara's father's men said needlessly. "We might stand and fight, but. . . ."

"But we are outnumbered. Clearly," Mara finished for him. It went against her every instinct, but there was no help for it—not with Earl Baldwin's murderous expression so clear for her to see. "Ride!"

The interlude with the earl and his party had lasted long enough for Mara's mare to catch her wind, and her guards' larger, stronger animals were yet fresh. It was a small enough fortune, but they had another.

Though her father's land and the earl's lay against one another like lovers, Ranulf's castle stood near his southern boundary. So did Baldwin's. He and his men had ridden a great deal farther than had Mara and her guards. And the earl's mounts had been ridden hard, as well. The distance between the hunters and the hunted closed, but slowly. Ullswater's formidable walls came into sight with the earl still trailing.

"Ullswater, to me!" Mara cried, leaning low over her

palfrey's neck. The mare's light mane streamed backward and mingled with her rider's own pale hair. "Gates! Close the gates!"

Hoofbeats thundered on the wooden bridge. The portcullis creaked downward noisily. Baldwin's stallion screamed as the earl hauled viciously on his reins.

She was just beyond his reach. She had escaped. Baldwin's teeth ground together, and his fists clenched spasmodically. Blood dripped from his horse's mouth, and bloody foam flecked its withers. As the red veil slowly lifted from the earl's vision, he touched his glove to a red smear on his horse's shoulder, then raised his fist to the barred gate.

"It will be your blood!" he bellowed hoarsely. "Ullswater's blood will be the next to flow. Oceans of it!"

Night did not fall so swiftly in the chill, early days of spring. The long winter nights were over, yet the evenings were cold enough still to welcome the warmth of a fire.

As had long been their habit, Ranulf and Beatrice sat by the massive hearth in the great hall and watched the failing light outside. They enjoyed the relative peace before the evening bustle, when all who resided in the castle, knight and vassal alike, gathered peaceably at the long, rough-hewn tables for feasting. It had not always been thus.

Beatrice closed her eyes and reveled in the warmth and failing light coming through the tall, narrow glazed windows of the hall. The windows had been one of the first gifts from her husband, when they had first wed. Even then he had feared for her fragile health, and he had ordered the costly glass installed to keep the damp and chill winds outside.

There were other things too that made Ullswater's hall one of the finest in the land. Tapestries woven by Beatrice and her ladies during the long winter evenings and blustery days of winter blanketed the stony walls. Fine banners hung between the high windows. There was pewterware for the high table; and chairs, cleverly wrought by the craftsmen of the thriving village that sprawled in the castle's shadow.

All was perfect. She had everything she ever wished, more than she had ever dreamed.

Most precious of all, however, was the peace at reign in the land, hard won and cherished. Armor grew rusty from disuse. Swords were unsheathed for sport or training only. But would peace continue? Would Henry's laws keep men like Earl Baldwin in check? Or had concord visited the land for too long? Was it soon to disappear?

"Are you chilled, my love?" Solicitous, as always, of the woman he had loved for nearly thirty years, Ranulf hovered over Beatrice when he saw her shudder.

"No. No, I'm fine. I was merely thinking."

"Of our daughter? Where could she be?" he asked, having missed the slight shake of his wife's head. "What's taking those fools so long to find her?"

"Perhaps she simply rode farther than usual, husband," Beatrice replied. "She was quite . . . agitated when she left. You know well her temper."

"Yes, and her will. When it's set for or against something, you're in for a battle." As if his words had brought the thought to life, Ranulf heard shouts coming from the courtyard.

"Ranulf. . . ." Beatrice began. But her husband was already gone, running for the door to the great hall. Heart in her mouth, Beatrice followed.

Mara had flung herself from the palfrey and grabbed a sword from the nearest knight. She ran to the portcullis, but Baldwin was already galloping his bloodied horse away. Trembling, she stood and earl's watched the retreating party disappear.

"Amarantha!"

Mara turned to face her father. He was a huge figure

silhouetted against the day's last light, a giant of a man. She smiled tightly.

"I apologize for the commotion, Father. I apologize also for my failure to immediately abide by your will, and the wisdom of it."

Lord Ranulf and Lady Beatrice, who stood next to each other, exchanged brief glances.

"I accept your choice of a husband, whoever he is. I accede to your wishes."

"Very well, Mara," her father responded at last, the question in his eyes, if not his tone. "And blessings be upon the union."

So why was there no happiness in his heart? Why did a sudden, icy chill run down his spine? In spite of the lingering warmth and his fur-lined cloak, Ranulf shivered.

He did not notice, as did his wife, the last rays of light that slanted through the high windows: Rusty red, they fell upon the rush-strewn floor, washing the hall in crimson and staining it like blood.

Chapter Five

The house, on the edge of town, was small and neat, very much like its owner. Stephen sat across from Millie Thurman in her tidy, cozy living room and forced a nervous smile.

"Your house is, uh, real nice."

"Thank you," Millie replied. She had a sweet smile, and her tiny hands were clasped on her lap. Lace surrounded her neck, the only decoration on her plain gray dress. The collar was, Stephen mused, much like the antimacassars that graced the arms and backs of the chairs, or the doilies under the lamps and the potted African violets: new but made to look old.

"My sister's told me a lot about you," he offered.

"She's talked to me about you as well, Stephen." That smile again, almost angelic. "She's told me you've had some difficulties the past few years."

That would be putting it mildly. Aloud, he said: "I've been, um, battling depression, I guess you could say."

"And the medical community has been unable to help you?"

The Circle of a Promise

He thought he should feel more uncomfortable. Actually, he didn't feel any discomfort or unease at all. "No, they haven't been able to help," he agreed.

"So you've come to see me." There was genuine pleasure in her tone. "Amanda explained to you what I do?"

Stephen nodded, strangely satisfied to feel at last the smallest prick of disquiet. "I have to tell you, though, I'm not . . . not too sure I believe in this reincarnation stuff."

"A flower doesn't have to believe in the power of the sun in order to bloom, Stephen," Millie replied gently.

"No, I . . . I guess not." He sat forward on the edge of his chair and folded his hands. "Sooooo . . . what do we do?"

"Well, I think the first thing I'd like you to do is try and relax."

Stephen eased back into his chair. It was a recliner, he noticed.

"Have you ever been hypnotized before, Stephen?"

He shook his head. "I don't think I'd be a very good subject."

"Perhaps not," she agreed pleasantly. "Some people are. Others are not. Would you like to recline your chair a little? It will ease the strain on your lower back."

Though his first instinct was to decline, he found himself adjusting the little lever on the left side of the chair. He did feel better.

"I understand your difficulties have been going on for a number of years," Millie said. Her voice was extraordinarily soothing. "Can you tell me at about what age they began?"

"Yes, I can. Definitely. Because it began so abruptly, with no warning." He liked talking to Millie. "I was twenty-two. I'd just graduated from college. With a business degree. I was ready to go out and conquer the world. Then . . ."

"Then what, Stephen?"

"I . . . I was just overcome with . . . sadness. I suddenly didn't want to live anymore."

"And you've been fighting this feeling ever since."

It was a statement, not a question. Stephen nodded again. He felt tears crowding the back of his throat.

"It would be nice at least to be able to relax for a little while, wouldn't it, Stephen? To be free of this burden for just a little while?"

"Yes."

"Would you let me help you try a little exercise?"

He nodded.

"Good. Then close your eyes. That's it. Now, I want you to think about your toes. All your toes. I want you to let them relax, totally relax. Feel the tension leave them. That's right. Now your feet, the tops of your feet, and the arches. Relax. And your ankles. . . ."

He felt so light, Stephen feared he might float away. Oddly, it was what she suggested.

"You're able to move about now, Stephen, even though your body will remain in the chair. You can float up to the ceiling. Just let yourself go."

He drifted.

"Are you there, Stephen? Can you see yourself sitting in the chair?"

"Yes."

"Good. That's very good. Now look up, Stephen. Do you see the sky? See the clouds?"

Yes. It was amazing. He could see it all. He was up in the sky.

"The clouds are moving, Stephen. They're moving faster and faster. Do you see them?"

Yes. Like a film in fast-forward. Faster and faster.

"They're moving because time is passing, Stephen. It's going backward, into the past. The years are falling away. And you can control it, Stephen. Stop it any time you want."

Yes. Yes, he could. He wanted to stop it . . . *Now.*

Chapter Six

The hare, after the fashion of its kind, froze into immobility. Its brown-ticked fur blended subtly with the forest shadows and fallen leaves, rendering it momentarily invisible. Yet the predators came on: lumbering, heavy-footed. The hare was frightened into movement once more. It leapt from its position, ears still flat to its head, and bounded away into the soft and woody gloom.

"There! There he goes! *Dinner!*"

The young, well-armed nobleman pulled up with a heavy hand on his stallion's reins, certain the prey had escaped.

His companion did not give up so easily. The wiry figure astride the smaller horse, unencumbered by sword or chain mail, sprang lightly to his feet upon his saddle. He nocked an arrow to his bow. A mere second later, the doomed hare leapt into the air and found an arrow through its heart; was dead before it fell back to earth.

"My lord." The small man, face as gray and pointed as a fox, removed his plumed hat and bowed deeply, still standing on his saddle. "Your dinner is practically served." Replacing his hat, the archer executed a neat somersault, landed on the ground, and dashed into the forest to retrieve his prize.

The more muscular, mail-clad rider shook his head and chuckled. Life was never dull in Jack's company, he mused. Nor were the two of them ever in any danger of starving. Although it irked him, he had to admit, that his small companion was a better provider of game than he.

Still, being bested in something was better than going hungry—and hungry was just what he would be if it were not for Jack. The young knight sighed. He himself could hack away all day with his sword, but he was not likely to serve up any supper with it. A bow was better for that, and Jack was a better shot.

Besides, his sword arm ached. Unconsciously, he clasped his left hand to his right upper arm and massaged. The skirmish on the border had been brief, but furious and bloody. He and his fellows had beaten back the Scottish raiders and sent them fleeing into the hills, minus a half-dozen of their stoutest fighters. It was doubtful they would return any time soon, but he had left his comrades to make sure of it. Stephen smiled inwardly.

Thomas and Walter had not needed to be asked twice to run down the remainder of the Scottish raiders. Thomas, young and ever eager, had been at the forefront of his knights. Walter, older, but not one whit slower, had been right on Thomas's heels. The balance of Stephen's knights followed those two with the kind of gusto peculiar to those who have not yet come to terms with the idea of their own mortality. Stephen rubbed his aching sword arm one more time.

He wished he could have gone with them. Or, at least, had them with him now. But he'd *had* to send them after the rebels. The Scots had not only butchered cattle but two entire families, raping the women first. Stephen would allow no threat against his people to exist. Especially now, with pressing business elsewhere and his thoughts in such a turmoil.

He must have groaned aloud, for Jack was at his side in an instant.

"Are ye all right, m'lord?"

"Of course I am," he replied brusquely, and straightened his shoulders. "Why wouldn't I be?"

The small man shrugged elaborately, a smile ghosting at the corners of his mouth. "Oh, I don't know. Too much on yer mind, mebbe. Havin' to leave yer knights behind an' all, t'finish yer business while you go a-courtin'. . . ."

The knight's dark and menacing scowl prevented Jack from saying more, but it did not prevent the man's smile from blossoming full grown. When the archer saw his lord bridle angrily, he raised the dead hare as if in self defense. "Your dinner, sir. Compliments of your most humble and devoted servant."

Stephen merely grunted by way of reply. His irritation with the other subsided quickly. It was difficult to stay angry with Jack as the man was, indeed, a most loyal and devoted servant.

His thoughts drifted back to the day they had met. Barely fifteen, Stephen had nonetheless been lord of the manor, and had been since his father's death. The older knights, like Walter, had helped guide and teach him, and the younger men, his boon companions, Thomas, chief among them, were among his best and bravest men-at-arms. He'd been content. But Alfred, his most senior knight, had insisted it was time Stephen take a squire as befitted his position.

Word spread, and the northern nobles applied for their sons. Though Stephen was young, he'd been well respected. He had set himself diligently to the task and legacy his father had left him, and had become known for his courage, honesty, and fairness. Many youths had been presented for his consideration.

Stephen, however, had been unable to choose, as politics seemed more important than other qualifications—and politics had never been a bit to his liking.

"How do you expect me to make a decision?" he had complained to Alfred as they sat in the high hall one sunny spring afternoon. "Every time I pick out a likely lad, you have some reason why another would be better."

"I merely point out the political ramifications," the old knight had replied evenly.

"Well, instead of 'pointing out,' why don't you just go ahead and pick for me?"

The day had been bright, and it beckoned with far more allure than the duty set before him, so without further ado Stephen had announced his intention to go hawking and had ridden out into the countryside with the closest of his companions. Just beyond a copse of slender yew trees, they'd flushed a brace of pheasants that took to wing in a flash of autumn color.

Before Stephen could loose his bird, however, the first pheasant fluttered back to earth, an arrow through its neck. An instant later, the second bird followed.

Swords were drawn from scabbards as Stephen's men prepared to defend him from the small man who appeared, like magic, astride a thin, brown gelding. A ridiculous plume of feathers bloomed from his wide-brimmed hat and, as they watched, jaws agape, he jumped to his feet in his saddle, removed the hat, and bowed low.

"My lord," the man said to Stephen, "If it was pheasant y'wanted for yer dinner . . . dinner is served."

Stephen had been too taken aback for a moment to speak. Not only had the little man crept up on them all unawares, he had dazzled them with the swiftest and most accurate display of bowmanship anyone had ever before demonstrated.

Stephen reluctantly smiled at the memory of that first meeting, recalling how his knights had wanted to hang

Jack as a poacher. But Stephen had been amused, and impressed, enough to hear the man out.

"If it's a squire ye're needin'," Jack had said, "y'need look no further. Not only kin I provide yer dinner, I kin cook it fair as any, I vow. Mebbe better. What squire'll serve you as chef as well as simple lance bearer and armor polisher? I kin do the boy's job ye be lookin' for, an' a man's job beside. Should strength of sword fail t'protect yer back, me arrows fly fleet, as ye've seen."

There had been no denying it. Additionally, it had solved Stephen's political problems by avoiding politics entirely. There had been only one question that needed asking and answering.

"Tell me something, Jack," Stephen had said. "Why? Why would a man of your obvious talents want to be both squire and steward? Squire, I understand, but . . ."

Stephen had hesitated, seeing the suddenly somber expression on the small man's hollow features.

"Well, ye might ask," Jack replied slowly. "An' I'll tell ye, for you're not just plainly of noble birth, but of noble and kindly mind, as well. Ye'll understand when I tell ye I had a son once. He wanted nothing more, ever, than t'be a squire. He attained his goal an' he come home once t'tell me all the fine and brave things he done, an' be doin' . . ." Jack had sighed deeply and continued, voice quavering.

"I was too busy drinkin' an' showin' off about me boy, the squire. I paid him no real mind. Not like a father should. He left. An' I never saw him again." Jack paused to clear his throat. He had looked Stephen straight in the eye.

"I know how t'do the squirin'. I *need* to do the servin'. As I shoulda served me boy. I'll look after ye in every way, an' none better."

Over Alfred's protests, Stephen had taken Jack on and had never regretted his decision. Well, almost never.

His thoughts having returned to the present, Stephen

eyed the rabbit held before him. "My thanks," he murmured grudgingly.

"Oh, you're most welcome, noble lord," Jack replied.
"Shall I prepare the feast? There's a clearing not far off
the road where we might comfortably spend the night."

Stephen turned his dark gaze down the rutted track,
as if he might see an answer in the distance. He ran a
hand through his thick, shoulder-length hair. It was not
far to his destination, only a few more miles. But truth
be told, he was more than a bit nervous about reaching
it.

"Perhaps it *would* be better to spend the night here,"
he answered, climbing from his horse. "Get a fresh start
in the morning. Better than to arrive a little late tonight
and disturb everyone. Under the circumstances, I'd
rather my reception be a pleasant one."

"Oh, yes. Far better to ensure our welcome is a happy
one," Jack echoed. "*Under* the circumstances."

Stephen gave his man a hard look before he led his
stallion off the road into the wood. He trod noisily
through the sodden leaves and undergrowth for a minute, then stopped to look back over his shoulder. "Mind
yourself, Jack. This is serious business and I'll have none
of your cheek."

The other man pulled a long face but wisely held his
tongue. Then dutifully he followed his master into the
small clearing. The situation was hard on his lord, no
doubt about it. It would be hard on any man, and Jack
was glad Stephen had decided to stop for the night. A
bit of roasted rabbit, a good night's sleep, and he'd be
ready to face whatever fate had in store. Tall one, short
one, buck-toothed or gap-toothed, a brunette with a trace
of a mustache, perhaps.

Jack giggled to himself. Or a fat one. *Oh, Lord.* . . . Jack
rolled his eyes heavenward.

Though, please, not one with a mustache.

"What's so funny?" Stephen inquired irritably.

"Oh, nothing," Jack replied. "I hope." Then he suddenly burst into peals of laughter.

Ignoring his servant, Stephen continued on into the woods. He had the uncomfortable feeling he knew exactly what Jack was laughing about.

For the hundredth time that night, Mara rolled over and curled into a new position. The movement dislodged one of her fur coverlets, and it slithered silently to the floor. She reached down to retrieve it, changed her mind, slipped from beneath the remaining furs, and crossed to the window. Trey padded at her heels.

The moon had begun its descent. Had her life, as well, begun a downward motion? Would she be doomed henceforth to while away her days in the women's bower, embroidering cloth, planning meals, awaiting her lord's pleasure?

And what of the man himself? Mara turned from the window, arms hugged to her breast. Her father had said he was comely, not unpleasant to look upon. But her father, she feared, would say anything at this point.

What did "not unpleasant to look upon" really mean? Not *too* fat? Not *too* short or *too* thin? What did this husband-to-be, this jailer, really look like? And where was he now, how close, how soon to arrive with the shackles of matrimony?

There were no answers. There were only the precious hours of liberty still left to her.

Mara paced from her bed to the window. The dawn was not far, nor the events it would bring. Her stomach spasmed, and her fingers curled into the palms of her hands. Her heart raced.

She shouldn't do it, she knew. The sun, and its exposure, was too near. She might get caught this time and tempt her father's legendary temper.

Yet something deep within her would not be still. It was more than simple restlessness, more than an urge to run and revel in the final hours of her freedom. It was a feeling almost of being summoned, and being unable to resist the call—a call so elemental it tugged at her very soul. Mara surrendered.

It took only moments to pull a woolen tunic over the linen chemise she wore. She picked up her boots and walked barefoot to the chest at the foot of her bed. Rummaging through its contents, the balance of her wardrobe and a few personal possessions, she extracted a large, iron key. Clutching it tightly, she tiptoed out her door.

Her parents' massive bed was limned by the predawn light. So closely entwined did they sleep, it was hard to tell one body from the other. How lucky they were in their love. How precious it was. How rare. Mara hurried on noiselessly, trying to swallow back the uncomfortable lump in her throat.

The great hall was the most difficult obstacle. Servants and retainers alike, knights with no families of their own, littered the floor and snored beneath rough wool blankets. Mara paused to pull on her boots and make sure all slept soundly. Trey trotted ahead, making a brief stop to sniff at Douglas, her father's old friend. The knight snorted and swiped at his cheek where the hound had laid its cold, wet nose.

"Trey!" Mara hissed, and patted her thigh. The dog obediently returned to her side, and they continued together across the hall.

Like most English structures of its time, the keep was built over a large storage area. Mara tripped down the steps into the night, key ready, and inserted it in the door to the undercroft. When both she and her hound had slipped inside, Mara closed the door and plunged them both into herb-fragrant darkness.

A secret door was cleverly concealed in the stone here, further hidden behind a large pile of market baskets. The hidden passageway beyond had been built long ago by the cautious and far-seeing Ranulf, and was forgotten by all but father and daughter. Mara squeezed behind the precariously stacked vessels and touched the wall where it was subtly indented. The stone portal opened.

Once again, Mara and Trey stepped into darkness. This time, it was total.

Often were the occasions, however, she had needed to slip past gate and guards unnoticed, and the way was familiar. Mara did not make a single misstep as she trotted along. When she emerged at last from the seemingly endless tunnel, behind a seemingly careless scattering of boulders, she was far beyond the castle walls, with its surrounding village, and was deep within the forest.

Aided by the imminent light of the sun, she jogged through the trees. It did not take long to reach her destination: the grassy bank of the small, woodland lake, far to the south of the Ullsmere.

Trey panted at her side. Paying no heed to the chill air, Mara removed her boots, drew her tunic and chemise over her head, then stood at last clothed only in the raiment God had given her. Before her mind had time to dwell on how achingly cold the water would be, she took a deep breath and dove cleanly into its dark and icy depths.

Stephen tossed and turned on the hard ground, his mind whirling in a hundred different directions. What, after all, had he gotten himself into? He had been quite happy as a bachelor. He had always had as many women as he wanted, and was just as happy to send them on their way when he was done with them.

Perhaps it was the way he had been raised, without a woman's tender ministrations. His mother had died birthing him and his father, already gray-haired when he had taken his young wife, had not lived past Stephen's eighth year. The boy had been left virtually alone with his father's aging retainers and their own sons. Those men were now his score of knights, all good and trusted friends, the men he had known since boyhood, and were left behind to protect his lands and his people. The masculine life was the only life he had ever known, ever wanted. So what was he doing now adding a female to the mix?

What I am doing, Stephen reminded himself sternly, I am doing for very sound practical and political reasons. He was no longer the boy who had puzzled over the correct choice of a squire. He was a man who had a duty both to himself and to the realm. Furthermore, alliances such as this were commonplace—to protect borders, increase lands, sway the outcome of inevitable disputes. This particular alliance would certainly aid and benefit all involved. He'd had no choice, really. Yet, at the moment, he found it difficult to dwell on the beneficial aspects of the impending union.

Despairing at last of sleep, Stephen rolled from his blanket and wakened his servant.

Jack groaned and curled into a tighter ball. Stephen nudged him with the toe of his boot. One of the man's green eyes opened and focused.

"Anxious to be off then, are we?"

"It's too early for your particular brand of humor," Stephen answered. "Get up and let's get moving."

They were packed and on the road by first light, and they set out at a brisk trot.

The day warmed steadily, and by the time the sun had crested the distant hills, Stephen's horse was lathered and the linens beneath his mail shirt were damp with sweat.

The shade of the woodland that bordered the road was irresistible. Stephen turned his horse off the dry, dusty track. He was rewarded immediately with a drop in temperature. And something else—not too far away, through the trees, the glint of sunlight on water.

Stephen licked his dry lips and tried to reach beneath

his collar for a good scratch. His stallion snorted and tossed his head.

"The horses could do with a drink," he said, half to himself. "It wouldn't hurt to lose some of this road dust either." Stephen turned to his servant. "What about you?"

" 'Tain't I who needs to be smellin' sweet as roses."

Stephen ignored him and guided his horse into the wood. When at last a small, secluded lake came into sight, he dismounted and handed the reins to his companion.

"The things we do for love." Jack sighed.

"Roast in hell," Stephen replied levelly. "If they can stand the smell of you down there." He really shouldn't take the time to indulge in a bath. He needed to be on his way, to do what needed to be done and return as quickly as possible to the men and lands he had left behind. Life had to go on, despite the unpleasant turns it occasionally took.

Yet it was more than simple procrastination that drew Stephen from his appointed path. He felt an inexplicable urge, almost as if some unseen hand tugged at him, pulled him down to the water's edge.

His mail shirt was heavy and difficult to remove, but under Jack's disgusted and disapproving gaze, Stephen laboriously pulled the thigh-length, steel-linked tunic over his head. Underlinens, breeches, and boots followed.

His smooth, broad chest glistening with sweat, Stephen looked longingly at the water. Careless of his nakedness, he strode quickly toward the inviting depths.

Mara floated on her back to rest and catch her breath. She had swum for nearly an hour, stroking back and forth across the tiny lake. If she had not managed to banish the dark cloud that hovered over her, at least she was now too tired to stare up at it. She had paused only once, to watch Trey bound off into the woods after some real or imagined prey. He hadn't returned yet, but he was close, she knew. He never strayed far, or for long. It was undoubtedly the hound she now heard making his way toward her through the forest undergrowth.

The sun had risen to cast its brilliant light over the surrounding hills and treetops. Mara closed her eyes to its brightness and turned onto her back, paddled lazily toward shore. It was time to return. Past time, as a matter of fact. The entire hall would be awake, the morning ale and bread set upon the trestle tables. Her parents would wonder where she was. She did not wish them to discover her long secret path to freedom.

Not that her freedom was going to last much longer.

Still, the swim had cleansed her spirit. If her escapade was uncovered, the key to the undercroft confiscated, so be it. The time she had spent in the lake was worth it. The lingering taint of her run-in with Baldwin was washed clean, and Mara was resigned—at least somewhat—to her impending betrothal.

Her toes found the grassy bottom of the lake, and her hands reached for the bank. She placed her palms downward on the green and fragrant ground and prepared to pull herself from the water.

Stephen had almost reached the lake when he noticed its surface broken by a series of ebbing ripples. He wondered idly which of the three possibilities—fowl, fish, or small animal—might have caused the disturbance. Then he pushed aside the last branch that barred his way and stepped onto the bank of the cold but enticing water.

At his feet, a naked woman heaved herself from the pool.

Chapter Seven

"When I count to three," Millie said softly, "you will awake feeling refreshed, better than you have in a long time. One . . . Two . . . Three."

Stephen blinked, but his eyes adjusted rapidly. The room was dim. Only a single shaft of sunlight fell through the parted curtains. "What . . . what happened?"

"Why don't you tell me, Stephen?"

He shook his head. "I . . . I . . . Oh, my God." Stephen suddenly held out his arms and looked at them as if he had never seen them before. "I was wearing some kind of . . . some kind of armor, I think."

"Yes. Go on."

"I rode a horse. And I had a . . . a servant." He shook his head again and dropped his arms. "No. No, it can't be. It's not possible. What did you do?"

"I did nothing, Stephen," Millie replied quietly. "Nothing but help you access a previous existence."

"No. You hypnotized me. Put something in my head."

"What's in your head, Stephen? Tell me. Where were you?"

The fuzzy memory came back to him with sudden clarity. "In the north of England. The Lakes District," he said without hesitation.

"Have you been there before?"

"No, never. I've never even been out of the state of New York."

"Tell me how it looked."

"Green, wooded. So beautiful. So clean and . . . and untouched."

"What year is it, Stephen?"

"I . . . I don't know. I'm not sure."

"Who is the king, Stephen?"

"Henry. Henry the Third." He sat up straight in his chair. Electricity seemed to prickle on the surface of his skin. "How . . . how do I know that?" he breathed.

Millie merely smiled. "Tell me how you feel, Stephen."

"I . . . I feel better. I feel *good*."

"I'm so glad."

"How . . . What did you do?"

"Would you like to come back?"

"Yes, I . . . I want to come back. When?"

"How about tomorrow at the same time?"

Stephen rose. He wanted to take Millie in his arms and hug her. "Th-thank you," he stammered instead. "Thank you so much."

"Until tomorrow, Stephen. Good-bye."

Chapter Eight

Mara raced back the way she had come. She paused only once, briefly, to don her clothes. She looked behind her before she ducked inside the concealed entrance of the secret tunnel, making certain she had not been observed. But she was alone. *He* had not followed.

She ran then, Trey bounding along at her side, all the way back to the door into the undercroft. It was late, and likely a servant would be about, sent on some errand from the hall. Mara used the greatest caution to push open the concealed door. Her luck held; no one was there. With her hand on Trey's neck, she ran to the outer door.

Various craftsmen and servants bustled about the courtyard, bent on their day's labors. No one noticed her slip from the undercroft and hurry up the stairs to the great hall. There was but one obstacle left.

Her mother and father sat side by side at the head table. They lingered over breakfast, shoulders touching. They had been speaking quietly together, but at Mara's entrance Ranulf turned his attention to the doorway. Lady Beatrice smiled.

"Good morning, my dear. Where have you—"

"Sorry," Mara interrupted. "I'm sorry. I couldn't sleep. I . . . I went for a walk."

Her mother's gaze held sympathy. Mara looked away guiltily.

"Would you join us for some breakfast, dear? You must be hungry, up and about so early."

"I'm fine," Mara replied, knowing it was probably the greatest lie she had ever told. Her hands trembled so violently she had to clench them behind her back as she walked past her parents. "I'll get something later. Thank you."

They looked at her quizzically. She was acting strangely, she knew, but she couldn't help it. Her parents would put it down to nervousness due to the pending betrothal. They would never—could never—guess the truth.

Mara dashed through her parents' apartments and into her own chamber. She slammed the door behind her and leaned against it heavily. Trey, who had not been quite swift enough, whined and scratched at the thick wooden barrier. She scarcely heard him. The image was before her still. Mara closed her eyes, but the picture only intensified. It wouldn't go away and, somewhere deep in her heart, she knew it never would. She would remember him forever. Unaware of her rising pulse and quickened breath, Mara surrendered and let the memory invade her completely.

He was a god. He had to be. One moment she'd been alone, the next she had pulled herself from the water and there he was: naked, perfect, the most beautiful man she had ever seen. Thick dark waves of hair fell to his broad and muscular shoulders, shoulders as well muscled as his chest, a chest that seemed sculpted from marble. His skin was white, smooth, untouched by the sun.

But it would not be untouched by a woman's hands, Mara had realized in a disconcerting rush. Unaccountable jealousy had flared in her breast and her gaze contined downward to a narrow waist and firm, flat hips.

Mara sucked in her breath at the recollection. A crimson blush spread from her breast to her neck, her cheeks. Down and down her gaze had licked him, down to that man-part of him, pale as it lay against his thigh, framed in its halo of dark black hair. She had not been able to look away. Mesmerized by the sheer, masculine beauty of the stranger, she had felt her lower lip with her tongue and experienced a rush of heat in the secret, female heart of her body. Almost reluctantly, she'd pulled her gaze to the thighs that framed his manhood, well shaped and bulging with strength. His calves were covered with fine dark curls.

Mara's eyes had traveled upward once again—up to the impossibly handsome face where she had been momentarily captured, mired, in eyes of brown velvet, deep, soft, and rich. Those eyes had devoured her as hungrily as she devoured him.

She'd watched him drink in the sight of her, felt the warmth of his gaze. Her breasts tingled. There was a sudden dampness between her legs. Her eyes had been drawn once more to his tantalizing manhood, and lightning flickered through her limbs as it moved slightly, growing . . .

Mara had regained her senses then, as suddenly as if she had been doused in cold water. She'd bounded away like a startled deer, a hind who had unexpectedly encountered the great gray wolf. She had run, bolted, fled as if fire burned at her heels. Somewhere along the way Trey had caught up with her and bounded playfully at her side. As the dog seemed to sense no menace, she had stopped to pull on her clothes, hands shaking, breath hitching in her throat.

Then on again she went, running, running, until she

was safe within the castle walls, safe within her room.

Safe from any who might wish to harm her.

But never again would she be safe from the image of the man who, in one burning moment, had seared himself into her soul.

For perhaps the first time in his life, Jack was totally at a loss. Stephen's behavior was totally inexplicable. After mere moments at the lake, he had returned. His skin was dry, his hair still dusty. And there was the most unusual expression on his face.

Stephen glanced once over his shoulder, in the direction of the lake, brow furrowed in puzzlement, and asked: "Did you . . . Did you see anything?"

See what? But without further elucidation, Stephen turned and disappeared once again into the trees. He returned minutes later with his peculiar expression unchanged.

Jack pressed for an explanation, but Stephen remained silent, almost as if in a trance. The knight dressed, slowly and thoughtfully, then mounted. Soon they were on their way again.

But what had *happened*?

Jack fidgeted in his saddle. He was not fond of long silences and had absolutely no patience for mysteries. In all the long years he had known and happily served his baron, neither of those situations had ever been a problem. Until now. He couldn't stand it any longer. He cleared his throat.

Stephen took no notice.

Jack tried again. "My lord baron. Ahem. Are you there? I wonder if I might have a word with you."

Stephen at last rewarded his servant with a distracted glance. Jack swiftly took advantage of it.

"You must tell me what you've seen, lord," he demanded in a tone he would not ordinarily dream of using. "I cannot help you if I do not know the facts, and as you most obviously need help, you must tell me at once what has affected you so. What happened? What did you *see*?"

His master's gaze returned to his distant vision, and Jack feared he had lost him. But then Stephen spoke.

"A goddess," he whispered. "I've seen a goddess."

Jack was momentarily nonplussed. "A . . . a what?"

"A goddess. She rose right up from the lake. Right in front of me. All cloaked in the most incredible hair, sort of the color of moonlight. Her eyes were . . . her eyes were like gems. And her form . . ."

Jack heard no more, for the memory of that magnificent body was Stephen's alone. Never, never would he forget it. When she had risen from the lake it was to stand nearly eye-to-eye with him, and he himself was tall among men. Her frame was large, heavily boned, yet beautifully balanced. Her breasts and hips were full and womanly, her waist small, her legs long and elegantly formed. He'd clearly been able to see the strength in them. Her amazing musculature was obvious.

Her femininity had been clear as well, her curves as generous as the muscles that corded beneath her pale white skin. His eyes had moved back to her face, the most beautiful face he had ever beheld, framed by the most incredible hair of a color he had never even imagined could exist.

And it was the same hue as the triangle between her thighs. That sight had left him quivering with the most overpowering desire he had ever felt. The vision of the woman from the lake had stunned him. Taken his breath away.

And then she was gone, running, swift as a forest creature, leaving him with a memory that would haunt him for the rest of his life.

Stephen held his stallion to as slow a pace as possible. He no longer had any desire whatever to reach his destination. Taking a bride would now be a very sorry affair, indeed. His heart had not exactly been in it in the first place. Since his vision at the lake, his heart would forever be in only one place. He would forever compare his wife, no matter how lovely she might prove to be, to the one matchless woman of whom he had just caught such a brief glimpse. The woman of the lake had been a woman to stir not only the senses, but the mind and heart as well. She'd been the kind of woman who would not be content to sit in her bower at the loom, but who would only be happy at a man's side, hunting and hawking with him, joining him as an equal. She was a true mate—a soul's mate.

No, he no longer looked forward to meeting his bride-to-be at all. There was only one love for him, he now knew, and she would burn in his memory forever.

Mara's pulse returned to normal. Whoever the stranger was, wherever he had come from, he was gone now. He could not affect her life, only her dreams. She eased herself onto the edge of her bed, then sprang up instantly at the knock at her door.

"Yes? Who is it?"

"May I come in, Mara?"

"Of course, Mother."

Lady Beatrice entered with her usual grace and dignity, the hem of her gray wool dress trailing on the ground. She noted the expression on her daughter's face but attributed it to events that were currently unfolding. Unfolding, suddenly, at a very rapid pace.

"Mara, are you sure you don't wish to eat? I could have Bridget bring you something before . . ."

The tone of her mother's voice caught Mara's full attention. "Before what? What is it, Mother?"

"We've had news." Beatrice touched her daughter's cheek, smoothed an errant tendril, and tucked it behind her ear. "Riders approach Ullswater. They bear the colors of Bellingham, and it is assumed it is the baron himself. Your father has gone out to greet him."

"I see." A pall seemed to settle on Mara's shoulders. She felt dull, weighted. "And this baron, he's . . . He's the one?"

"Yes, Mara," her mother replied evenly. "He's the one. We weren't certain when he would arrive, but it is a good sign he has come so quickly." She smiled gently. "He will be eager to meet you."

Mara's expression did not alter. Her gaze focused on something far away.

"Are you all right, daughter? Everything has happened rather swiftly, I know."

Mara summoned herself back from her distant place, put on a brave face, and took her mother's hands. "Of course I'm all right. Please don't worry about me."

Reassured, Beatrice returned the pressure of her daughter's fingers. "You're a good girl, Amarantha. You always have been. And I'm very proud of you." All at once, bright tears burned at the corners of her eyes. Before they could spill, she said: "Come. Come with me. I have something I want to give you."

Mara followed her mother into the next room and watched her kneel, stiffly, by the decorated wooden chest at the foot of her bed. Lady Beatrice opened it, and the fragrance of the herbs and dried flowers packed among the clothes wafted into the room.

"Here, my dear." Mara's mother unfolded an intricately embroidered chemise and draped it over her arm to display the workmanship. Dozens of tiny pink roses ran from the neckline down each flowing sleeve, then scattered in a seemingly random pattern across the skirt.

"It's . . . it's beautiful, Mother," Mara breathed. Although she had never had much time for finery, she genuinely admired the exquisite craftsmanship. "Is it for me?"

"Of course. And there's more. Here, look."

Lady Beatrice laid the shift on the bed and unfolded a tunic woven of soft wool of the same shade as the tiny pink buds of the chemise. The tunic would open down the sides to reveal the chemise's embroidery when worn over it. A head drape, along with a silver circlet to secure it, completed the set.

"Thank you, Mother," Mara whispered, and stroked the tunic's fine fabric. "Thank you."

"I'm just sorry that all this has happened so fast, my daughter. I haven't had time to do all I planned. You should have had a proper trousseau."

"Other things are far more important," Mara replied simply, honestly. "You've been good to me."

"Go on." Beatrice blinked back a new flood of tears. Turning her daughter toward the door, she added, "Go on and change into your new clothes. The lord baron will be here any moment—and you do wish to make a good first impression, don't you?"

Ranulf's first impression of Stephen, made over a year ago at a gathering of the northern barons, had been a good one. It was reinforced as he watched the young man dismount his imposing chestnut stallion.

"My lord baron," the young man called, and respectfully inclined his head. "I am Stephen of Bellingham. I came with haste, as you requested."

"And you have my gratitude," Ranulf replied.

Stephen motioned to the other rider. "This is my servant and loyal companion, Jack."

Directly upon the heels of his introduction, the smaller man vaulted from his saddle, landed on the ground at Ranulf's feet, and swept a courtly bow, plumed hat in hand.

Somewhat taken aback, Ranulf gestured for the pair to follow him to the hall. "If you will follow me, I make you welcome here."

"After you, kind sir," Stephen replied politely.

But as he trudged up the steps slowly in Ranulf's wake, making an effort to concentrate on his host's amiable banter, Stephen's mind was drawn, again and again, to the memory of the girl by the lake. He barely took note of his surroundings as they entered the great hall, barely noted the long, cavernous room was far more pleasant than most. Then he did see.

The windows were fitted with real glass; fine tapestries warmed the walls, and pitchers of wildflowers decorated each trestle table. At the head of the room, near the massive fireplace, stood several chairs. Stephen accepted his host's offer and sank into an elaborately carved armchair near the huge hearth. No fire burned at the moment, but none was needed.

"Once more I bid you welcome and extend to you every hospitality of Ullswater Castle," Ranulf said. "I also thank you again for being so prompt in your visit."

"We agreed this alliance would serve both our interests," Stephen answered his host. "I also know you would have this union made before the Cumbrian earl makes further issue. As I am a man of action, and no friend of the earl's, you find me at your doorstep."

He smiled at Ranulf without effort. He liked the man. He was sorry Ranulf's daughter would not now, or possibly ever, receive his full attention.

The Lord of Ullswater smiled back. "There are many matters we must needs discuss, Stephen. But the night is long, my ale is good, and your curiosity—I hope—is whetted. What say you we make the introductions without further ado?"

Stephen nodded. "I'd say you are a man of action like myself. Please. I look forward to meeting your lovely daughter."

Ranulf rose.

As if on cue, Lady Beatrice came through the door from their apartments. Mara trailed in her mother's wake, head bowed and eyes downcast. Her newly acquired rose-colored kerchief concealed her shining hair, and her hands were folded demurely at her narrow waist, clasped tightly by a silver girdle. She approached her father's chair without looking up, heart in her throat.

"Baron Stephen," Ranulf began, "I take great pleasure in introducing my daughter, Amarantha. Mara, meet your bridegroom, the baron, Lord Stephen of Bellingham."

Mara felt as if a great weight pressed upon her back and shoulders. It was an effort to lift her head, but slowly, slowly, she raised her eyes.

Chapter Nine

Beatrice unconsciously held her breath as her daughter raised her gaze to the man who would be her husband. She remembered clearly the moment she had first looked into the eyes of her own husband-to-be. There had been magic between them at once, a rare and wondrous connection. She dared not even hope for such a miracle to be visited upon her family twice in one lifetime, merely prayed the couple would find each other pleasant, at the least. A good first impression was so much easier to build upon than an unfortunate one.

The moment stretched, and Beatrice found herself growing increasingly uncomfortable. Why did neither of them speak? She watched her daughter's eyes widen, as if with shock, then glanced at Stephen to see his jaw drop. What was the matter with the two of them? Totally bewildered, she looked to her husband. Ranulf appeared equally perplexed.

"Mara?" Beatrice tentatively touched her daughter's arm. "Mara, are you all right?"

The sound of her mother's voice came as if from a great distance. Mara was unable to understand the words; she could only stare at the man who stood before her. The man she had thought never to see again. The one she knew she could never have, yet wanted so much.

The man who stood before her now, miraculously the one she was going to wed.

Here was the man with whom she had just shared the single most intimate moment of her life: The two of them as naked as the day they'd been born, nearly touching, eye-to-eye, breast to breast. What was she going to say to her parents? How was she going to explain how they'd met?

Mara was not the fainting kind. She had never done so and would have scoffed at anyone who suggested the possibility. Yet she suddenly found herself short of breath, dizzy. So dizzy she felt herself sway.

"Mara!" Beatrice cried. Her daughter had gone from a crimson flush to a waxen pallor in mere seconds. Now the girl appeared unsteady on her feet, as if she might faint. "Ranulf, help me. Take Mara's arm."

Ranulf reacted quickly, having watched his child with the same growing alarm. He caught his daughter in his arms and wondered, with guilt and dismay, if the stress of the betrothal had indeed caused in her some sudden illness.

Stephen watched with increasing unease. The shock of seeing her again—his goddess, his vision from the lake—nearly overwhelmed him. When she had raised her head at last and he had looked once more into her incredibly blue eyes, when he recognized her, he had been so stunned it seemed his heart would halt in his breast.

It was clear her reaction was similar. But was it from the simple shock of recognition, or was she horrified? Had their intimate encounter so frightened and embarrassed this woman that she would never be able to look on him as a wife must a husband?

Both Ranulf and Beatrice turned when they heard him groan.

"Good God," the lord of Ullswater rumbled, still supporting his daughter. "Now there's something wrong with the both of them. Help me, Beatrice!"

His wife found herself again with Mara as her husband turned to their guest.

"Sit down, lad," he ordered. "Sit. Bridget!" he called to the wide-eyed serving girl. "Fetch some ale. And be sharp about it!"

"I'm . . . I'm all right," Stephen managed. But he took the seat his host indicated.

"As I am," Mara echoed, extricating herself from her mother's embrace. "I—I just felt a bit dizzy for a moment."

"Perhaps you should come and lie down, rest awhile," Beatrice suggested in an undertone. "I know this is most stressful for—"

"No!" Mara shook her head. If she left them alone, what might Stephen say? Would he confess to their lakeside meeting? "No, I . . . I'll stay. I'm fine. In truth."

"Well, then sit and have a cup of ale," her father directed gruffly, still worried that the introduction was a terrible failure.

Mara sank gratefully into a seat near Stephen. When Bridget handed her a goblet, she raised it to her lips.

Stephen did likewise. And seeing her beautiful eyes over the rim of her cup, staring at him, importuning him, pleading silently, his own eyes widened in response. He didn't understand.

Mara set her cup on the table and, seeing her parents distracted, looked Stephen straight in the eye. She gave a swift but firm shake of her head.

Comprehension was instantaneous, and the flood of relief that washed through him was a tangible warmth in Stephen's veins. It was not him she feared, but the exposure of their secret.

He understood; she knew it. Their secret was safe. Her parents would never have to know. It would be between them, only them, forever.

It was also a bond, a beginning. A start with the man who would be at her side for the rest of her life, this most incredible man she had ever laid eyes upon.

The smile started in her eyes. Stephen saw the sparkle. Mara lifted her cup again, but the motion could not disguise the curve of her lips. When she returned the goblet to the table, the smile effervesced into laughter. She raised a hand to her mouth, but the young woman couldn't hide it, was unable to stifle it.

He was infected instantly. She was so lovely, so breathtakingly gorgeous. He had thought he might have to spend the rest of his life yearning for an ethereal vision he could never have—yet here she was, the woman he was to marry. And the incident by the water was not, after all, cause for fear and humiliation, but a secret bond between them. He responded to her mirth with a sudden and hearty laugh of his own.

"Look," Ranulf muttered to his wife. "What's the matter with them? One minute they're gaping at each other, Mara's in a swoon, and now . . ." He gestured helplessly at the couple seated before the hearth, shoulders shaking with laughter. "Now they're laughing? I don't understand, Beatrice." The old baron's arms fell back to his sides. "I don't understand at all."

Neither did Beatrice. Not completely. But she had a good idea, and it filled her heart so full her eyes brimmed. "Come, husband," she said quietly, laying a hand on his arm. "Let us leave them alone for a while to talk and get to know one another."

"Do you really think that's a wise idea, wife?" he asked. "Mara might be ill. You saw her. I'm not sure about this any longer. I—"

"Ssshhh, husband." Beatrice put a finger to his lips. "Mara will be fine, I promise you. Now, come. Come and sit with me for a while. Talk to me about the day *we* first met. Do you remember?"

"Of course I remember."

"Good." Beatrice took her husband's arm and guided him from the hall. "Then we'll talk about the past. And the future." She glanced once over her shoulder at her daughter and the man who would be her husband.

Yes, she sighed to herself. The future.

Mara waited until she was certain her parents had departed. "Thank you," she whispered.

The sound of her voice was so soft, so low, so enticing. Stephen leaned nearer and caught her scent, the faintest fragrance of dried rose petals. She obviously did not disdain the habit of personal cleanliness, as did many of their time. It reminded Stephen that his own bath that morning had been aborted. He was probably as rank as a ram in rut. Afraid to offend, he sank back in his chair.

Had she said something wrong? Mara's smile faded.

Stephen noted her expression, recalled her words, and found his tongue at last. "You're . . . you're welcome," he stammered. "If you mean for keeping our . . . secret. But I must apologize. I— After I saw you, I didn't . . . I mean, I know I must stink to high heaven," he finished lamely.

"That's what you were doing down by the lake!" Mara realized. Her smile returned. So, they had that in common, too. "You'd gone to swim, as I had."

Stephen nodded. "After I saw you, I must confess, I forgot all about it. I simply got on my horse again and rode here—thinking all the while that no matter what my future bride looked like, she would never be . . ."

He shut his mouth, appalled by what he had been about to say. But Mara's smile widened.

"I, too," she confessed quietly. "I ran all the way home thinking the very same thing. That my husband-to-be would never look as you. He might be ugly—"

"Oh, yes!" Stephen interrupted with a chuckle. "I

feared that also. That you might have a . . ."

He stopped again, but this time they both laughed. They laughed until they noticed they had caught the servants' attention. Mara put a hand over her mouth, and Stephen cleared his throat.

"I . . . Your father's castle is most impressive," he said at length, his tone sober for eavesdropping ears. "My own was built by a Norman lord and differs greatly. I would be pleased if you'd show me the grounds."

"It would be my pleasure," Mara replied. She longed to be away from this hall, to walk with this man and talk with him where others might not hear. "Come."

He followed her, newly amazed by her grace. For such a tall woman, she moved as gracefully as a doe.

Mara blinked in the bright sunlight outside. Arm in arm, they walked down the manor steps.

"So your castle is Norman," she began hesitantly. "I've seen only English manors."

"The architecture differs, of course. Also, the French style does not encompass all these outbuildings." Stephen stopped to gesture around him. "But my mother loved our home. She was Norman, and the land passed to her through her father. My name, in fact—the one she gave me—was *Stefan*." He used the foreign pronunciation. "It was my father who preferred the English version."

"Truly? My mother also is of Norman blood. Her name was Beatrix," Mara explained, herself using the French inflection. "But my father preferred to Anglicize it."

"It seems we have much in common."

Mara hated the blush that rose to stain her cheeks, but she could not prevent it—just as she could not stop the trembling in her knees. He was so close, and his nearness was nearly overpowering. He was so tall, broad, and masculine. The way his hair lifted off those muscular shoulders in a passing breeze—Mara had to move away.

"We . . . we have other things in common, I'll warrant,"

she said in a desperate attempt to hide her nervousness.

"For instance?"

"Like . . ." Mara bit her tongue. She hadn't meant to tell him, to perhaps alter his good opinion of her, but she found herself trapped. They were passing the mews, and she indicated the low stone building. "Like hawking, for instance," she blurted. "My father has many fine birds, and I—"

"You like to hawk?" He hadn't meant to interrupt, but Stephen was amazed.

"Yes, I—I must admit." Mara halted, arms hanging limply at her sides. Her gaze was downcast.

She had shocked him, she knew. He had discovered she was not the lady wife he had undoubtedly envisioned. "I confess I love to hawk. And hunt," she added honestly. She might as well get it all over with at once. "And I love to ride."

She lifted her eyes, her expression almost defiant. If he was going to be done with her, she might as well give him as many good reasons as possible. "My only quarrel with riding is that my father insists I ride a palfrey when I would much prefer a stallion. I should ride a charger, like a man. A stallion is a *true* mount."

Stephen felt his jaw drop. Could it be true? Was it possible? Was this actually the woman he had dreamed of but had known could never exist? Was this unbelievably gorgeous creature also, possibly, the soul mate who had previously lived only in his fantasies?

It was true, Mara thought miserably. She had done it. The heat of her unguarded tongue had scalded her once again. What must he think?

Sadly, she turned away. Stephen caught her arm.

"Wait! I . . . Is something wrong?"

She boldly looked Stephen in the eye. There was nothing more to lose. "I fear I should ask of you the same. I know none of these pursuits are ladylike. I have offended you. I doubt it not, that I have changed your good opinion of me. If you had one to begin with, that is."

Stephen shook his head slowly, with wonder. "Oh, my lady." He sighed. "You have no idea the opinion I hold of you. We have only just met, yet. . . ." Could he say it? Dared he speak what already he felt in his heart?

She had been honest with *him*.

"My opinion, my regard, is of the highest degree," Stephen said finally. "I've never known anyone like you. Not only are you the most beautiful woman I've ever seen, but the most remarkable. I can tell you, truthfully, I never imagined someone like you might exist. A woman who could ride at a man's side, share his interests, his life, his . . ."

He had been about to say "passions," but he was afraid he had said too much already. The heat he felt rise to his face was an unattractive blush. He had never blushed in his life!

The smile on Mara's face, however, reassured him.

"I—I apologize," Stephen stammered. I didn't mean to—"

"No. Don't." Mara's fingers longed to touch his lips, stay his words. But she knew to touch him would overwhelm her entirely. "Never apologize," she whispered, and she cast her glance away from him, embarrassed by her sudden and incomprehensible tears. "My lord . . ."

Neither noticed Jack and Trey, who had followed them as far as the bottom of the manor steps. The little man now sat on the bottom stair, elbows on his knees, chin on his hands. The huge dog sat beside him and nudged his shoulder.

Jack's hand strayed to the animal's massive head and idly scratched the shaggy ears. "Looks like you and I may have just lost our best friends, old boy," he murmured.

The dog whined, and the man patted him.

On the other side of the courtyard, Stephen and Mara slowly resumed their walk.

Chapter Ten

It seemed it was going to be a rainy spring. For the third time that week, the afternoon sky opened with a rumble of thunder. The new-leafed trees and neatly manicured lawns were achingly green. Lightning flashed, and the air crackled with the peculiar smell of ozone. Stephen continued to stare out the living room window even when he heard his sister come into the room and walk up behind him. When she laid a hand on his shoulder, however, he covered it with one of his own.

"How's it going, Steve?" she inquired softly.

"Good. Good, I think."

"You went to see Millie again today, didn't you?"

Stephen nodded. He listened to his sister sigh.

"Is it . . . Is she helping?" she asked tentatively.

It was Stephen's turn to draw a deep breath. He let it out slowly and turned to face her. "I'm not sure what to tell you, Amanda," he confessed.

"I'm sorry, Steve," she replied quickly. "I didn't mean to pry."

"It's not that. It's not that at all." Stephen stood and walked over to the window. He stood so close his breath fogged the glass. His brow furrowed, and his hands found his hips. "It's just that I don't know how to explain what happens," he continued thoughtfully. "It's so strange. I go into a . . . a kind of trance, I guess."

"Do you remember anything? When you come out of it, I mean?"

"Yes. And no." Stephen's vision blurred as he watched individual raindrops streaking the glass. "I . . . I remember certain things. I retain memory of scenery, for instance. Or what I was wearing."

"Like what?" his sister asked impulsively.

"Like chain mail," Stephen said slowly.

"Chain mail! As in armor?"

"Yes. And I ride a huge horse."

"So, this . . . This really could be the same period as your dream? You could be visiting that lifetime?"

"I don't know, Mandy," he replied, frustrated. He turned at last to face her. "I just don't know. I don't recall many details, people, things that happen when I'm . . . when I'm wherever I go. I only know that I feel . . . well, *good,* I guess you could say. It feels *right* somehow. Like I belong there. Like I really belong."

"Do you—I'm not quite sure how to ask this." Amanda tapped a forefinger on her upper lip. "When you're in the other time—in your trance or whatever—do you have any connection to this lifetime at all? I mean, do you have awareness of going there from here?"

Stephen shook his head. "None at all. At least, I don't think so. From what I do recall, everything seems completely natural. I'm living my life, going about my business."

"And you said you feel good?"

"When I'm there, wherever 'there' is, yes. Yes, I do feel good."

"Then maybe this wasn't such a crazy idea after all,"

Amanda said. She was gratified to see her brother smile.

"No, Mandy. Maybe not." He walked over to her and brushed his lips against her forehead. "Thanks for not giving up on me."

"Never, baby brother." Amanda hugged him. "I know there's an answer to all this. A solution. I just know it."

Stephen hugged her back. He was starting to believe.

Chapter Eleven

The sky was blindingly blue. Scattered patches of high white clouds scudded overhead. Their shadows moved across the land as a lofty wind blew southward. A field of corn was in sunlight, then shadow; a flock of sheep moved in and out of the light, soaring clouds moving swiftly over the verdant meadow; a herd of cattle raised their heads as the sky darkened, and a moment later returned to their placid grazing in the light.

The earthbound winds were not steady as those aloft, but fitful and brisk. In the warm and brilliant sunshine, Mara felt the dampness of sweat start beneath her woolen tunic. Then the spring breeze rose to cool her flesh and whip errant tendrils of hair about her face and neck. Laughing, she pulled her palfrey to a halt.

Beside her on his stallion, Stephen raised his face to the wind. Perspiration trickled from his temples. His chain mail glittered brightly.

"It seems the day cannot make up its mind," Mara said. "First hot, then cool. Shadow and sunlight."

"Too much sunlight. Not enough shade." Her betrothed wiped his brow.

"Shall we make for the woods?"

Stephen turned in his saddle and glanced at Jack, who rode a discreet distance behind them. Mara's great gray dog flopped to the ground and panted mightily.

"I don't think Jack or Trey would be averse." He directed his attention to the long, downward slope of the hill in front of them, and the welcoming gloom of the forest beyond.

Without hesitation, Mara put her heels to her mare. "Race you!"

Stephen watched for a moment as he held his prancing, eager stallion on a tight rein. Mara amazed him. Everything about her delighted him; her wit, her charm, her forthright innocence and honesty. Now he watched her race her mare, riding as lightly and easily as a feather borne on the breeze. Her prowess on horseback was undeniable. He would win the race only because of his more powerful animal. With a grin, Stephen gave his mount its head.

Mara heard Stephen's charger pounding the ground behind her. In seconds she would be overtaken. She had no chance on her smaller, slower mare, but she would not give in without a fight.

Stephen almost caught the dappled palfrey. Had he reached out, he might have tangled his fingers in the strands of her flying tail. He would easily reach the forest first. But then something incredible happened, something he would not have believed if he had not seen it with his own eyes.

Mara crouched low on her horse's neck and eased herself forward over the front of her saddle. She transferred both reins to her right hand and, with her left, reached down to grab the buckle that secured the saddle's girth. It was a dangerous maneuver, but the equerry who had taught her to ride had been a thorough teacher.

Helen A. Rosburg

"If you're being pursued, lass," he had told her, "and flight is your only hope, you need every bit of speed you can muster. You'll need to give your mount every bit of advantage. Shed all the weight you can, girl, including your saddle."

The buckle was quickly unfastened. Clinging tightly to the mare's shoulders, high on her withers, Mara gave her saddle a shove. Stephen's stallion had to leap over the obstacle.

Mara lashed her mare's flanks with the ends of her reins. Free of the heavy saddle, the horse leapt ahead as she felt the smart slap. Her ears pinned, her nostrils flaring, the palfrey reached the shady edge of the forest a full length ahead of the chestnut stallion.

Breathless, Mara tugged on her reins. Stephen pulled up beside her, a crooked grin on his handsome mouth.

"You win," he conceded. "And if that wasn't the most remarkable feat I've ever seen, I'd call it cheating and demand a rematch."

"Cheating?" An outraged Jack appeared on his own lathered brown mare. "That was courtin' death!"

The nimble man slipped from his mount. He had retrieved Mara's saddle and carried it to her dappled palfrey. "I'll admit, my lady, that you're a wonder on a horse. But my hair's gray already and the only thing left for it to do is fall out. If you don't want your lord havin' a bald servant, please don't be doin' that sort o' thing again."

Stephen silently agreed with Jack. This girl was a risk-taker, no doubt of it, as competitive and courageous as any man. Perhaps more so. But the thought of something happening to her made the blood run cold in his veins.

"At the very least," he said, dismounting, "these animals could do with a nice, sedate walk."

Jack volunteered. "I'll take them, m'lord. You and the lady catch yer wind and follow along later."

"Thank you, Jack," Mara said with a wide smile.

The little man blushed as he took her palfrey's reins.

70

It was no wonder, he thought, that his young baron seemed already besotted. Not only was the young lady beautiful and brave—if somewhat foolhardy—she could probably charm fish out of a lake.

Mara watched Stephen's servant lead the horses away, thankful for his kindness. There wasn't much left of the day, and she wanted to draw out and savor every moment with Stephen she could. She gazed up at her betrothed, a smile in her eyes.

"That was quite a feat of horsemanship," he repeated dryly. "I suppose you're going to tell me next that you can defeat me at swordplay as well."

Mara blushed. "I doubt I could best you," she replied honestly. "But I might just hold my own against you."

Stephen felt his jaw drop. Although, he realized, he shouldn't be at all surprised by now. This was a woman of many wonders.

"What's wrong?" Mara asked, suddenly apprehensive.

"Nothing." Her fiancé shook his head. "I must say, however, that I am glad you are to be my wife, if only so I will never have to face so formidable a foe as you in battle."

Mara laughed. "Quite so, my lord. You will never have to face me over the point of a sword. But know that, should you ever need it, my sword will be at your back."

He didn't know why, but a sudden chill ran down Stephen's spine and something cold clutched his heart. To lighten the darkness that threatened to settle on his soul, he forced a laugh to his lips, pulled his sword from its sheath, and tossed it hilt first to his lady.

Mara caught the weapon easily, as if it had no weight at all, and balanced it in her hand. "My arm for you, Lord Baron. And my life."

She had meant the comment, and the moment, to be lighthearted, and was dismayed by the expression on Stephen's face. She lowered the sword, and he took it from her.

"No," Stephen murmured as he resheathed his weapon. "Rather, my life for yours, lady. Always and forever, my life for yours."

The moment shuddered between them. It was only a moment, seconds, yet it seemed to last a lifetime. Mara felt her heart beat to a rhythm that surely matched Stephen's own. They were one—she felt it. Knew it.

And then the instant was done. Over. They were released from its spell.

Together, as one, Mara and Stephen set off on a faint path through the trees, headed back toward the castle. Trey plodded behind, too tired to chase the squirrels that chittered angrily at him from overhanging branches. The two walked in silence for a while, the only sounds around them the squirrels, the occasional scrape of a branch as they passed, and the crunch of their footsteps on the littered forest floor. From time to time, Mara glanced at the man beside her from the corner of her eye and was filled with the wonder of the remarkable day they had just passed.

Following their intimate moments in the courtyard, Mara had been overcome with shyness. She could hardly believe she had just told Stephen he must never apologize to her. She was not even sure *why* she had said it. Nor had she been prepared for the impact of his response.

"You are right," he'd said, softly but firmly. "I should not have to apologize to the woman who will ride at my side for the remainder of our lives. For I shall never do anything to harm you, anything to require apology."

Mara had felt scalding tears rush to her eyes. When she had dared to look up at him at last, she noticed that Stephen's eyes glistened as well. They'd held each other's gaze for a long, lingering moment, and she could not help feeling a pact had been made. A bond had been forged. He was her lord; she was his lady. He would keep her unto him, safe, for always.

It was Trey who had brought the moment to its inevitable end. He caught sight of a butterfly and began pursuit. He had leapt straight at Mara and Stephen, eyes upward on the fluttering insect.

Jack shouted in the nick of the time, and Stephen grabbed Mara and pulled her to one side. Trey crashed past and ran into the side of the stable. The butterfly flitted over the castle wall and flew away. It was once they had been able to stop laughing that they had decided to come on this ride.

Mara had changed into a dark blue tunic and leggings, her usual riding costume. With Jack and Trey as chaperones, she and Stephen had set off on a tour of her father's vast estate.

Long slow lopes across green fields and meadows had been interspersed with quiet walks past the grazing livestock, and around great stands of trees planted as windbreaks. They had talked companionably for hours, about horses, dogs, hawking, and hunting. She told Stephen of her childhood, how she had learned to ride a pony before she could even walk, and how she had wielded a wooden sword from its broad little back. The pony had been her destrier, and she was a knight, brave and true. She even admitted to Stephen her great and eternal disappointment in having been born a female.

"And now?" he had gently inquired, looking down into her eyes.

"Now I bless the kindly Fates that made me what I am and led me to where I stand at this instant in time," she had whispered. And she had meant it. For the very first time in her life, she thanked God He had not made her the man she had so often wished.

Stephen, too, had shared his past, his boyhood. He had confessed his loneliness, despite so many male companions, his longing for the mother he had never known. He'd told her of the love he bore his father and the grief he had suffered at the man's passing.

Eventually, it seemed they had known each other all their lives. Mara even told Stephen of her recent encounter with Baldwin.

He had reined his horse to a halt, expression dark. "I like this not," he said tersely. "The Earl of Cumbria is a dangerous man."

"I agree. But my father does not think he will make a move against us. Ullswater is impregnable, my father's strength renowned, and King Henry's laws strict."

Stephen had nodded slowly, hesitantly. "But our good Henry has his hands full with Simon de Montfort. Surely you know this."

"I know Montfort has become the leader of the king's opposition. But the barons are not behind him. What strength has Montfort without them?"

"The arm and will of the people," Stephen replied. "There may yet be civil war. Distracted, Henry may not keep a stern eye on his barons."

Mara had smiled, unwilling to think of Baldwin any longer on such a beautiful, perfect day—the most momentous, perhaps, of her life. "Trust that my father will keep me safe. Trust also that Baldwin is too great a coward to make good any threats, king's justice or no," she had finished dismissively.

Stephen had reluctantly fallen in beside Mara, and she'd urged her mare into a jog. Moments later, she had remarked on the heat of the day and the race ensued. Now Mara wished only for the lightness of their mood, and the peaceful beauty of the day, to continue.

She looked over at Stephen, who walked at her side in the dappled shade of the forest, hands clasped behind him. "So, did I acquit myself?" she asked lightly.

"Acquit yourself?" Stephen stopped, a puzzled expression creasing his face.

"You know, riding."

His slow smile blossomed into a grin. "Let me only say this, my lady: I am simply glad that it is as you say, I will never have to cross swords with you but have you at my back instead."

Mara laughed, and the sound washed over him like the warm and welcome mist of summer rain.

They resumed their walk beneath the leafy canopy, and Stephen caught himself wondering anew at Mara's beauty. Pale yellow beams of daylight pierced the densely woven branches above and fell upon her hair, paler as it was than daffodils. He stopped and shook his head with amazement.

"Is anything wrong, Stephen?"

"On the contrary. Everything is right. So right it almost scares me."

"Yes, I know," she replied softly. "But I also know, for a certainty, that nothing will ever scare me again." She looked away from Stephen for a moment, but when she returned her gaze to him, Mara's eyes sparkled with humor. "Nothing will frighten me anymore, that is, except running into a naked man by the side of the lake."

"I *did* frighten you then," Stephen exclaimed, dismayed. "I'm sorry, I didn't mean to. I—"

"No, no—you didn't frighten me at all," Mara interrupted, eyes still alight. "You startled me. You can surely understand why. But even as I ran, my only fear was that I would never lay eyes on you again."

Once again her forthrightness rocked him. Here was no coy, demure maid who would hide the secrets of her heart. There was no guile in her. In truth, he felt the secrets of Mara's heart, her very soul, already lay open to him. It was a trust he cherished, and he returned the gift.

"It was as you say for myself also," Stephen admitted. "When you ran, I thought I would never see you again. Not knowing it was you who awaited me, I no longer wished to ride to Ullswater to meet my bride. I knew I should forever find her wanting, for no woman might ever match you."

Mara had meant for the mood to remain light, but once again these sincere admissions were stunning. What had she done in her life, she wondered, to deserve such a man, such a mate as this?

Not wanting him to see the tears that blurred her vision, Mara turned and continued along the forest path. Stephen fell into step beside her.

They walked in silence for a time. Trey, recovered, trotted behind them, bounding away occasionally to pursue a squirrel. Jack had followed and trailed at a distance, leading their mounts, his footsteps nearly soundless in the forest's moldering, leafy carpet. The woodland peace fell upon them all.

Mara luxuriated in another glance at the man beside her. The dappled shadows softened the hard planes of his face. Light and dark, light and dark, sunlight and shadow moved over him as they walked. The fitful breeze lifted his blue-black hair from his mail-clad shoulders. Mara watched and marveled, fascinated by the tilt of his head as he bent to avoid a branch, the reach of his hand to pull another from her path.

Feeling her gaze at last, Stephen smiled. Mara's lips curved in response.

"Tell me something," he asked abruptly, "did you really mean it?"

"I always mean what I say. At least when I say it. There's always the chance I'll change my mind later."

Stephen's lips twitched in amusement. Everything she said enchanted him. "So you mean you might change your mind about hawking. You said you loved hawking."

"I love many things." She laughed. "But I don't think I'll change my mind about hawking. I enjoy it more than most pastimes."

"Such as embroidery?"

"Especially embroidery!"

Stephen laughed, too. Mara saw his teeth were very white and even. "So you will not be content to sit in your

76

bower and await my return from the hunt?" he teased.

"No, I will not. I'll return to my father at once. Unless, of course, you take me hunting with you."

Stephen bowed with mock courtliness. "As my lady desires."

"And I do so desire."

They looked long at one another, wondering at the kindly fate that had brought them together.

"All this talk of hunting and hawking," Mara said at length. "Did I tell you I can also throw a dagger with accuracy, wield a broadsword as you have already seen, and handle a crossbow?"

Stephen chuckled again. "As I've said before, thank heaven I will be your ally, not your enemy."

How she loved the sound of his amusement. Golden lights shone in his dark eyes, and she found herself longing to touch the crinkles at the corners that appeared when he smiled.

A jay scolded suddenly from the branches above, and Trey barked loudly. The spell was shattered, and Mara felt in its place an odd unease.

Perhaps it was because the sunlight barely touched the tops of the trees any longer. In minutes it would be gone beyond the distant hills. The breeze had turned chill.

Something was wrong. Stephen sensed it, would have known even had he not seen the barely perceptible narrowing of Mara's eyes. "What's wrong, Mara?"

She shook her head, not because she did not wish to tell him, but because she did not know. She shrugged. "I don't know. I'm not sure. Maybe I only fear this day's end. And our . . . Separation on the morrow."

"I'll not be gone long, Mara. I swear it. If there were not things I must do in order for us to wed, I would not go at all. You know that." Then another thought occurred to him, and his brow furrowed. "Or is it Baldwin who does, indeed, concern you? If it is, believe me, I will—"

"No, no. Baldwin doesn't frighten me. I've told you."

Mara appeared as confident as before, but Stephen was not so certain. The earl was a vindictive man. He would neither forgive nor forget his humiliation at this young woman's hands. And, as he had warned, the king had his eye elsewhere.

Their separation would not be long, however, as he had promised. In the meantime, Ranulf had assured him he would be at his most vigilant. The mighty gates would be locked, the walls manned night and day. Preparations that had not been seen in a long time were already under way at Ullswater castle.

Seeing the lines of worry form on Stephen's smooth, high brow, Mara found herself longing to reach out and touch him, to soothe away his trouble. But she feared the intimacy of the touch, was afraid her hand might linger, trace the curve of his cheekbones, the lines that parenthesized his mouth. That mouth smiled at her now.

"Just be careful while I'm gone," he admonished her. "No more early morning swims."

The simple mention of their morning's beginning brought a stain to Mara's cheeks. But the boldness of her gaze belied the flush. "Not without you," she replied frankly.

Her ingenuousness, lack of affectation or pose, her totally guileless sensuality, nearly overpowered Stephen. He was forced to swiftly banish the memory of her by the lake, when she had risen, dripping, clothed only in her silvery hair.

The urge to crush her in his arms and devour her lips was almost beyond the remains of his failing self-control. But he could not. Would not. He must not do anything that might damage the fragile bond they had forged between them. It was far, far too precious.

No, he would court her slowly, carefully, Stephen vowed. And he clenched the hands that had nearly reached for her. He did not want to compromise the untouched purity of her lips with his kiss until he had made her his bride.

"Your word," he said at last, his voice husky. "Give me your word. Promise me also you will go nowhere without *him*." Stephen nodded at Trey, who sat nearby, tongue lolling.

Mara chuckled, relieved her betrothed had finally spoken. "I never do go anywhere without *him*."

"Good. Then I shall only have to worry half as much."

The calm of the forest enfolded them once more. The only sound to accompany Trey's panting breath was the faint, high twittering of birds settling in for the night.

The sun neared its setting. The cool of evening had banished the last traces of its yellow warmth. It was time to return to Ranulf's hall. Stephen quirked an eyebrow. "We must return, my lady. The hour grows late."

Mara glanced about, as if surprised by the sun's absence and the gloom of twilight under the trees. "I suppose we should," she admitted reluctantly. "My father plans modest festivities in the hall tonight."

"To celebrate our betrothal."

"Yes. Our betrothal."

Only an owl noted their passing. It hooted mournfully to the falling night.

Chapter Twelve

Millie Thurman was concerned. This case had been different from the first. She had never before had a client who had suffered for so long, or who had experienced absolutely no relief whatsoever from the medical community. Although she believed that current-life problems were often rooted in past-life traumas, she did not always like to take on such difficult cases. It had been her policy, for instance, only to take on clients who were spiritually inclined as she was, and who believed in reincarnation. By his own admission, Stephen was a skeptic.

Yet Millie had known Amanda for several years. She knew the family in general was stable, apparently grounded and well adjusted. That was why, in spite of Stephen's skepticism, she had agreed to attempt a regression. She had not expected him to go back so readily, so easily, or to become so totally immersed in the life he visited. She had never had a client quite like him. There were other differences as well.

Almost all her other clients narrated what they experienced; they told her time, place, and what was going on at the moment. Stephen did not speak at all. He withdrew to his other world and appeared to be living in that time and place, oblivious of the present. He spoke to the people who inhabited his past life, although she scarcely understood what he said. His words were mumbled, and from what she was able to comprehend, he spoke with a thick accent in a dialect she could only guess was medieval English.

There was also the dream to consider. Millie had heard the details of it, which were not remarkable in themselves. She had heard of other recurring dreams similar to this. Stephen could be reexperiencing a past-life trauma, or simply a nightmare conjured from the depths of his own imagination. If the event was from a past life, however, she worried about how he would cope with it when—or if—he reached that point in his regression. Everything else so far had been so unusual, so unpredictable. How was he going to react to the event itself? Would he be able to resolve the conflict, the tragedy, and go on with his life? Or might something happen that was not within Millie's scope?

Using tried and true relaxation techniques, Millie calmed her mind and focused her attention on her client. He appeared to be in deep conversation with someone. As usual, it was almost impossible to understand what he was saying. At one point he seemed agitated, and Millie was tempted to bring him out of the regression ahead of time. But his serenity returned; he appeared, in fact, almost blissful.

The apparent end of Stephen's conversation coincided with the end of Millie's allotted time period. Millie cleared her throat.

"When I count to three, Stephen, you will awake feeling refreshed and rested. One, two, three."

A prick of apprehension nipped at the base of Millie's spine. Stephen didn't respond. She repeated her command, a little louder. Stephen's eyes fluttered open, and he smiled at her.

"How do you feel?" Millie asked.

"Wonderful," the man replied. "I feel wonderful. Did I say anything this time—that you could understand, I mean?"

"It was largely incomprehensible, as before. Do you recall anything, anything at all?"

Stephen's brow furrowed. "It was a beautiful day. I was with someone I care about deeply. I . . ." His face went slack. The creases in his brow disappeared. Then the corners of his mouth turned down.

"What is it, Stephen?" Millie asked. "Is there something that distresses you?"

"I . . . I made a promise," he stammered. "I made a promise to someone. I have to keep that promise, Millie! I have to keep her safe! I—"

"Deep breaths, Stephen," Millie said evenly. "I want you to concentrate on taking three very deep breaths. That's it. That's good. One more."

Stephen felt relaxation flow through him. The tattered remnants of his disturbing memory blew away. He felt good again, better than he had in years. He smiled again at Millie. "I'm fine. I'm fine. I can't believe how much better I feel." He moved to the edge of his seat. "Same time tomorrow?"

Millie hesitated. "Stephen, I . . . I'm not sure we should go on with this," she said finally.

"But why?" A fear so sharp it was physically painful stabbed Stephen's chest. "Why, when I'm getting better?"

He was getting better, it was true. Amanda had said the change in him was remarkable.

"Please, Millie," Stephen begged. "We can't stop now. Not when I'm headed in the right direction."

Was he headed in the right direction? That's where the problem lay. Millie didn't know. She had never experienced anything like this.

Outwardly, however, the man was definitely improved. Isn't that what everyone wanted? How could she turn him away now? What would happen, moreover, if she did?

"All right, Stephen. We'll continue. But only as long as you continue to improve and I think it's safe."

"Thank you, Millie. Thank you!" Stephen enveloped her in a bear hug, easily done as she was so tiny and he so tall. He picked her up off the floor and set her down again gently. "I'll continue to improve, I promise. We're doing the right thing. I know it. I know it with every fiber of my being."

"I hope so," Millie murmured. As she watched Stephen hurry to the front door she added, "With every fiber of *my* being, I hope so."

Chapter Thirteen

Maggie had lain awake long before the first pale rays of dawn had lightened the sky beyond the tower window. She lay very still, knowing the slightest movement would waken the man who slumbered noisily at her side. Awake, depending on his mood, he would either reach for her roughly or send her back to the kitchen with a curse and a slap, perhaps a kick. She sighed softly and closed her only eye.

She didn't mind. Not really. To be able to sleep in this wonderfully soft bed with its linens and furs was eminently preferable to the stone floor in a dank corner of the kitchen. She didn't even mind the brutal sex or occasional beating. She had long ago become inured to the cruelties of life. Her widowed mother, crazed with drink, had tried to stab her to death when Maggie was only four. She'd lost an eye in the attempt, as well as her mother. Reeling through their hovel, bloody knife poised, looking for the terrified child who had gone into hiding, the addled woman had stumbled into the fireplace. She had been too drunk to get up.

Maggie had been too horror-stricken, too wounded, and still too fearful of her own life to go to her aid. Her mother had roasted alive.

The stench had been the worst part, worse even than the screams. When a kindly cook had taken her in to work in the earl's kitchens, Maggie had feared to relive that hideously sweet odor each time a haunch of meat was spitted in the massive hearth. The odors were not the same, however, and over time she had lost her fear.

She had lost her dreams as well—if she'd ever had any. There was only day after day of endless drudgery in those dim and grimy kitchens, a few scraps to eat, and a corner in which to sleep. Maggie had clothed herself in rags and attempted to keep the tangles from her long, dark hair with a bit of thorny branch. She had become used to the sobriquet One-Eyed Maggie, and in her wildest imaginings never envisioned herself in a man's bed.

Then, one day when Maggie was eleven, one of the table servants had abruptly dropped dead at a most inconvenient time. Dinner had been laid in the hall, and all knew the earl's temper if it was not served in a timely manner.

"Pick up that platter!" the frantic cook had directed. "Make yourself useful. Serve the earl first and be quick about it."

She had been so afraid, Maggie's eye had remained downcast the entire time she had stood at the nobleman's side. Holding the tray with trembling hands, she had not seen his prominent and watery eyes appraise her, or the grim smile on his thin mouth. Maggie had been astounded, therefore, when she was summoned to the earl's sleeping chamber high in the dungeon tower. She'd been even more amazed when she realized why she had been called; when his soft, pale, long-fingered hand had reached to tear the rags from her body. . . .

Dawn gave way to the full light of day, and still the earl slept at Maggie's side. It might be best, she thought, to slip away before he roused. Carefully, the girl rolled onto her side and propped herself on an elbow.

Her lord and master's countenance, she had to admit, was bleakly unattractive. But her own visage was not much to gaze upon either. It was her body, she knew, that was her greatest asset. Her breasts were heavy, her hips wide, and her flesh—because she was not yet twenty—still firm. Her form, no doubt, helped to keep the earl's interest and explained the taste he had developed for her in his bed. Maggie also suspected, however, he took a perverse satisfaction in having someone around who was uglier than he. That was all right.

What wasn't all right, and what was the reason Maggie ultimately decided to remain in his bed, was the talk she had heard lately of the earl taking a wife. She gazed once more at her slumbering lover.

A wife would change everything for Maggie. There'd be no more nights in this great bed. At least not at first—and not ever, if the lady took exception to her husband's philandering. Maggie would no longer have the privilege of finishing the scraps from the earl's fine meals.

The threat loomed large on Maggie's horizon. Her lord had talked quite a bit lately of taking a spouse. He had done more than merely talk; he had raved. Whoever the lady was, the one with the strange name vaguely similar to her own, Earl Baldwin seemed obsessed with her. Maggie was frightened.

As if he had read her mind—which Maggie sometimes suspected he was able to do—the earl's eyes opened. He was instantly and completely awake.

"What are you staring at?" he snapped.

"Nothing, m'lord. Wasn't lookin' at all. Was just admirin'." Maggie gave him her most winning smile. It worked.

The hard glare softened to a lascivious gleam. His hands roughly fondled her breasts. He pulled her down over him.

Maggie's smile never faltered.

The Circle of a Promise

*　　*　　*

The view from the tower was breathtaking, and that was the reason he preferred to have his quarters here rather than in the manor proper. Baldwin gloated each time he stood at the slitted windows and gazed over his domain. Everything was so neat, well manicured, and prosperous. Even the village was tidy and thriving—not one of those hodgepodge hamlets that sprawled about the strongholds of the lesser nobility and boasted only the meanest of trades, dirty little villages that eked out existence in subservience to some minor lord. No. Here was a veritable hub of commerce. His craftsmen were the finest. People came from all over to trade at the village of the Earl of Cumbria. Some came simply to gaze upon his magnificent castle.

Baldwin chuckled mirthlessly. No mean little fortress was this, crouched on a hilltop. No ugly fortifications, moats, or drawbridges. His keep had none of the trappings of those poor, weak little nobles who quarreled endlessly among themselves, who grabbed each other's lands, then retreated inside the safety of their ugly stone walls to await the consequences of their actions.

No, indeed. There was no such ill-favored architecture here. Only a great, grand manor built in the most modern style around a massive courtyard. Oh, there was a wall, surely. But only to keep out the riffraff who would beseech him incessantly for favors. He had no need for fortifications. His wealth was vast, his power entrenched.

Feeling momentarily beneficent, Baldwin turned to the woman who still lay upon the disarray of his bed, and he smiled. "You've been particularly attentive of late, Maggie." He inclined his head in his most gracious manner. "Even after all these years, you continue to amuse me. I am pleased with you. So pleased that I've decided to share something with you."

Not a flicker of emotion showed on Maggie's scarred features. Inwardly, however, she cringed. Baldwin often "shared" things with her—usually the subtle or overt cruelties he intended to inflict upon one of his numerous victims in repayment of some real or imagined slight. Sometimes, however, she herself was the recipient. She wondered which lay in store.

The earl did not make her wonder for long. "You well knew my intention to take a bride," he began jovially. "As you also knew, I had selected a most suitable candidate."

Baldwin paused to watch for the slightest reaction, the least trace of emotion, on Maggie's face. In his disappointment, his smiled faded.

"Her father, however, finds some . . . some northern *baron*," he spat, "preferable to myself." Clouds formed on his brow. Maggie shrank against the bed linens.

"As it happens, I have changed my mind about taking a wife. What do I need with a wife when I have you, my little one-eyed wench?"

This time she couldn't help it; Maggie blinked.

"Ah, I thought that might please you." The earl's scowl faded, and his smile returned. He crossed his arms over his skinny chest. It had been three days since the blond witch had humiliated him. Baldwin's temper had cooled, allowing him time to dwell more rationally on the perfect revenge.

"I should tell you though, Maggie," he continued. "I've decided it would be most pleasant to have, shall we say, a *change* from time to time? And the blond beauty, Ranulf's daughter, will do quite nicely, I believe."

Baldwin positively beamed at her. Maggie did not move a muscle.

"This is much better than marriage—don't you agree, my ragged little tart? After all, a wife would most probably banish you from my bed, if not from my hall altogether. You'll much prefer this arrangement. Won't you, my Maggie!"

She nodded slowly, as she was expected to do.

"Ranulf, of course, is not going to like this," the earl

88

went on in a businesslike tone. He turned his back on her and focused his gaze somewhere beyond the window. "So I have developed a plan. Brilliantly simple, really. And who's to stop me from carrying it out? The King?" He uttered a sharp, derisive bark of laughter. "I think not."

Baldwin steepled his fingers and touched them to the point of his chin. "Henry, our noble monarch, is currently occupied with his nemesis, Simon de Montfort. Most convenient, I must say. Oh, do remind me, Maggie dear, to wish Simon luck with his new nationalist party. Quite original, isn't it? 'England for the English,' is his motto I believe. In truth, his ploy is simply to rouse the little people against us. He has even accused us—the *nobility*—of pursuing a 'selfish class policy.' "

Baldwin laughed. "Well, of course we are!"

"Still, I'm grateful to the man. Although Henry will undoubtedly deplore my action, what is he going to do about it when all his time and attention is devoted to my good friend Simon? Not a great deal, I'll warrant. Not enough to worry me. No. All will go well," the earl said. "All will happen just as I've planned."

He strolled to the window and, when he turned back to Maggie, she saw a smile light his features even as the sun haloed his head. His grin was feral, and his yellowed teeth gleamed moistly. "No more of this dealing and bargaining," he snarled. "No more offers of land or wealth in exchange for a mere woman. No. I am simply going to take what I want. And what I want, Maggie, is everything."

His tone, as much as his skull-like visage, chilled her. Maggie pulled a fur up over her naked breast as a frisson of fear ran down her spine.

"Everything that belongs to Ranulf of Ullswater," the earl went on evenly. "His lands, his chattel, his daughter. His life."

89

Chapter Fourteen

Ullswater Castle had been built by Ranulf's father, a man
of great wealth, energy, and dreams. Though Ranulf was
his only surviving child out of seven, he had envisioned
founding a long line that would populate Ullswater for
generations to come. As a result, no cost had been spared
in the castle's construction. The manor was large, well
laid out, and it supported within its perimeter walls all
necessary services. Mara lifted her hem out of the dust
as she hurried behind her mother in an inspection of
one outbuilding after the next, and wondered how her
frail parent kept up the pace. She herself was exhausted.

Beatrice stopped abruptly and turned to her daughter.
"You recalled the workings of bake house and buttery.
Shall we visit the pantry and kitchens next? You must be
sure to remember what to lay in store, how to keep fresh
goods, as well as how to direct the cooks to prepare
them."

Mara took a deep breath—only because she was tired,
however, not because she was averse to her mother's sug-

gestion. Since meeting Stephen, she'd found herself taking genuine satisfaction in knowing the practical aspects of running a manor. She would always rather visit a litter of puppies in the kennels, or inspect a new hawk in the mews, but caring properly for a household; a husband; had taken on a more special meaning.

At the moment, however, what Mara really wanted was a long, cool drink of ale and a cool, damp cloth on the back of her neck. But she smiled gamely. "Whatever you think, Mother."

There was a smudge of dirt on Mara's cheek—probably from the brewery, where she had been so fascinated by the process of ale making she had pushed up the long sleeves of her tunic and assisted the ale master. Beatrice found herself smiling and shaking her head at her daughter.

"Actually, my dear, I think it's time to rest and take some refreshment. In the garden, perhaps? We've gone over a great deal this morning, and there is time enough later to attend to the remainder of our tasks."

Mara nodded gratefully and, arm in arm, she and her mother strolled from the dusty yard back to the welcoming shade of Lady Beatrice's garden.

The walled area, attached to the keep, ran its length and extended out to the parapets. Under Beatrice's care for many years, it was lush with flowers both domestic and wild; pink, white, and red roses, both in beds and climbing the stony walls; the harbingers of spring, bluebells, cowslips, tulips, and maggiellis; and even a small fruit orchard.

In the shade of a pear tree whose buds were ready to burst, a stone bench had been placed. Beatrice and Mara sat side by side on it and enjoyed for a few minutes the fragrant serenity of the retreat.

The loyal and ever-present Trey lay near his mistress's feet, forepaws extended, panting beneath the warmth of the midday sun. His eyes were half closed, and with each breath the dog's head moved a fraction closer to the ground. A bird sang from atop the wall, and from the stables came the distant whinny of a horse.

The peace of the day was a balm, a gift, a rare wine that flowed warm and smooth through the veins. Mara felt her own eyelids grow heavy.

Gently, Beatrice took her daughter's hand. "It's hard to believe you'll soon be leaving," she murmured. "I'm going to miss you, Mara."

"Mother, I—"

"Do not misunderstand," Beatrice said quickly. "I do not say this with sadness or regret. It is a simple statement of fact. Your father and I will miss you."

"As I will miss you," Mara whispered. There was nothing more to say. There was only a huge lump in her throat that made it nearly impossible to breathe, much less to speak. The prospect of leaving her home had become very real, all at once. She was not just going to be married; she was going to leave everything, everyone she had ever known, behind. Unexpected and unaccustomed tears rose to her eyes.

Misinterpreting the reason for the tears, Beatrice dropped her daughter's hand and put both arms around her shoulders. "Mara, dearest child, how well I understand your fears. But you and the baron have made a good beginning, have you not? You told me you have much in common."

Dismayed by her own tears, Mara dashed them away. "We do, yes," she replied swiftly. "There couldn't be anyone more . . . more kind or understanding than Stephen."

"I'm so glad to hear you say that, Mara. Because there are other aspects of marriage that require a very great deal in common if husband and wife are to be truly one."

Mara knew exactly what her mother referred to, and she felt a blush rise all the way to the roots of her hair. Since their meeting at the lake, she didn't think there would be any problem with the "other aspects" of her and Stephen's marriage, and she certainly did not wish to speak about it. Her mother was perceptive and might too easily access the realms of her secret heart.

"I think I understand," Mara replied at length. "Among many other things, Stephen is as well educated as I—even in Greek. He . . . he even knew the meaning of my name." Mara's gaze lost its focus as she went back to that moment in time.

Her betrothed had come to the hall shortly before dawn, from the gate tower where he and his odd little servant had spent the night, to take leave of her. His road was long, he had said, and his haste great. He had much to do to prepare for the wedding and its accompanying festivities, all of which would take place in Bellingham castle, his home. Further, he wanted to make well and truly certain the Scottish rebels had been put down.

"For, if I will not suffer insult or injury to the least of my people, how can I abide even the vaguest of threats to the greatest?"

Mara smiled at the memory of Stephen's words.

"When I am certain the rebels are crushed, then will I return to escort you and your parents to my lands in the north. My proximity to the Scottish border must in no way ever tempt them to come south again. I must know my bride will be safe."

The time of parting arrived. Her parents had drawn away to afford them a private moment. They would have been alone, however, had they been surrounded by an army of knights.

"I shall miss you," Stephen had murmured.

"And I you."

"I'll not be gone long. Sooner than you think I'll return for you and take you to Bellingham."

For our wedding, Mara thought silently. She'd feared a heated blush would roar to her cheeks, but it had not. She'd returned Stephen's gaze steadily, confidently.

"Mara. Amarantha," he had whispered then. "It's from the Greek, isn't it? It means immortal."

Mara nodded, delighted but not surprised by his knowledge.

"As our love is immortal, Amarantha," he had murmured, his dark gaze reaching so deeply into her own that it was as if she felt him touch the very wings of her soul.

He had almost reached to touch her then, but had stayed his errant hand. Soon enough Mara would know the power of his touch, the pressure of his lips. Soon the amazing man would be hers.

Soon.

He had left swiftly, with a final farewell to the lord and lady of the keep. Mara had watched him ride away on his great chestnut stallion, Jack trailing on his plump brown mare. Jack had waved his plumed hat once as they crossed the drawbridge.

Then Mara's father had ordered the gates closed, as he had promised Stephen he would keep them. Mara would be kept safe, safe from Baldwin, safe from any harm until Stephen returned to claim her. . . .

Beatrice watched her daughter's faraway gaze and decided there was really nothing more to say. Nothing of importance, certainly. Not compared to the message she had just read in her daughter's dreamy countenance.

So that is how it is, she thought. *As it was with Ranulf and me.*

Beatrice kissed her daughter lightly on the cheek and left the girl to be alone with the bud that was slowly and surely blooming in her heart.

The warmth and beauty of the cloudless day had helped to maintain Baldwin's unusually fine mood, although he was generally unaffected by weather of any kind. He had strolled his castle grounds leisurely, hands clasped behind his back, a faint smile curving his mouth. He knew such tours made everyone nervous, and he reveled in them. All applied themselves a bit more diligently to their labors when he made such rounds.

Truth be told, though, this time he had barely noticed the people he passed. His mind had been elsewhere, honing his scheme, planning for contingencies, anticipating the sweetness of revenge.

Now he was ready, and he went to his thronelike chair at the head of his hall and eyed the twenty knights who were his personal guard and the mainstay of the small army he could summon at will. The same smile he had worn all day remained with him, and he noticed more than one man fidget nervously. He chuckled inwardly. Outwardly, his expression was grim.

"Wulfric!" The earl's hard stare pinned a large man who stood near the back of the group. "And you and you." His nod appointed two others. "Set away your armor and find something . . . common to wear. Try to blend with the masses, if it's not too great a strain on your intellect to figure out how, and ride to Ullswater. Take small arms only. I want you to be inconspicuous. Do you understand?"

The three men nodded.

"Good." His quirky little smile reappeared, and Baldwin steepled his fingers. "Watch the castle and learn its routine. Note its strengths and weaknesses. Particularly its weaknesses. Have you got all that?"

Again the three men nodded.

"How unusual," Baldwin quipped. "Well?"

Three sets of brows rose in nearly perfect unison.

"Well . . . get on with it, you idiots!"

The earl slapped his palms down hard on the arms of his chair; his eyes bulged and there was a brief scramble for the door. The men who remained in the hall shuffled their feet edgily. Baldwin had never been known as the sanest of men, and his behavior of late had been more erratic than usual. When he began to giggle to himself, they exchanged glances and, one by one, slipped quietly away.

It was a long time before Baldwin even noticed he was alone.

Chapter Fifteen

Stephen awoke in a cold sweat. He threw back the covers and sat up, legs over the side of his bed. With his elbows on his knees, he buried his face in his hands. Unfashionably long, dark hair fell forward over his shoulders.

It wasn't the dream again. But what was it? What was wrong with him? He walked to the bathroom, ran the cold water, and splashed it on his face. He stared into the mirror.

A two-day stubble darkened his angular jaw. He hadn't felt like shaving. He hadn't felt like doing much of anything, as a matter of fact, except going to see Millie. Since he seemed to be improving, Amanda didn't mind. But was he still getting better? Stephen continued to stare into the mirror, as if mesmerized.

Within the past twenty-four hours something had changed, gone wrong. It wasn't like before, not that god-awful feeling of hopelessness and depression. It was more like . . . Anxiety, he supposed. Yes, that was it. Anxiety. Apprehension. Something was going to happen. Or, he *feared* something was going to happen. But what? And to whom?

The intensity of Stephen's stare into the mirror was so great his eyes burned. He hadn't even blinked. But his thoughts focused.

He had promised. As he had told Millie, he had promised to keep someone safe, someone he cared about very much. But he was worried now. Worried. Why?

Even though it was well after midnight, the urge to call Millie was almost overpowering. Stephen actually found himself looking for his robe so he could go down and use the phone in the kitchen.

But he couldn't do that. Millie was already having second thoughts about regressing him. He couldn't risk putting her off completely. It was too important to be able to keep going back.

Why?

And what was wrong?

Feet planted wide apart, Stephen stood in the middle of his room and pushed the heels of his hands into his eyes. He had to think, to remember. Amanda had told him once that people could actually regress themselves if they concentrated and tried hard enough. She had told him the story of a friend of hers.

The woman had been terrified of flying. No traditional therapy had been able to help. A past-life regressionist had been unable to help her access a previous life trauma, either, so the woman had been advised to concentrate, meditate, every time she flew.

The woman realized she felt differently when flying over water as opposed to land. She was only afraid while over water. She concentrated on that aspect of her fear. Then one day, coming in for a landing over water, she slipped into a previous existence. She'd been a World War II fighter pilot, a man. She'd been flying in formation off the west coast of England. Her plane had developed engine problems, and she'd gone down. Although she'd survived the impact, her canopy would not open. She'd drowned. She remembered it all clearly then.

Stephen concentrated with all the power of his being, concentrated on his fear. He feared his promise might be broken. He feared . . . *what?* He feared . . . *leaving her.* That was it. He feared having to leave her alone for a time, until he could return to her. But he had to ride away. . . .

Chapter Sixteen

By the time she was three, Mara had been able to competently ride a pony; by six she could handle a horse; at ten her instructor declared he had nothing more to teach her. She had learned the art of falconry on her father's knee and the lore of weaponry by the time she was eleven. She could pick the best pup from any litter, accurately judge a fighting man's mettle, name all the kings of England, and draw an accurate map of her country. She could read both Greek and Latin. At the moment, however, she was completely bewildered.

Her formerly neat, somewhat austere sleeping chamber was a scene of chaos. Mara sat cross-legged in the center of her bed and looked about her in dismay.

Under Lady Beatrice's instruction, two of her serving women went through each item of Mara's apparel. Clothes were strewn everywhere, over the bed, the modest chest, the window seat. Beatrice examined each piece, discarded some and passed others, created a third pile that consisted of items in need of repair.

"Oh, Mara." Beatrice held up a linen chemise with a large, three-corner tear, and shook her head. "I had no idea your wardrobe was in such a state. Here, Agnes." She handed the chemise to a woman who had entered the room bearing needle and thread. "Start with this. Ordinarily I'd throw it away, but there's so little left already . . ." Beatrice sighed. "My dearest child. I have been remiss in my duty as your mother, haven't I? I had not realized you had so little . . ."

"In the way of feminine attire?" Mara finished when her mother faltered. "It is not your fault, but mine. It is I who wished to dress and act as a man."

"And it is your father and I who allowed it. Think no more of it, Mara. I see already that you no longer rail against the fate that made you what you are."

Mother and daughter exchanged a brief look, and Mara hung her head guiltily. Wardrobe, her appearance in general, had never been a priority. She supposed it must become so. She recalled how pretty she had felt in the tunic and chemise her mother had made for her. She had not missed the approval in Stephen's expression each time his eyes had caressed her. She had liked it. She knew she would wish to dress carefully for him in the future.

Or would she need as little in Bellingham as she had needed here? She had her basic tunics and the leggings she wore for riding. What more would she need? The life they intended to live would be spent mainly on horseback during the day. And at night . . .

Mara squeezed her eyes tightly shut, as if she might banish the images that recurred all too often of late, but her inner vision would not obey. The images remained bright and vivid behind her eyelids.

Day's end. Their chamber in his castle. A wide bed covered with furs. Stephen, his mail tunic gleaming with dull light in the candle's glow. Her husband, drawing the armored garment slowly over his head, revealing to her hungry eyes once again that sculpted chest, narrow waist . . .

Restless beyond endurance, Mara uncurled from her position and slid from her bed. Trey leapt eagerly to his feet.

"Mara, where are you going?"

"For a walk. I don't know. To the garden."

Beatrice curbed the response on her tongue. So far Mara had been remarkably compliant, and Beatrice did not wish to tax her by demanding too much. The girl had been used to many freedoms. It wasn't fair to curtail them all at once.

Only one thing really worried Beatrice. Baldwin. There had been no word from him since his last encounter with Mara. It was not like him. She did not trust the man's silence.

She did, however, trust her husband, and Ranulf had done everything possible to make the castle secure. His dozen remaining knights, though aging like their lord, were yet stalwart and trustworthy. Their armor had been polished, their swords and daggers honed. Servants who lived within the castle walls had been armed. Guards walked the parapets, and the stout wooden gate was opened only briefly once each morning and again at dusk. As long as Mara stayed within the walls of Ullswater, there was nothing to fear. Beatrice smiled at her daughter and waved the girl on her way.

The pear tree had blossomed. Its fragrant and delicate white flowers bobbed gently in the soft spring breeze. Bulbs planted along the edge of the flagged walkway had pushed up through the dark earth and waved like tiny purple and yellow banners.

Trey trotted ahead. He paused from time to time to look back expectantly at his mistress, but Mara ambled along slowly, hands clasped behind her back. What good was it to hurry? There was nowhere to go. Across the garden and back. To the stables, perhaps, or the kennel. A foal was due soon, and two litters of hound pups had recently been whelped. Two or three looked promising, and she wanted to keep her eye on them.

But those were sedentary activities. What she wanted to do was run, ride, swim.

A smile touched Mara's mouth, a flush kissed her cheeks. Would it always be thus when she remembered that instant by the side of the lake?

The thought, coupled with the fantasies that had disturbed her of late, did nothing to curb her already restless spirit and repressed energy. Mara's step quickened. If only she could go out, leave the castle for an hour or so. What harm could there be? Despite constant vigilance at the walls and gate, no one suspicious had been seen; no unusual activities had been noted. Baldwin had obviously retreated to his lair to lick his wounds. Deep ones, she hoped. He probably wouldn't come back any time soon. There was nothing to fear.

Yet she had promised Stephen she would not venture out. And she couldn't if she wished. With her own ears she had heard her father order the guards to let no one enter or exit without his permission. He would certainly never let her out, even for a ride accompanied by his men-at-arms. Unless, of course, she simply—

No. Mara shook her head. Yet at the same time, she gazed at the undercroft with longing. If she went out for only a little while, very early in the morning, what could happen?

The late afternoon sun no longer reached down through the trees, and William Aettewater felt the chilly approach of evening. It was nearly time to rendezvous with Rand and Wulfric at their small campsite, deep in the forest on the far side of the Ullsmere. He grunted. Here was the end of another fruitless day spying on Ullswater and its environs.

103

William rubbed the back of his neck and felt a cool tremor pass through his limbs—but not because of the sun's withdrawal.

Baldwin was not going to like the information the three men had gathered for him. Ullswater Castle was locked up as tightly as a convent expecting Vikings. Happily for Ullswater, unfortunately for William, the castle seemed prepared for assault. The earl was not going to like that. He was not going to like the men who brought him that message. The thought made William a trifle less eager to hurry back to the campsite.

Rand and Wulfric were ready to return to their lord, despite the news they bore. They were fools. William would just as soon put it off. His footsteps lagged until he came to a halt. It wouldn't hurt to stop for a time and ponder the dilemma. Put off the inevitable for a while longer.

A patch of grassy earth caught William's eye. It looked promising. It was at the foot of a hill with enough slope to make the reclining position comfortable. Also, it was out of the wind in the lee of a large pile of boulders.

No, it wouldn't hurt to linger here, to rest a bit. Because most peasants were too poor to own a horse, Baldwin had forbidden his spies to ride their animals. As a result William had walked many miles afoot. He was tired. He stretched out.

The only other movement he made throughout the entire night was to curl into a fetal position when the sun, and its warmth, finally dropped below the horizon.

Mara awoke before dawn, as she had known she would—she had done so almost every morning of her life. This morning was different in another way, however. It would be one of the last in her own bed, her own room, in her father's house. It was also one of the few remaining mornings she would awaken alone.

The furs were suddenly too warm. Mara swung her legs

over the side of the bed and encountered Trey's coarse gray coat. The dog got up, padded to the door, and whined.

"Down, Trey," Mara said irritably.

The beast dropped to his belly but fixed her with a mournful eye. Mara turned away and rolled atop her furs.

The fantasy returned at once to plague her: Stephen, lying in bed beside her. Their bodies touched, warm where flesh met flesh.

She knew what would happen next. She had never been sheltered from the more basic aspects of castle life; the breeding of horses and hounds, cattle and sheep; the nightly scufflings, murmurs, and moans under the blankets of those who slept in the great hall.

But how, exactly, would it come about? Would he kiss her? How would Stephen's lips feel against hers? Mara put a finger to her lips, imagining.

Would he touch her? Touch her face? Let his fingers trace the line of her jaw, slide down her neck? Her hand moved to her throat.

What would happen next? How would he love her? Gently?

How would his hands feel when they touched her? Would his caress be warm, lingering?

And why, why did she experience these strange sensations in her body she had never before known? Why the heat in her belly that spread like molten fire through her limbs and left her weak and trembling?

Mara bolted upright. Her breast heaved and pale strands of hair, escaped from their plaits, clung to the sheen of moisture on her arms and shoulders. She could not remain still another moment, could not bear the claustrophobic nearness of the walls around her. She had to escape, feel the fresh clean air against her skin. Just for a little while.

Trey grinned in canine fashion, his long tail swinging.

He stayed at his mistress's side throughout the familiar journey to the undercroft, waited patiently while she fumbled with the key.

Mara muttered a curse. Of all times to lose the connection between her brain and her fingers! Her father had posted an extra night guard, and that guard had picked this particular moment to cross the courtyard to the castle keep. She heard his measured steps approach. Another second and she would have to abandon her plan.

The key slipped smoothly home.

Perspiration had dampened Mara's linen shift and the thin tunic she had thrown over it. The sun had not yet appeared to warm the chill night air, and a fitful breeze stirred. Mara shivered as she stepped into the still, fragrant air of the undercroft. Seconds later she ran along the dark passage—and experienced her first real fear.

The threat from Baldwin was genuine. Her father had not locked up the castle or posted the extra guards merely to amuse himself. Furthermore, Mara better than anyone knew how angry Baldwin had been. It was an anger that would simmer until it boiled and boiled over.

Her father had been right to take extra precautions. Stephen was right to worry about her. She was a fool even to have contemplated leaving the castle.

Mara's steps slowed to a walk. She should turn around and go back. Immediately. She would . . .

After just one deep breath of fresh forest air. No one would see. No one would know. The boulders that concealed the entrance were only a few feet away.

There wouldn't have been time for a swim anyway, Mara realized. She had misjudged the time. Dawn had broken, for she could make out the massive forms of the trees that surrounded her. One deep breath and she would turn around and—

Trey growled. The sound was deep in his throat, low

and menacing. Mara knew the timbre of it. It was his warning. Of a stranger.

Mara whirled and saw him, asleep on the slope of the hill. But even as she watched, the man stirred, rubbed his eyes.

Before she could silence him, Trey barked. And then Mara was running, faster than she had ever run in her life. Making herself disappear, with a prayer on her lips that the armed stranger would think it had been a dream. Only a dream.

Chapter Seventeen

William woke in confusion. He expected to see the familiar faces of Rand and Wulfric. Instead, he found himself in foreign surroundings and had to pull himself together to recall where he was and how he had come to be there.

He shook his head and scrubbed his hands over the stubble on his chin. He had wanted to lie down and rest for a moment. That moment had turned into an entire night. Wulfric was not going to be pleased at all. At least he had not been discovered. That was something. Maybe Wulfric wouldn't be too mad—

A dog barked.

William froze. He couldn't afford to be found. Baldwin would have his head. There was only one course of action. Pulling his dagger from his boot, he let his eyes search the surrounding trees.

But there was nothing to be seen. There was no dog, not even the recent sign of one.

He had heard the animal. There was doubt of that. So,

where had it gone? It hadn't disappeared into thin air like smoke.

William swiped at the ragged scar on his stubbled chin. He was a cautious man, and he had grown up in the area. His father had been one of Ranulf's tenants, and William knew the lord raised deerhounds. Large, toothy, and aggressive deerhounds. If one lurked nearby, William wanted to know exactly where. He laid a hand atop the nearest boulder, carefully edged around its girth . . . and received the surprise of his life.

Mara did not stop running until she reached the door back to the undercroft. Habit forced her to pause and listen, and she was glad she had. Muffled voices came to her: the castle steward's and that of someone else, one of the cooks perhaps. She would have to wait until they had found what they sought and left.

Or did she dare wait? Had the secret been discovered? Did someone pursue her? Worse, were they at this very instant hurrying to tell Baldwin of the passage beneath the castle walls?

The full impact of what she had done, how she had compromised everyone's safety, hit Mara with the force of a blow. She needed time to think. Sheltered in the darkness, she put her arms around Trey's solid neck and leaned against the cold stone wall.

Forcing herself to remain calm, Mara tried to recall precisely what had happened. The man had clearly been asleep when she stepped outside. He had still been rubbing his eyes when she turned and fled. Surely he hadn't seen her.

But he had certainly heard Trey bark. Unless he was deaf. If he had become curious about the dog he might investigate. Investigation might well reveal the opening and the tunnel back here.

Mara knew she could not take the chance. She would have to tell her father the castle's security had been compromised. She would have to admit she had used the secret entrance—had used it, furthermore, when she had been expressly forbidden to leave the castle grounds. She did not relish her task.

There was silence at last from within the undercroft, and Mara entered cautiously. Footsteps dragging, she crossed the storage area and squeezed through the door into the bright sunlight. She had to shade her eyes as she trudged up the long flight of steps to the great hall.

As she climbed, her sense of urgency began to pass. In spite of her brief glimpse of the man, Mara remembered his peasant clothes. Whoever he was, he was surely not one of Baldwin's men. Thus, even if the passage had been discovered, it had been found by no one of great consequence. The worst the man might do was try to sell his information to the earl, or to some other thief or bandit. By then Ullswater would be prepared. Her former path to freedom would be sealed, but the castle would be safe.

Mara took a deep breath and pushed through the door to the great hall.

William had taken only a few steps into the passageway when he realized what he had chanced upon. The significance of the finding took his breath away.

William recalled rumors he had heard as a boy, that Ullswater had a secret entrance. He and his young playmates had spent many an hour searching for it, planned the raid they would make, the knights they would vanquish, the spoils they would take when the castle was theirs: A boy's fantasy, now a man's reality.

William could scarce believe his luck. He no longer feared to face his earl; he looked forward to it. He had the best possible news he could bring. Baldwin would reward him for it.

Without further hesitation, William turned back toward the sunlight. He would have to find Rand and Wulfric at once.

It was his lucky day, no doubt about it. Ahead and off to his left, William saw a flash of red approaching through the sun-dappled gloom of the trees: the tunic Wulfric had appropriated from some hapless peasant. He hailed the knight with a grin.

"Where the devil have you—?"

"There's no time to waste on your bad temper, Wulfric," he said. "Where's Rand?"

"Packing up. I came to find you. Where were you all—?"

"Look at this," William interrupted for the second time. "Come and look at this."

Wulfric's main strength was his prowess with a sword, and the power in the massive arms that he used to wield his weapon. He had never been noted for his cleverness. Yet even he could not fail to see the importance of his comrade's find. A smile spread across his broad, coarse features, and emerged from the gray-flecked dark of his beard.

"This is good, Will. You done good."

Even as William nodded in agreement, however, he experienced a twinge of apprehension. Where had that dog gone? From whence had he come? William cast about him again, keen eyes alert for any sign of the animal's recent passing. Nothing.

There was only one place from which the beast might have come, and disappeared again as quickly: the tunnel. It was the only explanation. Furthermore, the dog had probably been there in the first place because it had accompanied someone—someone who had been warned by the dog's bark. Someone who had seen William and fled back the way he had come. At this very moment, he might be sounding the alarm. In the space of a heartbeat, William saw his incredible good luck, his dream of success, turn to dust. Unless . . .

"Wulfric, listen. You're going to have to go without me. You and Rand ride back, fast as you can, and tell the earl what I've found. Tell him. . . ." William hesitated, allowing the plan to fully form. "Tell him to bring everyone, at once, right to the castle gates. Tell him that when he gets here, they'll open. If luck continues to be on my side, they'll open for the Earl of Cumbria."

"But, Will, what—?"

"Just go, damnit! Get the horses and ride!"

William waited only long enough to make sure Wulfric was well and truly on his way. Then he turned and, in spite of the tunnel's Stygian darkness, ran as fast as he dared. All that was against him now was time.

Mara had not found her father in the hall. Her mother claimed he had gone to the kennels to check on his favorite bitch, mere hours away from whelping. Almost able to see the question form on her mother's tongue, Mara hurried away. Not only did she not wish to have to admit her folly and disobedience twice, but her sense of urgency had returned.

Ranulf spied his daughter as she strode swiftly in his direction. A smile formed on his lips. It died almost at once.

"What is it, Mara? What's wrong?"

Mara faced her father and looked him squarely in the eye. "I've disobeyed you, Father. I've used the passage from the undercroft. More than once. Today may have been once too often."

Ranulf did not betray his dismay by as much as the flicker of an eyelid. "What has happened, Daughter?" he asked.

"I may have been seen. There was a man sleeping near the entrance at the foot of the hill. I'm fairly certain he didn't see me, but Trey barked. If he came looking for the dog . . ."

There was no need to finish, nor was there time. Ranulf had already gone into action.

"Douglas!" The lord of Ullswater waved at his old friend and companion, well past his prime, yet a willing and worthy campaigner. When the venerable knight had joined him, Ranulf explained the situation. He brusquely issued orders.

"Round up the rest of my men-at-arms, such as they are." Ranulf wondered silently if he was going to regret the attitude of laxity he had allowed to flourish during the present king's peaceful reign. "Put a half dozen more men on the walls. Bring the rest and meet me in the undercroft."

Although puzzled by the last command, Douglas knew better than to question his lord. Mara watched him hasten away to do her father's bidding, and she fell in step behind her long-striding parent.

Please God, let it have been only a curious peasant, Mara silently prayed. Then: *Hurry back, Stephen. Hurry.*

William felt himself teeter on the edge of panic. The totally lightless passage had finally ended in what he assumed was a door. But how to open it? Frantically, he groped in the darkness, knowing time might be growing short. If the alarm had been raised, someone would be coming at any moment. Perhaps it would be better simply to run.

Without the slightest sound, the hidden door suddenly swung wide. Even the dim light of the undercroft caused William to blink, but he did not waste time allowing his eyes to adjust to the light, or to wonder what he had pushed to effect his release. He stepped into the room, nudged the door closed behind him, and peered cautiously around a large pile of baskets.

Halfway down the long wall, William saw the door to his freedom, rimmed in the morning's light. He did not hesitate to wonder if he was going to make it or not; he knew he must simply move quickly, or be caught. He was mere steps from his goal when he heard the heavy tread of booted feet swiftly approach.

Ranulf threw the door wide and strode into the storage room. He looked in the direction of the concealed doorway, his attention so riveted on the heap of baskets he barely noticed the slight commotion off to his right. He glanced over his shoulder to see one of the servants kneeling to gather scattered potatoes into a bowl.

"Sor-sorry, m'lord," the man muttered. "Y' startled me. I'll be out o' yer way in a blink."

Ranulf did not bother to acknowledge the man. "The door's over there," he said to those who had accompanied him, and indicated the direction with the point of his sword. "Barricade it. Then search this room. Mara, come with me."

Their security had apparently not been breached. Mara's relief was so great she did not fear what was to come. Her father's harshest words would be nothing compared to the condemnation she had already heaped upon herself. Considerably lighter of heart, she followed her father from the undercroft.

Neither gave further notice to the faceless servant who slipped out behind them.

Chapter Eighteen

The fruit trees were fully in bloom; their frothy blossoms trembled in the late afternoon breeze. Roses, full blown, bobbed their heavy heads. Mara raised her face to the day's last sun, one hand atop Trey's big head, and closed her eyes. She breathed deeply in an attempt to capture the familiar peace of her mother's garden. It was futile. Mara rose and paced the flagstone path.

Her actions were inexcusable. No wonder her parents had insisted it was time to wed. She was spoiled and willful, not to mention irresponsible. It was not helpful at all to remind herself that she had confessed her disobedience to her father, or to know that precautions had been taken: Both the secret door in the undercroft and the tunnel mouth had been barricaded. No enemy would be able to take advantage of her indiscretion.

No, that knowledge did not help to soothe her conscience. Such precautions should never have been necessary in the first place. Silently berating herself, Mara turned at the end of the garden walk and headed back to the castle keep.

At least there had been one bright spot in her day: a message from Stephen. His preparations for the wedding were nearly complete. In a day and a half he would arrive with a small entourage to escort her and her parents to Bellingham. Her new life would begin.

A life of duty and responsibility, Mara reminded herself. A life far different from the one she had led up to now. The carefree days of childhood were gone forever. She was a woman, and must act like one.

Even Trey seemed affected by his mistress's mood. His long tail slowed its rhythmic swing and finally drooped between his legs as he padded slowly up the stone steps after Mara.

The tension was almost more than William could bear. Had he been a fool, after all, to think his plan might work? So many things could go wrong. The timing, for instance, had to be perfect.

The stable was quiet. The animals had been fed and bedded for the night. William listened a minute longer to be sure, and crept from the empty stall where he had spent the day in hiding. A glance out the door at the sun's angle, low on the horizon, told him what he needed to know. He had to make his move now.

William sauntered across the castle grounds with his head low, arms swinging loosely at his sides, attitude relaxed and nonchalant. It was a good act, although daggers of apprehension stabbed him with every step. What if the earl was late? What if he disregarded the message, laughed at the plan, and had decided not to come at all? The Earl of Cumbria was unpredictable at best. What had made William think such an impulsive act had a chance of success?

Greed. He had no hesitation admitting it to himself. As unstable as his lord might be, the man was usually generous with those who pleased him. Vanquishing Ranulf of Ullswater would please the earl very much indeed.

If the earl failed him, however, he'd be a dead man. William had little choice but to go ahead with his scheme, though.

No one paid him any heed. William slipped inside the gate tower unnoticed. He closed the door behind him with one hand and, with the other, pulled the dagger from beneath his tunic.

The anticipation of action and the comfortable feel of the weapon in his hand replaced his anxiety. He'd always been partial to the stealthy use of small, sharp blades, and the trace of a smile touched William's mouth as he crept silently up the spiraling stone stairs.

Preparations for the evening meal were supervised by Beatrice. Following a sharp discussion with the cook, she ordered the trestle tables and benches moved from their positions against the long wall and into the center of the room. She made sure Ranulf's cup of ale was full, and turned her attention to the arrangement of some lilies from her garden. Her favorite hour of the day had arrived, and she welcomed it. The day's tension had taxed her frail strength, but it was over now and they all would be safe.

Beatrice smiled, her hands on the lily stems. There were so many things to be thankful for, not the least of which would be a tranquil old age spent in the quiet company of the man she had always adored. The only cloud on her horizon had been her daughter's future happiness, and that now seemed assured. Within a few days Mara would be wed. Happily.

Lost in her reveries, Beatrice did not notice at first the sun's last rays as they fell through the tall, glassed windows. Only when the ruby light fell across her lilies, and stained them red, did she look up with alarm. With a shiver, she recalled the black wings of premonition that had touched her scant days before.

They enfolded her now, again, cold and dark. A shadow passed over her vision.

The connection between them was so strong, so true, Ranulf felt his wife's tension across the long room. He looked up in time to see the blood drain from her face, and had half risen from his chair when several things happened at once.

Mara entered the hall, Trey at her heels. Her waist-length braids were in disarray. Pale strands, escaped from the braids, clung to the shoulders of her dark green tunic. Her expression was grave, her eyes dark. Suddenly her dog whirled back toward the doorway and gave a short, sharp bark.

Douglas burst through the door. He was out of breath, cheeks unnaturally flushed beneath his graying beard. "It's Earl Baldwin," he gasped, without preamble. "Riding hard. I don't like the looks of it, m'lord."

"How many ride with him?"

"A score at least."

Ranulf didn't like the sound of it, either. Baldwin was up to something to approach so boldly. It wasn't his style at all. "Come to the bailey with me, Douglas," he ordered sharply. "Send another man to the gate tower. One with a crossbow."

"Ranulf, what—"

"I don't know what, Beatrice. But I shall soon find out." He turned to his daughter. "Stay here with your mother," he said. And then he was gone.

It was going to happen. It was all going to happen!

A curious and familiar elation flowed hotly through William's veins as he pulled the unsuspecting guard's head back with his left arm. With his right, he slit the man's throat. Never a sound. A warm gout of blood gushed over his hand, its brilliant crimson color magically alight in the sun's failing rays.

Reluctantly, William let the body drop. It was time to raise the gate. The earl had come!

The clatter of booted feet on the stone stairs momentarily distracted him from his task, but it didn't bother William. He could deal with whatever came at him now. Success was within his grasp. With renewed strength, he applied himself to the huge wooden gear that raised the castle gate.

The ponderous wooden structure groaned in protest. Cries of surprise and alarm arose from the courtyard. William applied himself more diligently.

And then it was the thunderous clatter of horses' hooves across the wooden drawbridge that came to William's ears.

He stooped to retrieve the fallen guard's sword. Both hands on the hilt, he held it pointed in front of him and prepared for the men who came charging through the door.

Ranulf and Douglas stood side by side in the castle courtyard and watched in shocked disbelief as the gate slowly, steadily rumbled upward.

It couldn't be happening.

But it was. And there was only one explanation: treachery from within!

Ranulf's flesh turned to ice, and an unfamiliar nausea churned in his belly as he heard Baldwin's exultant shout of triumph. It was then that he saw him.

His enemy rode hard on a light gray stallion, galloping over the drawbridge at the head of his men. Ranulf saw his destiny in the mad glint of the man's pale blue eyes.

Everything that followed, the last moments of Ranulf's life, happened in slow motion.

Almost all his men were posted on the walls, useless lookouts. Ranulf watched as most of them hurried to make their way down into the courtyard, but he knew they would be too late. *Too late.* Assured of victory, Baldwin rode at the head of his knights, straight in Ranulf's direction. Though the earl's short-sword was drawn, he would not strike the killing blow, Ranulf knew, but would leave that messy job for someone else. Someone with a strong arm and a long and heavy blade.

On foot, before an armed knight astride a war steed in full charge, Ranulf had not the slightest hope of defense or chance for survival. Neither could he turn and run, however. In a chilling flash of knowledge, like the stab of an icicle through his heart, Ranulf realized how his stubborn pride had brought down ruin on them all. He would die in atonement.

Ranulf pulled his great-sword from its scabbard in time to parry the mounted knight's first blow, but it rocked him. He wheeled in an attempt to hamstring the charger as it galloped past, but his stroke was ill timed. From the corner of his eye he watched his faithful Douglas unhorse another mounted man, and felt a faint glimmer of hope. It was short-lived.

His knights were too few, too burdened by their years. He watched as two of his small band were cut down, then another, and another, 'till only he and Douglas remained. And the knight who had charged him initially had managed to turn his destrier to come at him again.

"I have your back!" Douglas shouted.

"Old friend," Ranulf murmured under his breath, and turned to face his oncoming foe.

Then Douglas fell. Ranulf heard the sword that clanged against the knight's armor. Heard the clatter as Douglas dropped to his knees. He did not have to turn to see the killing blow.

Barely in time, Ranulf ducked out of the way of the charging warhorse. It was over now. All over. There was but one thing left: to see *her* beloved face once more. Although it grated against the very core of him, and his soul cried out in protest, Ranulf turned his back on his enemy and ran.

In single-minded pursuit of his goal, he pounded up the stairs to the great hall. He was oblivious of the sound of metal shod hooves behind him on the steps. His whole attention was on the door in front of him.

He saw it open.

Then he saw no more.

Mara had learned her lesson. Despite every instinct to the contrary, she had obeyed her father and shut the door behind him. One of the serving women whimpered in fear and was silenced sharply by Beatrice. Mara turned to face her mother.

"If something has happened, if something has gone wrong because of what I did, I . . ."

"Hush, child. Don't say another word." Beatrice gripped her daughter's shoulders. "Whatever Baldwin is up to is none of your doing."

Still steeped in her guilt, Mara was about to protest when she heard an all too familiar sound. The hair along Trey's back bristled. "Mother, that . . . That's the castle gate. It's opened!"

Mara fell silent. Her mother had already moved past her to open the door and let in the last light of the almost perfect spring day. She opened it onto a sight that would haunt Mara to the very last moments of her life.

Her father, in headlong flight, had nearly reached the top of the stairs. The mounted knight in pursuit had just urged his huge gray stallion onto the bottommost step.

Frightened, the animal balked. Then its rider brought the flat of his upraised sword down hard on the horse's flank and, with a startled snort, the stallion gathered its legs and leapt upward. Mara watched, frozen in horror, as one of the horse's huge forelegs caught her father a glancing blow and knocked him to his knees.

Like an animal Ranulf was, readied for the sacrifice beneath the descending sword.

Her mother's agonized cry went through Mara as

121

cleanly as the blade that stole her father's life. Helpless, Mara saw her mother fall to her knees in the doorway, arms outstretched.

Then the rider was upon Beatrice, too. The charging stallion knocked the frail woman aside and into the cold stone wall. She crumpled like a shattered doll.

Dimly, screams came to Mara's ears. As she turned, she had an awareness of people scattering, servants fleeing in all directions, running for their lives. She herself had no intention of running. She merely sought a better place to make her stand.

Without a pause in her stride, Mara pulled the dagger from the silver girdle at her waist and leapt atop the nearest table. When she turned to face the rider, Trey was at her side. As if of a single mind, they hurled themselves at the oncoming knight.

The man screamed as canine fangs bit deeply into his unprotected thigh. He reacted instinctively and swung at the beast with his blade. The top of Trey's head was momentarily obscured in a bright spray of red.

But the attack had given the blond-haired Fury the opening she needed. With a snarl as vicious as her hound's, she was upon her foe. Again and again she slashed the knight with her dagger. Most of the blows were deflected by his chain mail tunic, but a few scored his neck, and one opened his chin. Maddened, the knight dropped his horse's reins and swung at his attacker with his free hand. His animal reared, dislodging both struggling humans from his back.

The last thing Mara remembered was falling.

Chapter Nineteen

Bellingham Castle was far different from Ullswater. It was older, having been built by a long dead Normal lord during the rule of the Conqueror, William of Orange. The days and years of the subjugation of the Anglo-Saxon people had been brutal ones. The Norman king had shown no mercy to the English. The Angles had fought back bitterly.

As a result, Bellingham's sole purpose had been defense. It boasted few of the comforts or amenities of Ullswater Castle, and was a great deal smaller. It did not sprawl along a wooded slope down to a picturesque lake, but was perched upon a barren and windy hill. Its only buildings were the castle keep, a modest stone stable— half of which served as kennel and mews—and a high donjon tower.

It was an imposing structure, nonetheless, and appeared to watch over the surrounding bleak and hilly countryside, and the tidy hamlet at its foot, like the benign guardian that it was. The fields and meadows of its vassal tenants spread around it on three sides like a homey quilt in shades of green. To the northeast lay the Kielder Water—a dark, tree-rimmed lake whose river flowed to the sea.

The people of the village of Bellingham who served the castle, and who were served by it in return, were happy with the arrangement and pleased in particular with the lord of the manor, the young and handsome Baron Stephen. They had been delighted to hear of his impending marriage, and looked forward to the upcoming festivities. Despite the early hour, therefore, early even for such hardworking people, they had turned out en masse to call out their greetings and wish their lord well on his way.

Stephen was glad of the predawn darkness that hid his foolish grin. He was a knight, a proven warrior, hereditary baron of Bellingham, and feudal tenant of the king of England. It didn't seem quite right to feel such boyish elation. Or to be so completely unable to control the expression on his face.

Yet the respect and affection the people obviously had for him pleased Stephen. And the errand on which he embarked filled him with something more than mere pleasure.

It didn't take long to pass through the village. The chargers were fresh and eager to be away on the crisp spring morning. A last thatched cottage on the left, and the knights were on the open and lonely road. It was yet so dark they could not even see the surrounding hills. But the vision in Stephen's heart was bright before him.

The turn of events still amazed him. It was like the story an old woman might tell to children by the fireside at night. It was surely not something that happened in real life.

Yet it had.

Fresh as the new day, Stephen's great chestnut war stallion pranced ahead of the other three riders: two of Stephen's knights, and his ever-present servant, Jack. Now, as if reading his mind, Thomas Strong pulled even with his lord.

"It all seems almost too good to be true, doesn't it, my lord?"

"My very thoughts," Stephen replied. "I am indeed a fortunate man, as you will soon see."

Thomas chuckled. "Your descriptions have been so thorough, I hardly need to see her at all. You have most ably painted her picture."

"Still, mere words cannot do her justice."

The first pale hints of dawn lightened the gloom, and Stephen was able to make out the angular planes of his friend's face. He looked directly into Thomas's wide-set hazel eyes. "I am also most fortunate to have a friend like you. And to have had your assistance in winning over the others." He glanced back pointedly at Alfred, who rode beside Jack, then shared a knowing look with the other man.

It hadn't been easy smoothing the ruffled feathers of the men who had lived the bachelor life with him for so long. No one had wanted the rather pleasant state of things to change. Alfred, in particular, had been difficult; the older man had served Stephen's father when Stephen was still a lad, and had been leery of such a hasty marriage. He was the knight who'd tried to assist Stephen in choosing a squire, and always espoused caution. Still, while Stephen admired the older knight's wisdom, he also knew himself to be a good judge of certain things. Just look how Jack had turned out!

"It was wise to bring Alfred," Thomas said in an undertone. "The honor has pleased him. And if the lady is all you say—as I am sure she is—she herself will win him more effectively than any words of yours. He, and all the others for that matter, have certainly not been able to deny the political wisdom of this union."

Stephen frowned and turned his gaze to the greening

hills now visible all around them. *Politics.* Up until now they had simply been a fact of life to be dealt with whenever necessary. Baldwin of Cumbria, already powerful, sought to increase his wealth and stature. To maintain the balance and curb the rapacious earl, the merger of Ullswater and Bellingham had been both desirable and necessary. Baldwin could not overcome their combined strength, either on a field of battle or in the king's court. Thus Stephen had agreed, albeit reluctantly, to the match with Ranulf's daughter.

That had been the political necessity, and it was now dealt with.

Thank God, he thought. Thank God Ranulf was an honorable man and loving father. Thank God Baldwin's offers had not tempted him for a moment, as they might have a lesser man. Stephen shuddered. The thought of Baldwin with his hands on Amarantha was like blasphemy.

"Something is amiss, my lord?" Thomas was always alert to the moods of his friend. "You look as if you felt a chill wind."

"In a manner of speaking, I did. I was thinking of the earl."

It was Thomas's turn to frown. "Never a happy thought. Particularly now. Do you fear he'll cause trouble?"

"I *know* he'll cause trouble. It's simply a matter of when and how, and that's one of the reasons I've taken such pains to expedite this marriage. With Mara well away from Ullswater and safely wed to me, the immediate temptation for Baldwin will be removed. Fearing reprisal from me may also make him think twice about any petty vengeance he might wish to visit upon Mara's father."

"So, why the long face?"

"Because she is *not* yet wed to me and *not* yet safely away." Without further explanation, Stephen kicked his mount into a mile-eating lope.

The hours passed, the riders alternately cantering and jogging their horses to conserve stamina, and the landscape subtly changed. For the first several miles, the rolling hills were gaily decorated with patches of purple and white heather. Farther on, an occasional stand of trees sprouted from the side or crest of a hill. Eventually, the hills flattened. The trees became windbreaks, then forest.

Sunlight glinted off of water here and there, and Stephen's party paused twice, briefly, to refresh both men and mounts. Although they made good time, their pace was still not rapid enough for their leader. A queer sense of foreboding had gradually settled on him throughout the course of the day. It was all Stephen could do to keep from kicking his stallion into a flat out run.

The sun was low when they crested the last ridge north of the Ullsmere. The castle was south of the lake and difficult to see. The dark and ivy-covered stone of its walls and buildings blended with the shadows of the great wood that surrounded it.

Though the sun was not directly in his eyes, Stephen shaded them and squinted. Beside him, the nimble and farsighted Jack jumped to his feet atop his saddle. He dropped into his seat almost at once, and laid a light hand on his lord's gloved and muscular forearm.

"Trouble, I fear, my lord."

Stephen tensed. Thomas and Alfred drew nearer. "What do you mean, trouble?"

"There's smoke, my lord. And 'tis not the smoke of hearth or chimney."

Stephen felt his blood grow cold. He registered no other thought or feeling, even fear, before he was in motion. Ears pinned flat, nostrils dilated, and tail streaming, his gallant chestnut stallion thundered down the road to Ullswater Castle.

The day rapidly waned. The sun was a mere reddish glow on the western horizon, but the band of riders did not

127

hurry. They did not increase their pace. Rather, they slowed as they entered the village of Hawkshead.

The daily market had closed. Vendors and clients had returned to their modest homes. The bustle in the street had died.

It quickly revived when the people realized it was their earl and his knights who had returned from some foray into the countryside. They streamed from their cottages, curiosity overcoming caution.

Baldwin relished the reception. The faces that turned to him wore expressions of awe mingled with fear. Fear, because they had long lived in the shadow of the earl's castle. Awe, because of the sight to which he treated their eyes.

Baldwin allowed himself a tight, smug smile and looked first at William Aettewater, who rode on his right hand, then behind him at the prisoner who had captured the villagers' openmouthed attention.

Mara did not acknowledge the earl's regard by so much as the blink of an eye. Neither did she look to the right or left of her, although she was aware of the townspeople's presence. Baldwin had brought her through Hawkshead on purpose, she knew. To parade his prize. To humiliate her.

But she would not give him the satisfaction. Although her hands were bound in front of her and her hair wildly disheveled, though her face and bodice were streaked with blood from the gash on her temple, Mara held her head high, chin upthrust.

The village fell behind them at last. A few ragged children and barking dogs ran along behind the mounted band for a way; then the group outpaced their straggling followers and the earl signaled his men to pick up the pace. His knights broke into a canter.

An avenue of trees passed in the periphery of Mara's vision. Gates loomed ahead, opened, and they went through them.

Hooves clattered on a cobbled surface, voices babbled, dogs barked, someone shouted over it all—Mara barely noticed. She maintained her stiff and erect posture and rigid self-control. She blessed the accompanying numbness. If she allowed herself to think, to imagine, to dwell on whatever fate the earl had in store for her, she feared she would lose her mind.

William held the earl's horse and kept a careful eye on his lord as Baldwin dismounted. He was well aware of how tenuous his new position was, and knew he must remain alert to Baldwin's every mood. He watched the earl eye his splendid prisoner, and smirked.

"She'll not be stickin' that haughty chin quite so high in the air when you've had your way with her, will she, m'lord?"

Baldwin smiled slowly. "No. No, she won't." He dragged his eyes from her bloodied but still noble form, and turned to his new right-hand man. "See that she's taken inside. Take her to my apartments in the hall and have one of the women . . . No, have *Maggie* clean her up. Then have her brought to me." He beamed. "In the tower."

Though it took great effort to resist one more look at his magnificent captive, Baldwin kept his attention firmly on the path before him. It was going to be an interesting evening.

Far more interesting than Mara could dream.

Chapter Twenty

The four men rode at what speed they could, but soon the going was difficult. The road was clogged with men, women, and children, all laden with satchels and bags full of their meager belongings. Their expressions were haggard and frightened. A few limped, or bore other signs of recent injury. All tried to melt into the woods as the riders approached.

Despite the desperate sense of urgency that drove Stephen, he slowed his mount and lifted a hand in greeting. "Fear not, people of Ullswater," he called. "I am the baron Lord Stephen of Bellingham. I am friend to Ranulf, Lord of Ullswater."

Terrified children clung to their mothers' hands and huddled against their skirts. A few of the men exchanged glances. At last, one burly peasant stepped forward.

"If you are friend to our baron Ranulf," he began, "and have come to aid him, you have come too late." The man gestured behind him, toward the plumes of smoke that still rose from the gray and stony walls. "All lies in ruin. All are dead."

A bolt of lightning seared Stephen's soul. His hands tightened on his charger's reins, and the animal danced nervously in place. He had to force the words from his throat. "And Amarantha, Ranulf's daughter?"

The peasant hung his head and shook it slowly. "I know not." He raised his bleak and bloodshot gaze once more. "I know only our homes have been destroyed, our livestock slaughtered. There is nothing left. Nothing."

Without another word, the man sidestepped Stephen's stallion and continued down the road. The ragged and bloodied vanguard fell in behind him.

Thomas rode to his baron's side. "My lord."

Stephen paid him no heed. He loosened his reins, and horse and rider bounded away to the gates of Ullswater Castle. In spite of the peasant's warning, he was not prepared for the horror that greeted his eyes.

Stephen's knights followed. They pounded across the wooden bridge and into the castle courtyard. There, greeted with the smell of smoke and death, Stephen's charger slid to a halt and reared on its hind legs. Stephen's three companions drew up beside him.

"Oh, my God. My God," he whispered.

Thomas pulled his horse up next to his friend, but he remained silent. The magnitude of the devastation robbed him of speech. Even Alfred, who had seen much, found his eyes stinging from more than the acrid smoke. It was Jack who finally broke the spell of horror.

The spry little man climbed slowly from his horse and moved from one fallen man to the next. "All dead." He shook his head sadly. "All dead."

Even the dogs from the kennel had been taken out and butchered, puppies thrown down onto the cobbled yard, their small skulls shattered. The bodies were strewn across the blood-soaked ground, the kennels burned, as well as the mews. Only the stables were intact—but all the fine horses were gone, stolen. Jack returned to his master.

Stephen did not look at him. His attention was on the door to the great hall and the huge, broad-shouldered body sprawled before it.

All eyes were on Stephen as he dismounted. They followed him as he trudged up the stairs.

"Ranulf," he said softly, and knelt by the lifeless body. It was obvious the man had been cut down from behind. Stephen laid his hand on the big baron's shoulder, then rose.

It was an effort to move. Never in his life had he dreaded anything as much as he feared to enter the great hall. His feet moved nevertheless. They carried him across the threshold.

"No. Oh, no."

Beatrice lay where she had fallen, head at an odd angle. A trickle of blood ran from the corner of her mouth and stained the bodice of her pale yellow tunic.

Stephen closed his eyes. Someone gripped his shoulders from behind, steadied him.

Jack slipped past into the hall. "I'll look, m'lord. But I doubt she's here. He'll have taken her, y'know."

Stephen nodded, eyes still closed, while his servant made a quick tour of the long room and its sleeping apartments. There remained nothing but three serving women, throats slit, and what must have been Ranulf's steward. The man had been decapitated. Also, everything that might have value and was portable had been stolen. Furs were gone from the beds and tapestries from the walls. Clothing was scattered about as if it had been picked through. Jack inadvertently kicked a fallen pewter mug, and it rolled across the floor. He returned to Stephen's side.

"She's not here, m'lord. He must have taken her."

He had known it. In his heart Stephen had known. Yet the long sigh of relief escaped him anyway. She was alive. In terrible, desperate trouble, but alive. Now he had to think. To plan.

He turned abruptly and started down the steps. Thomas and Alfred exchanged glances and hurried after him. When he put his foot into the stirrup, Thomas put a hand on his arm.

"Stephen, wait."

Stephen tried to shake him off, but Thomas's grip was firm.

"Tell me what you plan to do."

"Do? Are you mad? I'm going after her!" Again, Stephen attempted to mount his horse.

Again, Thomas restrained him.

"Let go of me, Thomas!" he snarled.

"No. Listen! And think. There are only four of us against . . ." Thomas gestured at the horrific scene in the courtyard. "How many did it take to do this?"

Stephen reluctantly removed his foot from the stirrup. He did not, however, let go his grip on his stallion's reins. "So, what do you suggest? Let Baldwin have her? Let him get away with this?"

"Of course not. But we do need more help before we go after your bride. We also need to do something about . . . about all *this*." Thomas's nod indicated the carnage.

Stephen's hold on his reins relaxed. He hung his head. "You're right, Thomas. You're right." Stephen rubbed his eyes, and lifted his gaze to his old friend. "I'm not thinking clearly. Tell me what we should do."

Thomas breathed a small sigh of relief. "Send Alfred back to Bellingham with word of what happened here," he said. "Let him bring back help, every able-bodied man who is willing and who can be armed. Baldwin is obviously going to claim Ullswater as his. It was a mistake for him to abandon it in the first place. We must take advantage of that. He can't lay claim to Ranulf's land and chattel if we hold the castle."

"That's all well and good," Stephen growled. "But what about Mara? As long as he has her, he can lay claim to anything he wants. And if he forces her to wed. . . ." Stephen was unable to utter the words. "No, I cannot, will not, wait for Alfred to return. *You* wait. I've got to do something."

Jack's eyes flickered as Stephen reached one more time for his stirrup. "Wait, m'lord, I . . . I think I have an idea."

All attention was directed to the little man, who removed his plumed hat and turned it nervously in his fingers. "You'll have noticed the earl had everything he thought might be of value removed. From what I remember, it's quite a bit, what with tapestries and all. Difficult to carry. It won't be men on horseback takin' all that loot back to the earl's castle. Somewhere there's a cart, loaded up and goin' slow." Jack squinted one eye and cocked his head. "It's not dark for another hour. If we ride hard, m'lord, you an' me, and Thomas to take the horses when we catch up with the wagon—"

"You're brilliant," Stephen interrupted. "I know exactly what you have in mind, and it's perfect. Let's not waste another minute."

Stephen quickly filled Thomas and Alfred in on the details of Jack's plan, and issued orders even as he mounted his horse. "Also, find one of my peasants who is willing to ride to the king. Give him a horse, one of my best. Tell him it is his if he rides straightway to Henry and tells him of Baldwin's perfidy."

Gathering the reins, Stephen put his spurs to the animal's flanks. Thomas and Jack were left to run for their own mounts. Within seconds their lord had disappeared out the gate.

Baldwin's great hall was larger and more lavish than any Mara had ever seen. The fact registered on her senses without actually touching her. Nothing would ever be able to touch her again. She was numb. Dead. As cold and lifeless as the family and friends she had seen slaughtered before her very eyes.

Trancelike, Mara followed the one-eyed woman through the hall. Even her will to resist was strangely absent. The two men-at-arms who trailed behind her were unnecessary.

Built after the fashion of the time, the sleeping apartment of the manor was off the end of the hall. It, too, was more luxurious than the usual chamber, with tapestries on the walls and a rare silken coverlet on the bed. Despite the furnishings, however, the room seemed curiously empty. There were no lingering scents, no small personal objects scattered carelessly about. It felt as if no one had lived there for a very long time.

"There now. Sit yourself down, an' we'll set about cleanin' you up." Maggie indicated a stool with a nod of her head. Mara remained motionless.

This noble woman really was a pitiable sight, Maggie had to admit. The initial jealousy she had experienced had seeped away. The woman was remarkably beautiful—that much was obvious. She must have been quite an imposing figure. But now . . .

Maggie shook her head sadly and pushed the thick, dark waves of her hair off her shoulders. The poor thing was in such a state she hadn't even reacted to Maggie's deformity. She barely seemed to notice her surroundings. Her hair was matted and tangled, her clothes soiled and torn, her face bloody. Her dark blue eyes stared vacantly into space. This was the woman who would supplant her in the earl's bed?

Maggie clucked her tongue. There wasn't much to worry about. *Yet.* In the meantime, she'd best follow her master's orders. She'd seen the excited gleam in his eye, put there no doubt by the day's bloody events. His appetite for more would be as keen as the edge of a blade.

Maggie took a shift and a soft woolen tunic from a tall wooden cupboard, and felt her jealousy temporarily return. These clothes had belonged to Baldwin's mother.

She'd never been allowed to touch them until now; they had been saved for the lady of the manor.

Maggie's single dark eye flickered in Mara's direction, and a terrible heaviness descended upon her heart.

Baldwin paced the length of his tower room, hands clasped behind his back, and halted near one of its four narrow windows. Night had fallen, and the sliver of a moon revealed nothing for his greedy gaze. Nevertheless, he smiled.

Everything had gone perfectly. Ranulf, as well as his pale and puling wife, was dead. He, Earl Baldwin of Cumbria, had everything of value that had once belonged to Ranulf; his personal effects, his land, his castle. He reminded himself to send a contingent back to secure it.

But best of all he had Ranulf's daughter.

Baldwin allowed himself a tremor of pleasure and hugged it to his narrow breast. Revenge had been sweet so far. So sweet, in fact, it had whetted his appetite for more. He had what he wanted from Ranulf. Now he would take what he wanted from Ranulf's daughter—and more besides. He would take away the very dignity she had once sought to steal from him.

Baldwin rubbed his thin, dry hands together. Oh, yes, he was going to have everything he had dreamed of. And more.

When the knock came at his door, he hesitated to savor the moment. Then he slowly turned.

"Yes?"

" 'Tis me, m'lord. Maggie. An' the lady."

"Enter."

It wasn't real, couldn't be happening, Mara thought. Here she was, entering Baldwin's bedchamber with no doubt about what was to happen. Her parents were dead, savagely murdered; she would never see Stephen again; she was now the property and toy of the most brutal and repulsive man in all of England . . . and she felt nothing. It had to be a dream.

"Come here." Baldwin crooked his finger. "Come closer."

When Mara didn't move, Maggie grasped her hand and pulled her nearer the earl. He dismissed Maggie without taking his eyes from his captive.

"Leave us," he ordered brusquely. "But remain outside the door."

Maggie hurried to do as she was bid. She ducked her head so he would not see the wonder and dismay in her expression. When she had closed the door behind her, she hesitated, unsure whether she wanted to hear what was to follow or not. In the end, Maggie pressed her ear to the heavy wooden door. It was long moments before she heard another word.

Baldwin circled his prisoner, index finger pressed to the point of his chin. He let his eyes caress Mara slowly. There was an ugly, purpling bruise at her temple, and a jagged gash. But that did not detract from her magnificence. The mass of her pale hair fell to her waist and gleamed in the candlelight. Her eyes, though dull, were as deep and dark as the sea. Despite her captivity, the girl's stature was undiminished. Never had there been such a woman.

And she was his. To do with exactly as he pleased.

Baldwin completed his circle and halted mere inches from Mara. She could smell his rank breath. His hand touched her arm, traveled upward. His fingers curled around the neck of her tunic. He smiled. And ripped the garment from her body.

Mara gasped and Baldwin laughed. Despite the fire that hissed in the hearth, the air was chill and Mara's nipples pressed against the thin fabric of her chemise. Baldwin's gaze devoured her with renewed appreciation.

"You're lovely, my dear. But you know that, don't you? You've always had quite a high opinion of yourself." Baldwin reached out and chucked Mara's chin. The action was neither playful nor gentle. "And now you've reached the pinnacle, haven't you?" he continued. "You belong to me, Earl of Cumbria. You wear . . ." He chuckled. "*Wore* my mother's clothes. Soon you'll be my plaything. You will sleep in my bed. Won't you, my dear? You've reached a station in life you never thought to attain. Mistress of the Earl of Cumbria."

Yellow teeth gleamed in the firelight as Baldwin grinned. "And, yes, you did hear me correctly. I did say 'mistress,' not 'wife.' Marriage is no longer a privilege I care to bestow upon you. No. No, you will simply occupy my bed from time to time. Until I tire of you, of course."

Baldwin let his watery gaze devour Mara's clearly visible breasts. They were exactly as he imagined them to be, full, heavy, tipped with rosebuds. He watched them rise and softly fall with the rhythm of her breath. He felt the stirring in his loins. Smiling, he lifted his eyes to her face again.

Proud. Haughty. Unbowed. The sapphire stare regarded him without so much as a blink of apprehension. He felt his manhood become flaccid once more. Felt the red rage begin to build in his breast.

But he must not let it. With every ounce of his being, Baldwin fought to retain control. She must not win. Not this time, not this battle. She was his now. She would learn that.

Baldwin turned and walked to the fire. He folded his arms across his chest. "But not yet, my dear," he went on. "Not quite yet. There is something you need to learn first." He stopped in front of the hearth and put one hand on the warm stone mantel.

When he turned to face her again, the blessed numbness that had protected Mara was momentarily pierced by Baldwin's expression of absolute cruelty. She trembled.

Baldwin eyed his captive for a long moment. He would

break her. *Yes.* He would strip away her pride and leave her clothed only in fear. Then he would cleave her with his sword.

"You need to learn humility, my dear. You need to know what it is to be cold, so you will appreciate the warmth of my bed. You need to experience hunger, so you will relish the scraps from my table. You need to be alone, and very, very lonely, so you will smile when you are brought into my presence. Do you understand, my pale-haired whore? That is what you will be, you know. You will grovel for my attention, my touch. And if you are very, very good, I shall reward you with my . . . affections."

The earl's thin hand reached as if to caress Mara. But his fingers had barely grazed her breast when they were suddenly at her throat. The grip was tight, painful. It cut off her breath.

As suddenly as he had grasped her, Baldwin released Mara and slapped her smartly across the face.

"Witch!" he hissed. "You will learn what it means to cross the Earl of Cumbria! Maggie! Come here!"

Maggie slipped inside the door and tried to make herself as small as possible. "Yes, m'lord?"

"Take the *lady* to her rooms." The lines of brutality that etched the earl's face were unrelieved by his smile. "To her rooms in the dungeon."

Chapter Twenty-one

Amanda knocked again. No response. Knowing it would be locked, she tried the handle anyway. It turned uselessly in her hand. She knocked harder. "Stephen!"

Nausea churned in the pit of her stomach. She forced herself to remain calm.

John was in the kitchen. She could get him to come and open the door. But did she want him to see how much Steve had deteriorated? Maybe it was better to handle it herself at the moment—at least until she saw what shape Steve was in. The door wasn't really a problem.

Tim had accidentally locked himself in the bathroom once when he was three. She remembered what John had done with a wire hanger. It didn't take her long to open the door to Steve's bedroom.

Her brother was sprawled on the bed. The stubble on his chin had almost grown into a beard, and the unpleasant odor of stale sweat permeated the room. The first thing Amanda did was open a window. Stephen groaned and rolled over.

"Get up, Steve. Come on. This has gone on long enough." Amanda stood over him, hands on her hips. "Steve, do you hear me?"

He did hear her. But it was so hard. He didn't want to leave where he was. He didn't want to come back, not yet. He had something important to do. Perhaps the most important thing he had ever done in his life.

"Can't . . . can't, Mandy," he muttered, face turned to the pillow.

"Can't what, Stephen?" she demanded. "Can't get up? Take a shower? What's the matter, Steve? If you're sick, I'll call a doctor."

No, no doctors. Stephen managed to rouse himself. He rolled over and squinted at his sister. "I'm fine. Fine, Mandy."

"No, you're not. You're not fine." Amanda had reached the limits of her patience. "You haven't left this room in four days. You haven't eaten. You obviously haven't bathed. I don't know *what* you've done, except lie here. This can't go on, Steve. You can't just lie here until you *die.*"

"I'm not going to die," he said tiredly.

"Well, it sure doesn't seem like you want to live."

Oh, but he did. He did. He had never felt so alive before. And if she would just leave him alone, he could return to that life. "I'll be fine, Mandy. Please. Just let me sleep." He turned over again.

"You've slept long enough," Amanda snapped. "I've had it, Stephen. I'm going to have to do something."

He was groggy, already prepared to slip into the twilight world where he was happiest. But something in the tone of his sister's voice had managed to penetrate his consciousness. He was in danger. He had to do something to protect himself. He had to be able to return. To return to *her.*

Stephen sat up and shook his head. It was always so hard to remember when he was fully awake. He felt the pull from the . . . other place. But he couldn't recall it with clarity. At least he couldn't before.

It was clearer now, however. He had to get back. *Had to*. She was in trouble.

But so was he.

How long had it been since he had eaten? He felt dizzy and light-headed when he stood up. He stumbled to the bathroom and splashed cold water on his face. Mandy. He had to talk to Mandy.

Stephen took the stairs slowly, holding on to the handrail. Maybe he'd eat something, take a shower. Have a talk with Mandy. She needed to know how important it was for him to rest now, to be able to go back to wherever it was he went. Because the answer to everything lay in that other place. He knew it. He had to go back and take care of . . . *her*. Then everything would be all right.

He heard voices when he reached the bottom stair. Voices coming from the kitchen. John and Mandy. He stopped.

They were talking about him. But he couldn't quite hear. He moved quietly around the corner, into the dining room.

"—always supported you, Amanda. I'm not going to stop now."

"I know, John. And I'm so grateful, honey. I can never tell you how much I appreciate what you've done for Stephen. But I . . . I just don't think we can care for him here anymore."

"That has to be your decision, Amanda."

"I know, I know."

Stephen heard the sorrow in his sister's voice. He knew what she was going to say next. He was right.

"I . . . I think I should call Dr. Krieger. Maybe he was right after all. Steve needs to be hospitalized. It's perfectly obvious *I* haven't been able to help him. I don't know *what* I was thinking, sending him to Millie Thurman."

He didn't wait to hear any more. Time was of the essence now. He had to get away, had to get back. If they stopped him now, put him on drugs, he wouldn't be able to reach her again. There would be no more second chances. The promise would be broken forever. He would be doomed.

Stephen sprinted up the stairs.

Chapter Twenty-two

Stephen had never been more miserable. His impatience to reach Baldwin's castle was nearly intolerable. Fear for Mara's safety gnawed at him. It was a searing pain in his gut, and the physical discomfort increased with every turn of the cart's wheels. He glanced at Jack, who sat beside him, hands loosely holding the horse's reins. The small servant was apparently unaffected by the constant jolting and side-to-side sway. Stephen wondered how he stood it. He himself longed for the solid, sturdy feel of his chestnut stallion beneath him.

But their mounts were back at Ullswater by now. And Thomas, who'd returned with them, had promised to recruit what locals he could to bury Ullswater's dead and restore the castle and grounds as much as was possible. Alfred had been sent to Bellingham for reinforcements. The man who had originally driven Baldwin's cart full of plunder, an innocent peasant who had once supplied wheat for Ranulf's mill, had been sent happily home to his family. The guard who had accompanied him, one of

Baldwin's men, had been summarily dispatched. Everything, so far, had gone according to plan. The most difficult part, however, was yet to come.

Stephen stared into the darkness ahead as if might see the path to the future. Would their plan work? Would they even make it through the castle gates? And, if they did, would they be able to find Mara? Alive? Whole? Untouched by Baldwin's filthy hands?

His thoughts were devastating, debilitating. Stephen knew he must banish them or lose his mind. He could allow himself to think only about rescue. Escape. It was likely more than an army of knights could accomplish, much less a single man, but he had to try.

A few lights still burned here and there in Hawkshead; then the village was behind them. He and Jack were alone together in the black of the night with only the steady *clip-clop* of the horse's hooves and the rickety creak of the cart. And then they were alone no longer.

"Ho! Who goes there?"

A horse whinnied and two riders appeared. They were well armed and well mounted, and Stephen assumed they were the earl's men. As Jack hauled on the reins, Stephen called his own challenge.

"Who are you to interfere in the business of the Earl of Cumbria?"

"The earl's men-at-arms," came the immediate and insolent reply. "Now speak. Who are you?"

"Only a poor farmer," Jack said quickly, with a sidelong glance at his master. "Pressed into service by yer lord. Jack, I be called. An' I bring the treasure from Ullswater Castle with this guard here, as I was bid."

A brief discussion between the riders followed. Then: "All right. Follow us. Move it along. Sharp now!"

Stephen had to muffle his long, deep sigh of relief. With an escort of the earl's own men, they were assured of getting past the gate guards and through. Luck seemed to be with them.

Minutes later the castle loomed before them, so massive and dark it was silhouetted, black on black, against the midnight sky.

"Open for the earl's men!" one of the escorts cried, and proceeded to identify himself. A groan, a rumble, and the heavy gate lumbered upward.

"Hup!" Jack slapped his reins on the cart horse's broad back, and the animal set its load into motion once again. Stephen's right hand gripped the seat until his knuckles were white.

They were inside.

Cold. She was so cold. Mara hugged herself and shivered uncontrollably. Her teeth chattered. She squeezed her eyes shut and prayed for the dawn to come, the sun, and its warmth. She longed to feel it on her face. Feel it seep into her bones and relieve the awful, aching chill that leeched the warmth from her very blood.

It was better if she kept moving, and Mara rocked, careful not to touch the cold and damp stone wall at her back. The straw-filled pallet she sat on rustled, and an unpleasant musty odor rose from it. It was not nearly as bad as the stench that rose from the shallow trough that ran through her cell, with its trickle of vile, contaminated water. She turned her face to the small, barred window.

Her damp and dank cubicle was built into the foundation of the tower, but it was not completely below ground level. Her window, an inch or so higher than her head, looked out on the castle courtyard. Sunlight and fresh air. She kept her eyes fixed to the tiny opening until she was able to discern a lessening of the darkness.

Soon she would feel warmth again.

But only warmth, nothing else. No life, no emotion. The numbness was her blessing. Baldwin would eventually send for her again. Better that she did not care what happened to her.

Better she never thought of Stephen again.

The Circle of a Promise

*   *   *

Light was the enemy. All had gone well under cover of darkness, but in the bright light of day the game might be over. It was one thing to masquerade as one of the earl's men in the dark; it was quite another to keep up the charade in daylight. As the world around them slowly took on form, Stephen shrank into the shadow of the tower door.

Jack stood in front of him, arms casually folded, and gazed about the courtyard as if he hadn't a care in the world. He actually had several. The cart had been unloaded, and any moment someone was going to notice and send him on his way. Jack winced when their horse snorted impatiently and pawed at the cobbled ground.

"I may have t' leave you soon," he whispered out of the corner of his mouth to Stephen. "If I do, I'll get back in somehow. There's bound to be lots of traffic in an' out durin' the day. No one'll notice an extra body."

"It's too risky," Stephen hissed back. "If I find Mara, I'm going to have to run for it. I don't want to have to worry about you, too."

"On the other hand," Jack replied softly, "I may not have t' leave at all. Look here."

A familiar clank and rumble came to their ears as the great gate opened. A minute later, the first of several carts rolled into the courtyard. Stephen smelled fresh bread, and his mouth watered. His heartbeat quickened with renewed hope.

The village of Hawkshead provisioned Baldwin's castle. There would be a great deal of activity throughout the day. There were not only villagers and their goods, but mounted guards who rode among them, examining wagon loads and keeping order. Stephen would be able to move about with at least a modicum of freedom. He might even be able to locate Mara's whereabouts.

"Go stand by the horse," he instructed Jack. "Try and look busy. I'm going."

As Jack sauntered casually toward their cart horse, Stephen melted into the rapidly growing crowd.

Mara stood beneath the window and gripped the ledge when the sun finally topped the castle walls. Her body warmed slowly, and she moved from her post only once.

Soon after dawn, Maggie appeared with a mug of water and piece of stale bread. She hastily put the meager meal on the ground inside the door and withdrew. The bread was too moldy to consider eating, but Mara's thirst was almost unbearable. She drained her mug and returned to the window.

Her mind was still numb, and the day passed in a haze. From her vantage, Mara saw little but booted feet, horses' hooves, and wagon wheels. A subdued din came to her ears, aromas of bread, baked meats, and spices to her nostrils. Once, a stirring breeze lifted the hair from her temples. Yet her senses registered little but sun and warmth, blessed warmth on her flesh. Then, in mid-afternoon, the clouds rolled in.

Mara didn't notice at first. The bright light winked in and out as clouds blew past the sun. But finally their gray, purplish mass obscured the glowing disc altogether, and Mara felt the chill.

Had she the tears, she would have cried. The sun was gone, and the smell of moisture rode the air. A low rumble of thunder sounded in the distance. Mara leaned her forehead against the cold stone wall and wondered if she would be able to bear another night.

The day neared its end, a spring storm threatened, and the courtyard had almost emptied of its daily bustle. Even Jack had finally been forced to leave, no longer able to find excuses for his loitering. Stephen knew he had to act now or never. As the last cart clanked and rattled its way across the wooden bridge, he made his move.

The long day had not been totally wasted. Stephen had

learned at least one important fact: Baldwin slept not in the manor, but in the tower. And where Baldwin was, Mara must eventually be.

The tower's huge and heavy wooden door was recessed in its smooth, stone wall. Stephen kept to the shadows as he made his way to the entrance. No guard stood outside, but he knew there was one inside, for he had seen him once when he had admitted a one-eyed woman bearing a laden tray: The earl's supper, probably.

Stephen had also caught glimpses of men at the arrow-slit windows above him, and along what must be the spiraling stairs to Baldwin's chambers. How he was going to deal with them, find Mara, and flee with her he had no idea. He only knew he had to try.

He had almost reached the doorway when he caught movement out of the corner of his eye. He melted into the wall and recognized the woman he had seen earlier. This time, she carried a bucket of water that sloshed over her shabby skirt. There was a length of linen cloth draped over her arm.

Stephen stood stock-still, barely breathing, and prayed the shadows camouflaged his form. But the woman appeared not to notice him. Her good eye was on the side away from him. Her vision was restricted and, for the moment at least, he had the advantage. He had to use it.

Maggie knocked twice, and the guard opened up. They engaged in a brief conversation, door still wide, and Stephen edged closer. He heard the woman's voice.

"Thanks to ye for takin' me bucket," she said. "Think m' arm was gettin' longer."

"Let me call someone else down here to the door so I can help—"

"Oh, never mind that. 'Twill take but a minute. Mind y' don't spill any more."

Footsteps then, receding. Downward. Into the dungeon.

It was incredible luck. Stephen slipped past through the door.

Maggie was grateful for the help. Her arm was stiff, her back ached, and her heart was heavy. Her lord's words echoed in her head.

"Make her presentable. Even Ranulf's daughter will not have fared well after a night in my dungeon." He had been seated in a chair by the window. He had rested his chin on steepled fingers and smiled. "I like the wares to be clean before I sample them."

Maggie had dropped her gaze to hide her chagrin. But the earl missed little.

"Oh, now, Maggie. Don't look so forlorn. I'm merely sampling, I told you. What if she's not to my taste? She will no longer warm my bed, and you will still have your place in it, won't you? That *is* what you're worrying about—isn't it, Maggie?"

Somehow she had managed to nod, though his words had not helped at all. How could he not find the lady attractive, desirable? She would not only become his bed-mate, but possibly his wife as well.

Dismissed at last, Maggie had hurried from the room to do her lord's bidding before he could see the tears that tracked down her grubby cheek.

Now, as the guard opened the cell door for her and returned her bucket, the lady Mara turned toward them. The faint spark of hope that yet flickered in Maggie's heart went out completely.

Never had the good Lord created a woman so beautiful. Not even a night in the dungeon had bowed her. Lower lip caught between her teeth, Maggie put her bucket on the floor and set about her labors.

Stephen was ready for the guard when he returned. The man trudged slowly up the last few steps, expecting no one, treachery the furthest thing from his mind. He did

NAME: _____

ADDRESS: _____

_____

_____

TELEPHONE: _____

E-MAIL: _____

_____ I want to pay by credit card.

__ Visa   __ MasterCard   __ Discover

Account Number: _____

Expiration date: _____

SIGNATURE: _____

Send this form, along with $2.00 shipping and handling for your FREE books, to:

Love Spell Romance Book Club
20 Academy Street
Norwalk, CT 06850-4032

Or fax (must include credit card information!) to: 610.995.9274.
You can also sign up on the Web at www.dorchesterpub.com.

Offer open to residents of the U.S. and Canada only. Canadian residents, please call 1.800.481.9191 for pricing information.

not see the tall, mail-clad figure pressed to the wall opposite the door. His thoughts were far away, on a pale-haired beauty, and the terrible waste of her on a man like the earl.

He did not have time to gasp for breath, much less cry out, when the hand went over his mouth. He struggled, but the grip that held him was like iron. Then a bright blossom of pain exploded behind his right ear, and he knew no more.

Stephen lowered the man gently to the ground. He would sleep for a long while—long enough, perhaps, for Stephen to take care of the remaining guards on the stairs. After that . . .

The earl was somewhere above him. Stephen raised his eyes, as if he might see through stone, and his hand tightened on the hilt of his sword. If Baldwin had so much as laid a single finger on Mara, he would die painfully. In the meantime, a blade pressed to his neck might persuade him to disclose Mara's whereabouts. He might then serve as hostage until they were clear of the castle.

It was a desperate plan, but the only one he had. Stephen took a deep breath and started up the stairs—then heard footsteps coming up from below.

He whirled. It might only be the woman, and she would be easy to deal with. If he hurried.

Stephen bolted down the spiral stairs, taking two at a time. Thunder crashed overhead and the gloomy evening turned darker still. He did not see the women until he was almost upon them.

Two feminine figures were all that immediately registered on his senses. He halted in a fighting stance, the point of his sword held out directly in front of him.

Then he recognized her, bruised and pale, clad only in a thin chemise. But alive. *Alive!*

Stephen's heart swelled, rose from his chest to his throat, and threatened to choke him. "Mara!"

Chapter Twenty-three

The guard startled Mara, standing there in a fighting pose. It roused her momentarily from her stupor, and she raised her eyes.

Stephen?

The shock was too great, more than she could comprehend in her state of perpetual dullness. Stephen? she wondered again.

He saw the amazement and disbelief in Mara's gaze. Saw surprise and fear in the single dark eye of the other woman. Knew in an instant she would scream and raise the alarm.

Mara watched Stephen's glance alight on Maggie. She saw the angle of his sword, and knew what he intended to do. He had no choice. Mara, too, knew what she must do.

Despite her dulled senses, Mara had observed something in Maggie. She used it now as her weapon.

The servant's eye was wide. Her mouth fell open as Stephen started for her. Mara raised her left hand, halting him, and put her right on Maggie's arm.

"Maggie, listen. Listen!" Mara repeated urgently. "This is the man I . . . I am betrothed to." She gave a brief glance at Stephen; then all her attention was focused on Maggie. "He's come to take me from Baldwin, to take me home. So the earl can't have me. Do you understand, Maggie? I'll be gone."

The girl's eye flicked from Stephen to Mara and back again. She remained silent.

"Please, Maggie. Please let me go!"

"He'll . . . he'll know," she said at last. "He'll hurt me."

Mara winced involuntarily. She could well imagine how Baldwin treated this poor girl. "How could he find out you let me go, Maggie? You could simply say I escaped."

Maggie shook her head. "He . . . he might even kill me this time."

Mara looked at Stephen with the plea evident in her gaze. He understood at once.

"Come with us," he said quickly. "I'll make it seem you're my hostage, my prisoner. Then you'll be out of his reach. For good."

Out of his reach. The words replayed in Maggie's head. But she knew, sadly and without a doubt, that she could not, would not, ever leave Baldwin. Slowly, she shook her head.

"No. I can't," she replied simply.

"Stephen." Mara's voice was scarcely more than a groan. "He *will kill* her."

"Not if he thinks she did her best to prevent your escape," the man said suddenly. "Not if she's injured trying to prevent the escape."

Maggie understood. And she did want Mara gone. It was worth the injury. Worse had happened and might happen still. But at least Mara would be gone; the earl would be hers again. She nodded.

"Thank you, Maggie," Stephen said quietly. Then, before she had time to be afraid, he caught her a glancing blow across her cheek with the hilt of his sword. Nothing was broken, but a cut opened. Blood trickled down her cheek, which soon would purple. Something within Stephen quailed, not because he had inflicted the injury, but to see how Maggie bore it—like a dog long used to its beatings.

Maggie raised a hand to her cheek. Then, "Go," she said in a curiously unsteady voice. "Go on now. Run!"

They did not need to be told again.

William thoroughly enjoyed the elevation in his status. Although nothing as yet was official, most of the men-at-arms looked to him for leadership now, and he took on as many responsibilities as possible. He wanted to consolidate his power and position while he was still in favor. When the earl's mood changed, as it inevitably must, he wanted to be a difficult man to dislodge. He enjoyed power, its perquisites, and intended to keep them.

One of the duties William had assumed was the end-of-the-day patrol of the vast castle courtyard. Built fairly recently, to the earl's specifications, the castle was less an island of defense than a lavish residence. It was shaped like a large oval, with the great hall opposite the main gate. The perimeter wall was interspersed with towers, six in all. And, as Baldwin loathed clutter of any kind, the sole outbuildings were twin stone structures positioned symmetrically at opposite ends of the long oval. One was a stable, the other a basic kitchen. As a result, the castle was provisioned almost entirely by the village. It was an arrangement that suited everyone, particularly William.

A stable boy held his horse's headstall, and William mounted. He was a bit slower these days, with the addition of some fine pieces of armor, only slightly dented. Although Ranulf's knights had been well past their prime, their equipment had been first-rate.

Comfortably seated, William gathered his reins and nodded at Wulfric, his chosen companion of late, and the two headed off on their rounds. So many people came and went during the day, on so many different errands, there were usually a few strays. The earl looked upon strays the same way he looked upon clutter: to be removed.

The two knights set off in opposite directions, to meet again in front of the great hall. The only people in sight were Baldwin's men-at-arms and those few who maintained the stables, the kitchen, and the earl's person.

William examined each face carefully. Just let him find a straggler. He knew what to do. The earl would be proud of his efficiency.

He had just passed the second of the towers south of the gate when he heard the commotion.

Maggie pressed the fingers of one hand to her wounded cheek, and intentionally crumpled against the wall. Stephen threw her a last sad glance.

"We're going to have to hurry," he said to Mara. "We're free. For the moment. But the castle is crawling with guards." He did not have to add that Maggie would not, could not, remain silent for long.

The strange lethargy in his betrothed's eyes, however, disturbed him. She had been sensible enough to reason with Maggie, but the curious lassitude seemed to have fallen upon her once more.

"Mara, stay behind me. Be cautious. And be prepared to do exactly as I say. Do you understand?"

She nodded dumbly. He wanted nothing more than to take her in his arms and hold her, to bury his face in her hair and make the world go away. But they had to flee. Now.

"Take my hand, Mara."

He had never touched her before. The moment should have been different. Mara didn't even consider it. Numb, she did as she was told. Stephen pulled her up the stairs behind him.

The guard was still unconscious. No one had discovered him. Stephen opened the outer door—and saw two patrolling knights.

The pair rode away from him, backs turned. The gate was still open.

Another incredible stroke of luck. He hesitated only an instant, to glance at Mara and see if there was comprehension in her eyes.

She, too, saw the guards, the gate. A spark of life flickered in her gaze.

"Run, Mara. Run!" Stephen hissed, and sprinted for the gate.

Mara matched him step for step. A shout went up from the walls.

The gate was close, so close. And the approaching storm had further darkened the evening. Concealing night would come soon. Rain would wash away their tracks. If they could just make it through the gate, they'd have a chance to run, maybe to find a horse.

But the alarm was given. Guards atop the wall pointed at them and continued to shout.

Legs still pumping, Stephen saw the heavyset knight nearest him wheel his mount. The animal reared as the man drew his sword and prepared to sweep down on them. Stephen pushed Mara behind him.

"No!" Her spark had become a fire. Her tone brooked no opposition. "Give me your short-sword. I'll stand at your side."

There was no time to argue, even had her tone allowed. Nor was Stephen sure he wanted to. Though clad only in her linen shift, her long pale hair in wild disarray, she was a spectacular figure. It occurred to Stephen, in a flash, that he would do well to have this woman fight at his side. He pulled his short-sword from its sheath and handed it to her.

She gave him the briefest of smiles.

Then Wulfric was upon them.

The knight did not fully grasp the situation. He did not know who the young, black-haired man was, or why he was with the earl's woman, apparently taking her away. He did, however, enjoy a good fight. Especially weighted on his side. He was on a horse. The couple was afoot. He grinned as he charged down on the foolish young pair.

Steel rang against steel as the weapons met. Wulfric was surprised at the man's strength. He hauled hard on his mount's reins and prepared to turn and attack again. His surprise turned to unpleasant amazement.

Mara hated to do it. She loved animals, particularly the magnificent and well-trained stallions skilled in the arts of war. But in a life-and-death situation, she had no sentiment. As Stephen met Wulfric's renewed attack, Mara moved behind the horse and, with one swift, accurate stroke, slashed the blade across the horse's hind legs.

Although Wulfric's mind worked slowly, he did realize his mount had been hamstrung when the animal sank down on its haunches. He kicked free of the saddle just as the huge stallion collapsed with a scream of pain.

Wulfric scrambled to his feet. He took his sword in both hands, pivoted, and prepared to fight on foot. He grinned when he saw William riding hard in their direction. In moments, guards from the walls and gate towers would also join them. He'd have to hurry to strike the winning blow.

Stephen and Mara stood back to back. William came from one direction and Wulfric, slowly and steadily, grinning ear to ear, from the other. When Mara saw William would easily reach them first, she stepped aside to give Stephen full use of his sword arm.

He used it well.

William did not anticipate a problem. Whoever the fool was who thought to steal the earl's prize—single-handedly moreover—was about to lose his head. The entire guard of the castle was against him. He didn't stand a chance. William had developed a fatal sense of over-confidence.

Experienced and able fighter that he was, Stephen noted at once the foolhardy brashness of his opponent's attack. He drew his sword over his right shoulder, both hands on the hilt, and when William reached him he gave a mighty swing.

The strength and force of the blow caught William completely off guard. The knight lost his balance, dropped his weapon, and toppled over backward. He forgot to let go of his reins. The gray stallion he rode reared when he felt the cruel pressure on his mouth. Already overbalanced by his rider, the great animal slowly, inexorably overturned.

William had no chance. He opened his mouth to scream, but only a terrified, strangled breath issued forth. An instant later, two thousand pounds of horse crushed him into the cobblestone courtyard.

Wulfric hesitated, momentarily stunned by the gruesome scene that had just occurred. It was the last and most important bit of luck Stephen and Mara required. As William's blood-flecked animal struggled to its feet, Stephen grabbed hold of the horse's reins and vaulted into the saddle.

"Mara! Your hand!" He reached down, clasped the girl's forearm and, as she swung her leg over the horse's back, pressed his heels to the charger's sides. They were in a full gallop by the time they reached the gate.

Events had transpired so quickly, the gate guard had barely had time to register them. When he belatedly realized he must lower the gate to prevent the couple's escape, the earl's prize and her rescuer were almost through.

His hands were quickly in motion . . . but too late!

Stephen and Mara pounded over the wooden bridge, just in time to hear the gate rumble closed behind them.

Seconds later the sound was drowned out by the throaty roar of thunder.

They had made it. Against all odds, they had made it.

Stephen longed to halt the stallion and take Mara in his arms, but they were not yet out of bowshot. Angry shouts came from the walls, and he did not have to look back to know arrows rained through the swiftly falling gloom. He urged the charger on, faster and faster.

Soon the gates would be opened again. Armed, mounted, and angry knights would pour across the bridge. He and Mara could not pause for an instant.

Yet it would take only seconds to do what he had yearned for since he had come upon her climbing the tower steps. Mere seconds, and perhaps the most precious seconds of his entire life.

The dappled charger was a massive animal, but expertly trained. As soon as Stephen applied pressure to the reins, the stallion slid to a halt. He shook his great head. Slowly, Stephen turned in the saddle.

Mara's eyes were nearly on a level with his own. They were dark—as dark as the night that enfolded them. He could not read her expression, could not see if the strange languor had returned. His gaze dropped to her mouth.

Her lips trembled. He longed to still them. Longed to crush her in his fierce embrace. She was safe, alive, Baldwin's prisoner no more.

Yet he could not know what was in her heart, a heart so wounded he could not even begin to comprehend the pain and anguish she must feel. So he cupped her face tenderly, so tenderly, in his hands. "Mara," he whispered.

She did not respond.

A patter of raindrops fell. Their stallion shook his head again, pawed the earth, and snorted. The rain fell in earnest.

Another miracle. He could not afford to waste the gift God and the heavens gave them, the rivers of rain that would wash away the signs of their passing.

Even as Stephen gave the stallion his head, thunder crashed and the full might of the heavens' downpour was loosed upon the earth. In seconds the pair was soaked, hair and clothing plastered to their skin.

Stephen felt Mara's arms snake about his waist. She clung to him, and they pounded away through the wild and stormy night.

Chapter Twenty-four

Baldwin had watched from his tower window. He had seen it all.

The shout from the wall had alerted him. He had hurried to the window in time to see Amarantha—his prize, his trophy—emerge from the tower door below. Her hand had been clasped tightly, familiarly, by a lean and muscular man. The quality of that man's mail, boots, and weapons marked him as a man of substance. A landed man. A baron? One of the *northern barons?*

His fists clenched, hard and white. The blood drained from his face. Baldwin knew who it was who escaped with the hard-won, silver-haired witch.

Bellingham. Stephen of Bellingham. The man to whom Mara was betrothed.

Even as he watched the melee below, even though the baron was only one man among many, a single knight amidst a castle full of knights, Baldwin knew he would triumph. His reputation as a fighting man cast a shadow across the whole of England. How he had come to be within these castle walls, had breached the tower and stolen away its most prized possession, Baldwin did not know and did not care. He knew only his treasure was lost.

The earl's jaws had clenched as tightly as his hands as he watched the drama unfold. He saw William and Wulfric make fools of themselves. He watched William die, crushed to death beneath his gray stallion. He had watched his treasure stolen away. Then he had watched the gate close behind the fugitives, making any timely pursuit impossible.

Fools! Idiots! Incompetents!

"Guards! Guards! Where are my guards?"

Maggie was halfway up the spiraling stair when she heard Baldwin's shriek. The guards who rushed out the tower door hesitated. Although the fight in the courtyard· was clearly over, no one wanted to face the earl's wrath. One of the two men looked away and knelt to aid his fallen comrade, the unconscious guard at the foot of the steps. Maggie did not wait to see what the other was going to do. She knew her place.

Baldwin did not answer her knock. Maggie entered the room anyway, and saw his back was turned to her. She closed the door quietly and leaned against it. Blood from the wound on her cheek stained her neck and bodice, but she made no effort to wipe it away.

Her earl's thin body was rigidly erect, arms stiff and straight, fists clenched and pressed hard to his thighs. Maggie had seen him like this once before, when a stable man's ineptitude had caused the death of Baldwin's favorite mount. What followed had been frightening. Maggie was frightened now.

The tension in Baldwin's body built until all he could hear was the sound of the blood rushing through his veins. His usually orderly thoughts whirled crazily, until there was nothing but chaos in his brain and a hot, red rage in his heart. He spun.

Maggie stepped aside with a small gasp. The earl did not seem to notice her. He yanked the door open and swept past down the stairs, his long black hair lifting from his neck in the breeze of his swift passage. The uncertain guards, who still milled about the open tower door below, pressed themselves to the walls. Baldwin did not appear to notice them, either. He strode past into the courtyard as the more drops of rain pattered on the cobblestones.

Someone had put the hamstrung charger out of its misery. It lay, throat gaping, in a pool of congealing blood. William's crushed form lay nearby. Baldwin headed straight for the gruesome corpse.

"Imbecile! Half-wit!" he screamed, and kicked the broken body. "You deserved to die!" Another kick. "Get up! Get up!"

Rage and hatred contorted the earl's narrow features. Saliva flecked his chin. He kicked the corpse of his minion again and again, to the accompanying roar of thunder, until his boots and the hem of his tunic were stained with blood. Over and over he shrieked at the dead man to rise.

One by one the onlookers turned away. All but Maggie. She no longer feared her lover might learn her part in his prisoner's escape. When the earl finally sank to his knees, exhausted, she came and knelt at his side. The rain quickly soaked them both.

After a time, he allowed her to lead him away.

Despite his double burden, the noble gray stallion galloped steadily through the downpour. Stephen kept to the muddy track, but did not fear pursuit. Their tracks would soon be obliterated, and they were headed on a westerly route as well. Baldwin, if and when he chose to search for them, would head directly northeast, for Ranulf's castle. He would not find them along the way.

They continued on through the heavy rain. Streaks of

lightning occasionally, briefly, lit their way through the stormy night. Eventually the stallion's heaving sides began to steam. Stephen slowed him to a walk and turned in the saddle.

"We're going to have to find someplace to spend the night," he said quietly to Mara. "We're far enough from Baldwin to be safe, and I'd like to spare the horse."

His betrothed remained silent and immobile.

"Are you all right, Mara? If you fear to stop, we'll keep on."

After a while she shook her head. Her hair and clothes were sodden, and she was so cold her body was as numb as her emotions. "I'm . . . I'm all right," she muttered hoarsely. "Stop. Please."

Stephen's stomach tightened at the dead sound of Mara's voice. He recalled, with vivid horror, the scene at Ullswater castle. Mara had undoubtedly witnessed the carnage. She had seen her parents brutally murdered. And what had she suffered as Baldwin's prisoner? Stephen dared not think. Not now, not yet. He had to find shelter.

The countryside around them was green and wooded. There were no villages, and only two or three widely scattered shepherds' cottages. Visibility was poor, and Stephen would have missed them entirely if they had not been close to the road. The feeble light from their small windows barely penetrated the soggy gloom.

Stephen feared to compromise the inhabitants by asking them to shelter fugitives from the earl's wrath, but Mara needed rest and warmth. Soon.

The deserted hut, set well back among the trees, would have passed unnoticed had Stephen's attention been less focused. As it was he almost missed it. He turned the stallion off the road and approached the small, tumbledown structure cautiously.

One wall was missing completely, the other crumbling. Barely half of the rotting thatched roof remained. Dead and moldering leaves littered and floor and banked against what was left of the walls. Nothing had ever looked so inviting.

Stephen dismounted and held out his arms for Mara, who fell into them. He steadied her and led her into a corner beneath the sagging roof.

The sudden cessation of rain beating on her head and shoulders was wonderful. Mara's daze slowly lifted. She looked around, took in the details of her surroundings, and sank to the leafy ground. She leaned back and closed her eyes.

Stephen watched his bride-to-be with concern. He knelt by her outstretched legs and lightly touched her shoulder. Her eyes flew open.

"Mara, are you all right?"

Her eyes closed again as she nodded. "I'm just . . . cold. So cold. And tired."

Although her body already relaxed toward an exhausted sleep, Stephen saw convulsive shudders tremble through her. He grasped her upper arms, and was aghast at how icy her flesh had become.

"Mara." He gave her a little shake, and her eyelids fluttered. Stephen rubbed her arms, trying desperately to ease the dangerous chill. "Mara, I'm going to find some dry wood, start a fire. I've got to get you warm. I won't go far."

She was too exhausted to reply. She thought she gave a small nod but wasn't sure. She was so terribly cold and numb.

Yet that was good—good because her mind couldn't summon the strength to remember the massacre, her parents' gruesome deaths, her part in the treachery that brought Baldwin's fist down on them all. Her fatigue was so great, all she could do was sit and listen to the small sounds Stephen made as he searched beneath the leaves for twigs and bits of dry wood. Then she heard him strike his flint, and she heard the flesh- and soul-warming sound of a crackling fire.

Mara turned her face to the warmth and saw the redness of the flames through her closed eyelids. She felt the frigid chill recede from her flesh.

Stephen returned to kneel at Mara's side. Purple bruises of exhaustion remained under her eyes, but some of the frightening pallor had left her face, and a hint of color touched her cheeks.

"I don't even have a cloak to give you," he murmured. "I'm so sorry. Sorry for everything." He looked away for a moment, lips compressed. He had to force himself to continue. "I . . . I rode with my knights to Ullswater, Mara. To get you. I know what happened."

She did not open her eyes. She turned her face away.

Stephen's concern deepened. He took her shoulders in his big hands. "I know you can hear me, Mara," he said. "If there's anything more I can do for you, please tell me. Let me help you, Mara. Please."

Mara opened her eyes slowly. She looked at Stephen squarely. "You can do nothing," she replied dully. "Unless you can undo what I have done."

"What you've done? What could you possibly have—"

"I am responsible for their deaths," she said, her voice toneless. "All of them."

"Responsible! For Baldwin's perfidy? You could not in any way be responsible, Mara. You would never knowingly invite this tragedy upon your family. I will not believe it." Stephen took Mara's chin in his hand and forced her to look at him. "Never forget that it was you who got us out of Baldwin's dungeon tower. It was you who stood at my side, you who fought at my side and saved us. I have never witnessed a greater act of courage. And I have seen many valiant deeds."

The fire's warmth seemed to have roused the gelid blood in her veins. Mara allowed memory to flow back into her.

She remembered seeing Stephen on the stair, the wonder of his presence when all hope had deserted her. She remembered Maggie and her brave sacrifice, their stand in the yard, the sword in her hand, the brief moments of the fight, their flight upon the great, gray charger. . . .

Something had stirred to life in her then. It stirred again now.

Stephen had come for her. Against all odds, he had come for her and rescued her from a fate too horrible to imagine. Her own part in the action was nothing. She had simply done what she had to do. The growing warmth in her kindled to a small flame.

He had come for her, risked his life for her, this man who knelt beside her with her chin tenderly cupped in his hand.

"Stephen, I . . ." The words caught in her throat. Tears pushed at her eyelids. The words that swelled Mara's heart, the thing that she wished to say was too big, too overwhelming, to give voice to. She wasn't ready. Not yet.

Instead, Mara tried to push to her feet. "The horse," she mumbled. "The horse . . . I—We have to take care of him."

Relief flooded Stephen like a wave. "I'll take care of him, Mara. Don't worry. He served us well. Stay by the fire and keep warm."

She sank back gratefully. Exhaustion still held her in its coils, but Mara no longer felt that weariness sucked her very life away. Through half-lidded eyes, she watched Stephen tend the stallion that had carried them so far, so fast.

The huge animal was docile. Stephen unsaddled him easily, and drew him out of the drizzle and into the flickering circle of firelight. He stroked the long, smooth curve of the horse's muscular neck.

Mara couldn't keep her eyes open any longer, could no longer seem to support the weight of her eyelids. They did not even open when the stallion lowered his head and nuzzled her shoulder. His warm breath blew against her neck. Blindly, she put a hand out to touch his great, damp head, and a faint smile curved her lips.

"You rescued us, didn't you?" she whispered. "I think I'll call you . . . Hero."

Stephen knew, when he saw her hand drop to her lap, that she slept. When he eased down beside her and put his arm about her shoulders, her flesh was no longer icy, but warm and vital. He allowed his own eyes to close.

The stallion stood watch over them both.

Jack had spent his day lurking as close to the castle gate as he dared. He abandoned the cart in a stand of ash and requisitioned its horse as his mount. He was ready to ride the instant he saw Stephen and his rescued bride.

But his anxiety had grown along with the lengthening shadows. It turned to fear when thunder rolled, and there was still no sign of his master.

Jack cursed himself for ever having left Stephen. What had made him think his master could effect such a daring rescue all alone? He was on the verge of risking all in an attempt to reenter the castle, when the most amazing thing happened.

He was near enough to hear the commotion. He sat a little straighter on his big, brown horse and watched the gate intently. Just as a light rain started to fall, a handsome gray charger pounded over the bridge. On its back were the two people Jack wanted most in the world to see.

Grinning ear to ear, Jack nocked an arrow in his bow and prepared to pick off at least the first person in pursuit of the pair. Then another amazing thing happened: The gate closed.

Jack lowered his bow. His jaw gaped. It was incomprehensible.

Yet it had happened. And Jack wasted no more time

pondering the imponderable. He set off at a canter behind the gray stallion.

His mount was slower than the charger, even with the charger's double burden, and his master's tracks were soon eliminated by the rain. But Jack had seen Stephen head west, and he knew Stephen's mind. He continued on the western road.

The rain lessened, but the ground was thick with mud. The cart horse plodded on slowly, and Jack dozed fitfully on the animal's broad back. He almost missed the faint light flickering through the trees.

Jack halted his horse and slid to the ground. He moved through the wood as silently as the fox he resembled. He had to clamp his hands over his mouth to keep from shouting with joy when he saw who it was in the ramshackle structure.

The two were sound asleep. Stephen's arm was around Mara's shoulders; her head was on his breast, one slim, elegant hand resting on his chest. Over his heart.

Only the gray stallion noticed Jack, and it pricked its ears curiously.

He backed away as quietly as he had come.

A smile lit his fine, sharp features. The rain was no more than a lingering mist. He would sleep in the open for the remainder of the night, the old brown horse his companion. He'd done worse.

Far to the east another pair slept, but not in peace. Tormented by his dreams, Baldwin tossed restlessly on his wide bed. Despite the chill in the air, his linen shirt was rank with sweat. An arm, flung to one side, caught Maggie on her injured cheek and she woke. It was not the first time that night.

"There, there," she murmured, and stroked the earl's pale, damp forehead. "Sleep, lord. Sleep."

The earl's lips continued to work in silent conversation. From time to time Maggie caught a word or phrase spoken aloud, and she knew why his body tried to flee from the dreams in his head. They were dreams of blood and death. Revenge.

She lay back on her pillow, but sleep eluded her the rest of the night. Mara was gone, yes, but her ghost haunted them. The earl would not sleep in peace again until he had recaptured his prize and taken his revenge. Maggie remembered the young man with the long, dark hair, the kindness in his gaze, the guilt and sympathy when he had struck her. She was sorry, truly sorry, he was going to have to die so horribly.

Chapter Twenty-five

Thomas could keep still no longer. His anxiety was too great, the impatience and inactivity too unfamiliar. For the tenth time that day, he toured the castle grounds.

No one would ever guess a massacre had occurred, bathing the courtyard in blood. Not a trace of the carnage remained. Thomas, along with the knights sent by Alfred, had been amazed by the outpouring of aid and sympathy from the people who tenanted Ranulf's estates. Once they saw the castle manned again, its defense against the earl secure, they had flocked to help.

The dead had been decently buried. Because the castle had no chapel or mausoleum, Ranulf and his lady lay side by side in Beatrice's garden, in the shade of the flowering pear. What was left of the kennels had been razed, the scorched stones hauled away to leave no reminder. The hall and sleeping apartments had been scoured and set to order, fresh rushes strewn upon the ground. The rooms looked empty, however, stripped of their luxuries.

A small staff of men and women, vassals whose homes near the castle had been destroyed, stayed to run the kitchen and look after Stephen's knights. All was set to rights, and in good time. It only remained for Stephen to return with his bride.

But as the hours of the second long day passed, Thomas grew increasingly pessimistic.

The weather did not improve his mood.

Yesterday it had rained. Though the present day was dry, the sky still threatened. Purple clouds hung low, without break, and a fitful, moisture-scented breeze stirred the air. Thomas felt it lift the thin and soft brown hair from his neck. He scrubbed at the faint stubble on his chin.

The day neared its end, and he didn't like to wait. He doubted he could stand another night wondering what had become of his baron and comrade. And he cursed himself for allowing Stephen to embark on such a desperate plan with such little hope of success. Splendid as she might be, no woman was worth losing one's life.

"Thomas."

He flinched, startled, and turned to see Walter approach. The knight, shorter than both Thomas and Stephen, was nevertheless broader and walked with the peculiar gait of a man with heavily muscled legs.

"The stables are in order," Walter reported. "All our horses are bedded. There was plenty of room. There were only a couple of palfreys left after Baldwin took what he wanted."

Thomas nodded. "Thank you, Walter."

"Thank me not. Merely direct me to the next task. You know I loathe idleness."

"We are of the same mind, old friend. But I . . ." Thomas hesitated. "Well . . ."

"You want me to have your horse saddled?" the man asked. He had the insight of long association.

The Circle of a Promise

"You know well my orders. I am to remain here, in charge, until the baron's return."

The two men exchanged knowing looks.

"I . . . I suppose *I* could go," Walter volunteered. A grin played at the corners of his mouth. "No one ordered me to stay put. I could take a few men, in case I ran into anyone needing assistance. I might even—"

Walter was cut short by a sudden and sharp bark.

But all the dogs had been butchered. They had both seen it. The men turned in unison toward the source of the sound.

The hound emerged from behind a pile of refuse near the kitchen building. His coarse gray coat was dirty and matted, dried blood covered his large head, and one eye was nearly swollen shut. He was lean from starvation and wary of the two men. His lip curled into an ugly snarl as he moved past them toward the gate. Once well away, he broke into a run and did not stop until he had reached his goal. He placed his broad forepaws against the gate and scrabbled at the wood, whining piteously all the while.

Thomas and Walter exchanged another glance. Then Thomas grinned.

"Well, I'll be damned," he breathed. His next words were shouted. "Open the gate! Quickly! Let that dog out!" To Walter, he said, "That hound knows something we don't."

"Let's find out what it is."

There was no time to go for their horses. As the gate lifted from the ground, the men sprinted for it in hot pursuit of the lean, gray hound.

The long sleep had left Mara's body rested, but she had eaten nothing in over twenty-four hours and she felt weak and shaky. The gash on her temple had closed, and the swelling had subsided, yet her head ached miserably and each step Hero took set it throbbing anew. Each step—bringing her closer and closer to Ullswater Castle.

The curious lassitude had returned. Mara had awakened to find Jack hunkered with Stephen by the small fire. She had been glad to see the loyal servant, and had managed a smile in reply to his cheerful greeting. Then Stephen had told her they would ride immediately to Ullswater.

"My knights hold the castle," he had informed her. "It's safe, Mara. You'll be safe there."

"Safe," she had murmured. "Yes, Stephen, safe. As long as there is no more treachery from within."

Sobs had threatened to choke her, and she buried her face in her hands. Stephen was at her side in an instant.

"Mara, what is it, what's wrong? What do you mean?"

She shook her head. It was too horrible. What she had done was too horrible.

But she had to tell him. The burden of guilt was crushing. She could no longer bear it alone.

Mara's hands dropped to her lap. She took a deep breath and looked Stephen in the eye. "It was all my fault," she said evenly. "Every death is on my conscience."

Stephen had protested, but Mara had continued with her tale. She told him of the secret passage, her disobedience, the peasant she had seen. She told him of her confession to her father, and the precautions that had been taken.

"But it was too late. Too late. Whoever that man was—and he must have been one of Baldwin's—he surely followed me back through the passage. It's the only way he could have gotten through so quickly, before the tunnel was sealed."

Mara recalled the incredible sound of the gate as it rumbled open. "It must have been him who opened the gate. Baldwin was able to ride right in . . ." She had been unable to say more.

Both Stephen and Jack had tried to dissuade her from her guilt. It was Baldwin, they said, who was responsible.

No one else. Stephen had even tried to console Mara by assuming his own burden of guilt. If only he had come sooner. If only . . .

But her heart was too heavy with sorrow to hear the reason in their words. Mara had not even been able to cry. Once again, she was numb.

It was a blessing, Mara told herself. How else was she going to pass beneath Ullswater's gate, return to the scene of the massacre? How else was she going to be able to withstand the terrible guilt?

She had tried once, briefly, to persuade Stephen to take her on to Bellingham. He had been gently firm.

"Bellingham is too far, Mara. You need food, proper shelter, and clothes."

He had gone on to assure her that Thomas and the other loyal knights would have put all in order. He did not elaborate, but Mara knew what he meant.

The bodies would be buried. The blood washed away.

Something had moved in Mara then, something huge and terrible. It had threatened the fragile stability she had been able to erect. She could not let it take over, could not allow the tears to fall. She had to be strong. She had to return to Ullswater and face the consequences of her actions. She had to return and atone for the tragedy she had brought upon her family. She must never cry.

For the tears might be a balm. They might wash away the guilt she must bear forever. It was her penance.

In the end, she had agreed to return to Ullswater, and now they made the grim journey. Even Hero seemed affected by his rider's mood, and the beast hung his head dispiritedly as he plodded northward. Stephen, at Mara's side, rode the brown cart horse. Jack was mounted on an aged red roan they had bought along the way.

No one spoke, mindful of Mara's sorrow and the ordeal she had to face. Stephen would have done anything to help her, anything to ease her awful burden, but he was helpless. If only she could cry, he thought, the tears might cleanse her soul and ease the pain.

But Mara remained upright in the saddle, gaze fixed on a horizon only she could see. She was silent, her eyes dry.

They continued on through the somber day. Clouds lowered and thunder rumbled. Mara did not look up when a raindrop splashed beside her nose and ran down her cheek. It was followed by another, and another. The sprinkle dampened the coarse tunic Jack had managed to obtain for her. Her hair matted and tangled about her shoulders. The grime that coated her fair skin became streaked.

Then the rain stopped. Branches drooped. The birds did not resume their singing.

The three riders continued onward. They were almost home. Although she tried not to look, the familiar countryside registered on her senses. They neared the castle, the castle where her family and friends had been butchered. All dead. Murdered. Betrayed. The litany played in her mind.

It was Jack, ever alert, who held up his hand and shouted, halting them. "Look there! What is it? A wolf?"

Stephen squinted and edged his horse closer to Mara. His hand went to the hilt of his sword. All three horses snorted and moved their feet nervously as the lean gray body hurtled in their direction. Stephen's sword was halfway out of its sheath when Mara gave a startled cry.

"What?" Stephen threw himself off his mount when he saw Mara slip from Hero's back. Had she completely lost her senses? A wolf that size—

But it was not a wolf. It was a deerhound, and it ran straight at Mara, planted its giant forepaws on her shoulders, and madly licked her face.

Something within Mara was desperate to be free. It was enormous, and it hurt terribly. She squeezed her eyes

176

shut and clung to her dog, fingers wound into his shaggy fur. *Alive! He was alive!*

The thing inside her moved. It surged like a tide, pushed at the very fiber of her being as it sought to escape and flow free.

A light rain began to fall. Neither Jack nor Stephen noticed.

The tears started slowly. They squeezed from under Mara's eyelids. A sob issued from her trembling lips, as if torn from her soul. Then the dam was broken, the torrent loosed. She wept until she choked on the sobs caught in her throat. She wept until the force of her weeping drained the strength from her limbs, and she sank to the ground. Trey no longer licked her face but nuzzled her, big head between her breasts, worried by her grief. She clung to him until the strength had gone from her fingers as well, and her hands dropped weakly to her lap.

Stephen did not realize he had clenched his fists. He did not know his own cheeks were wet until Mara's weeping had eased. When he looked up, at last, from the woman and the dog huddled on the road, he saw his friends, Thomas and Walter. Their eyes, as well, had a peculiar brightness.

Unable to speak, Stephen acknowledged their presence with a nod. They stood, silent and respectful, as their lord approached his heartbroken lady.

Stephen knelt at Mara's side. He stroked the shaggy hound and noted the blood-matted fur and swollen eye. "Another hero," he whispered.

A bright memory flashed through Mara's mind. The mounted knight who had struck down her father, murdered her mother. Her defensive position atop the table. The angel of death in his shining armor riding down on them. Trey's brave attack. The red rage that had engulfed her. The vengeance in her heart. Her own savage attack.

She had tried. Oh, God, she had tried. Her breath hitched on a broken sob.

She had not meant to be the author of all those appalling deaths. She had tried to avenge them.

The tears ran anew, but Mara's exhaustion was so great she could only manage a gentle weeping. This time it was not a raging storm of grief and guilt, but a summer's cloudburst that cleansed the earth and brought new life.

Mara did not resist when Stephen took her into his arms. His fingers twined in the tangled hair at the nape of her neck, and he drew her head against his shoulder.

His mail tunic was cool against her flesh, but his embrace was warm. So warm.

Stephen felt her arms steal around his neck. He held her, rocked her, and the healing rain continued to fall.

Chapter Twenty-six

Stephen woke to the sound of cars speeding past his window. Used to the sound of birds, it disoriented him. He attempted to sit up and realized how weak he was. He rolled to the edge of the bed and dropped his legs over the side.

He was in a motel room. He remembered now.

He remembered other things as well.

He had to pull himself together.

Like most motel rooms, this one had an excess of cardboard cutout advertisements for local restaurants and other attractions. The one closest to him was for a pizza joint. He dialed the number and ordered a large deluxe and a liter of Coke. Then he stripped, left his clothes where they fell, and took a shower.

An hour later only grease was left in the pizza box, the plastic bottle of Coke was empty, and Stephen felt better. He wondered how long it had been since he had eaten. Five days, maybe. He couldn't let that happen again. He had too much to do. He lay back down on the bed, arms crossed under his head.

It had been smart to walk to the bus station and take a taxi from there. If Amanda called the police, which she probably would, no one would recall an anonymous fare from the depot.

No one would remember him, especially in the shape he was now, thin, bearded, and haggard. The motel clerk had been half asleep in the middle of the night when he'd checked in. The man wouldn't remember a thing. He was safe, for a while at least. Until the money ran out.

That was Stephen's only worry. The cash had to last until he got where he needed to go, and he didn't know how long it was going to take. Things were good now. Better anyway. Mara would heal. He was going to take care of her.

It was why he had to take care of himself. Mara needed him. He had to be there for her. He had to return. He couldn't get back to her if he starved to death. Or if they locked him away and put him on drugs. He had to stay healthy. And free.

The lethargy was coming on him again, but it was all right. He had better control now. He could come back to the present whenever he needed to. He'd let hunger and thirst be his alarms. He and Mara had a long road to travel together.

Stephen's eyes were heavy-lidded. The sound of the traffic faded away.

He wasn't quite certain exactly where he was headed with her yet. Or how the dream figured into it all. He only knew he had to continue on down the road.

The sound of rain came faintly to his ears.

Chapter Twenty-seven

It rained and rained. The gray clouds hung low, hugged the earth, and the earth accepted the moisture as a gift. Spring crops flourished. Grass grew green and thick and the livestock fattened. Peasants who had fled Baldwin's destruction returned and rebuilt their homes. Ashes and blood were washed away.

Eventually the rain ended. A breeze sprang up and the clouds were torn asunder. The world was new again, the sky blindingly blue. The bright, fragrant days of spring moved toward summer. Mara moved on, as well.

Although it had taken almost a full day, she had managed to comb the tangles from her long hair. She no longer wore it in plaits, however, but in a single braid wound around the crown of her head. There were other changes, too.

Her step was slower. She did not hurry everywhere. She was not as quick to smile, and her smile was not as wide. Her laughter was not as joyous, if more profound, and when she spoke her voice was softer. Her posture, while always correct, was now more graceful than imposing, her carriage elegant rather than severe. More importantly, Mara *felt* different: more balanced, at peace with the child who was, at ease with the woman who had become. She healed.

Ullswater, too, had changed. When Mara had recovered enough to notice, she was immensely grateful to Thomas and the rest of Stephen's men-at-arms. They had done her and her family a great service. Their caring and assistance gave honor to the dead. All traces of the massacre had been removed, each body respectfully buried, every grave marked.

But in spite of its new inhabitants, the courtyard still seemed empty, the great hall lonely and abandoned.

Once she had her own life in order, Mara tried to restore the castle as well. She had the newly cleaned rooms freshened with the dried herbs and flowers her mother had preserved. She harvested summer's blooms from the garden and arranged them on the hall tables, as her mother had done. She tended the garden with the aid of a clever youth, the new cook's son, and it bloomed and blossomed with renewed fervor. Her parents' graves were neatly kept, and a new kennel rose from the ground.

But it was not the same. It never would be.

The realization had been slow but inexorable. Mara was at peace with it now, as she was with herself. The horror was behind her, the future ahead.

But what future? What did fate intend?

Stephen had been nothing but kind and caring. He had helped to tend the graves, and he'd offered his aid in every task she set for herself. He had been solicitous, alert to her every mood, compassionate, and attentive. And he had rescued her. Almost single-handedly he had breached Baldwin's castle. Alone, he had come for her. He was a bold, brave, noble man. His integrity was unmatched.

But what did he feel for her? What did he truly feel? For that matter, what did she feel for him?

The day neared its end, and the sunset was crimson. Like her parents, it was Mara's favorite time. She descended the steps of the great hall and headed toward the stable, as had become her habit at each gentle dusk.

Mara knew she had changed on some elemental level. She was able to recall, clearly, the anticipatory joy she had felt in Stephen's presence. She remembered how light her heart had been, how full of expectation and sensual delight she could only imagine. But what lay within her now? What did she feel for the man who would yet be her husband?

Something was hidden deep inside, something she could not quite touch, could not name. It was only waiting to be drawn forth from her. Did it lie within Stephen as well? Was it there, waiting, curled within his soul?

Trey padded at Mara's heels. She crossed the courtyard, nodded at Walter when they passed, and entered the stable's cool, fragrant gloom. Hero nickered a greeting.

Stephen had been closeted with Thomas in the newly erected kennels. He had had a hound bitch sent from his castle in Bellingham, and had bred it to Mara's loyal companion, Trey. A new generation was on its way.

Finished with his discussion, he glanced out the doorway and noticed the ruby light of day's end. Mara would be in the stable, as had become her wont. She visited Hero twice a day, without fail, at dawn and dusk, to bring him a tidbit from the garden, or a sweet bun from the kitchen. Stephen strode into the courtyard.

Over the passage of many days, Stephen had watched Mara heal. He had observed the changes in her. He had seen her not only resurrected but metamorphosed— from a glorious, exuberant girl into a stunning woman. The girl he had come upon at the lake was gone. In her place was a startlingly different human being.

Stephen had been infatuated with that girl. Her beauty, her bravery, her wit and charm had enchanted him. Now?

Now, he couldn't deny it; he found himself afraid to approach the woman Mara had become. The flower that had blossomed before his very eyes was perhaps too rare, too exotic, to pluck from its stem. Who was he, after all? A northern baron her father had deemed it politically necessary for his daughter to wed.

So he had come, and had been mesmerized by Ranulf's daughter. There had been a bond between them, of that he was certain. But it had been so new, so delicate and fragile. She had suffered much since then, and was no longer the person she had been. Did she still feel for him what had been in her eyes, her words, her laughter, that first day they had spent together?

Or was it gone, as dead and buried as the bodies of her friends and family?

There was only one way to find out, one way to know if she held in her heart what he knew he held in his.

Mara was unaware of Stephen's presence as he watched her stroke Hero's neck. She no longer started as easily as she once had, and turned slowly when she felt the hand on her shoulder. The sight of Stephen's familiar features, shadowed in the pleasant gloom, filled her with quiet joy.

"Walk with me awhile, will you?" he asked. "I'd like to talk to you."

"Of course."

At Stephen's signal the gate was raised, and they walked together out and down the road toward the Ullsmere. They had no fear of Baldwin at the moment. Stephen's men constantly patrolled the castle lands, and the loyal tenants who populated them were eyes and ears as well. No one, not a single stranger, could approach Ullswater without notice.

The low sun glinted brightly off the surface of Ullsmere's dark water. Tiny waves lapped at the rocky shore, and birds chorused in the surrounding trees. Mara sat on a boulder at water's edge and smoothed an errant wisp of hair from her cheek.

"Ullswater recovers well," Stephen began without preamble. He wasn't good at small-talk and didn't believe in it. "Your father was a good man, his tenants loyal. Thomas has overseen the estate matters for me and tells me there are no problems. The vassals will remain loyal to Ranulf's daughter and . . . and her husband."

Mara felt the first butterflies stir their wings in her stomach.

"Baldwin has been quiet. So far," he continued, arms folded across the mail tunic he habitually wore. "But we have absolutely no reason to trust him. While I doubt he'd try another direct assault on Ullswater with the bulk of my force here, I'd feel a little safer up north. Bellingham is remote, and I know I have the support of the other northern barons, as well as the Earl of Northumberland. I just, well . . . I wonder if you . . . if you'd be happy up there. In my home."

Mara inwardly sighed. There. He had said it. Or almost. He still, apparently, wished to marry her.

But why? The political necessity still existed, of course. United, they could stand against Baldwin.

But what was in his secret heart? She had to know. Mara raised her eyes to Stephen.

"I am still willing to marry you, as my father wished," Mara murmured. "If it is as *you* wish."

She seemed so calm, so serene. What was truly in her heart?

"If it is as I wish?" Stephen blurted.

The sun's last light haloed Mara's silvery hair. Her eyes shone like gems. Her pale, sculpted lips parted to reveal the tips of her white and even teeth. She was the most beautiful woman he had ever seen. And more. So much more.

Stephen was no longer able to bear the enforced restraint of the preceding days. He had nurtured her, cherished her, given his all to the process of her becoming. He could not stand it any longer.

He banished the distance between them, then abruptly halted.

Mara gazed up at him, so tall and broad and handsome. His thick, straight black hair stirred softly in the breeze, brushing the tops of his muscular shoulders. She recalled how he had looked that day she had first laid eyes upon him, and had realized he would live in her heart forever.

The memory surged in her, powerfully. Mara's lips parted and she brushed them with her tongue.

In the instant she had risen from the lake and beheld him, in that single burning instant, she had known his image would never leave her. She would forever compare all other men to the portrait that had been etched upon her soul. And when she had come to know him, in those few, short, precious hours, she had come to love him as well. It had not come upon her like a young maid's giddy first romance, but revealed itself as a certainty, a knowing deep within the essence of her being. She had not doubted it from the first.

So why, now, did she hesitate? After all they had been through together, all she felt for him, why did she not simply say what was in her heart? Had grief so numbed and maimed her that she was unable to tell this good, honest, loving man what he wished to hear?

Mara could hardly speak for the sudden and painful lump in her throat. Awash with shame, she nevertheless rose gracefully to her feet and looked Stephen directly in the eye.

"I will be very happy in Bellingham, Stephen," she replied in a barely audible voice. "I will always be happy wherever you are."

Stephen didn't realize he'd held his breath until he let it out. "Then you'll . . . You still want—you mean, you'll marry me?"

"Of course I'll marry you," Mara said simply. She had to smile at the boyish wonder etched so plainly on his hard, masculine features. "I love you."

Stephen remembered the vow he had made their very first day together; the vow not to kiss her until he had made her his wife, but too much had happened since then. Everything was different now, everything had changed. She had said she loved him.

As he loved her. Totally. Completely. Forever.

Mara's heart hammered as Stephen's big hands lightly gripped her upper arms. She saw him swallow, saw his lips part. The intoxicating male scent of him came to her as he drew her nearer still. She closed her eyes.

The whole of Stephen's being was concentrated in one spot. He lowered his mouth to hers. Covered it.

She was helpless. All of her life gone before was as nothing, and she opened to him like a flower to the sun. She welcomed him, and surrendered to him, all at once.

Stephen was dizzy, reeling. Mara was everything he had ever wanted. And now she was his, in his arms, her confession of love still ringing in his ears. But if he did not stop now . . .

He pulled away abruptly, leaving Mara breathless. His hands remained on her arms, but he held her away from him.

"We must—It must be soon," he said, every word an effort. "The wedding. I'd like to leave for Bellingham at dawn. There's an abbey along the way, and I know Father Gregory there. It's secluded, very simple, but he'll marry us. Unless . . ."

"Unless what?"

"Unless you'd rather wait until we get to Bellingham.

I did have a ceremony planned. Festivities, feasting." Stephen's disappointment was evident. "All the people of Bellingham have looked forward to it since they heard I was to take a bride. So I . . . I guess we should go ahead and—"

"Get married at the abbey," Mara finished. "The festivities may take place after the fact, as they would have done anyway."

Stephen was entirely unable to control his grin. "You're sure you don't mind?"

"The only thing I mind is further delay. I want to be your wife, Stephen."

"And so you shall be, Mara. So you shall."

It was done. As simply as that. All questions answered, all doubt banished. She loved him, wanted him, wished to be his wife. If words were not enough, he had felt the giving of her soul into his in that single embrace.

Mara was prepared this time when Stephen lowered his head to hers. Her heart had wings. Her spirit soared.

He loved her. He wanted her. The culmination of her entire life was in this moment.

Their lips met softly, fleetingly at first. Stephen murmured against her, words meaningless, lost in the passion that rose to engulf them. The meaning, however, was clear. The kiss became shattering in its intensity. The world faded away. The sun slipped behind the distant hills and they held each other, locked in an embrace that would transcend time.

Chapter Twenty-eight

It was the first day of summer, the most perfect day. The sky was faultlessly blue, the air warm and fragrant and filled with birdsong. Pale and delicate spring flowers had given way to the sturdier blooms of June, and they blossomed along the roadsides and in sunlit patches of forest in shades of red, orange, and purple.

The small band rode slowly out through Ullswater's gate, as if afraid to disturb the fragile, magical peace of the day. Once past the castle walls, however, Mara reined Hero to halt. She turned in her saddle and took a long, last look at what had been her home for so long.

Memories assailed her. They rushed and tumbled in her mind's eye as if the very walls of the castle called out to her, begged her not to forget.

She saw days of summer long ago, when she'd been but a child and had laughed and played, rolled with the hound pups, and charged about on her pony. When she'd been hugged and kissed and loved, and brandished her first sword, carved of wood.

She remembered evenings in the great hall, a warm and welcoming fire that crackled in the hearth during the long, sharp days of winter. Her parents' love for one another, and the way they had guided her so surely through the awkward time of adolescence. Ice on the Ullsmere and snow in the yard.

She recalled the crisp, bright days of autumn, the aroma of roasting venison, and the hearty taste of ale. Leaves of gold. Shedding her child's body and emerging into womanhood.

And she remembered all the springs, blossoms as dainty as dewdrops, her mother's laughter, forests greening, mares heavy with foals and ewes with lambs. Sunlight on melting snow and trickling streams. An icy lake, and a man who had planted a seed in her girl-woman's breast.

A seed planted in soil fertile and innocent. Bathed in blood. Steeped in sorrow. But a seed that had grown nonetheless, and flourished.

No one moved during Mara's long contemplation of her home. Trey sat in the dust, unconcerned. Horses indolently swished their tails. Mara straightened in her saddle and gazed at her husband-to-be.

She had still been a girl that day by the lake. Now she was a woman, and she loved like a woman. No giddy and giggling courtship, this. They'd be partners, for all time. Soul mates who had found each other, cleaved to each other.

Mara glanced over her shoulder one more time. The gray stone walls of Ullswater seemed warm in the sun, content, full of their memories and at peace with them.

She put her heels to Hero's sides and silently rode away.

It was nearly a day's ride to Bellingham. The Cistercian Abbey was almost halfway between Bellingham and Ullswater, just over the border on Stephen's estate.

Close by noon they were still on Ullswater's land. The

narrow road wound through a vast wood, and Mara welcomed the shade. The summer heat was upon them. She looked over at Stephen, clad, as usual, in his mail.

"How do you stand it?" she asked, and nodded at his armor. "Aren't you in danger of being boiled in your own juices during the summer?"

"Constant danger," he replied.

Mara laughed. "When we reach the abbey we might just be able to carve you up and have you for supper. Father Gregory would no doubt be glad of a nice roast for his table."

Stephen's expression sobered. "You know, I usually do send supplies to Father Gregory and the monks. I should have brought something with me this time. We arranged the journey in such haste, I forgot."

Mara reached over and briefly laid a hand on his arm. "He'll certainly welcome you, Stephen, with or without a gift. Especially if you've been generous in the past."

"Of course he will. I just feel bad."

They rode a few moments in silence. Then: "How long have you known Father Gregory?"

"Oh, a very long time." A half smile touched Stephen's lips. "Before I was born, my father was hunting with some of his knights. On the road to the forest, my father's horse stumbled and fell on him. His leg was broken. None of my father's men knew what to do—except send for help, naturally.

"Then a small band of monks came along the road. They were journeying, tired and hungry, but Father Gregory stopped to help. He was skilled in the healing arts. He set my father's leg and, from herbs and plants he'd found along the wayside, concocted a tea that soothed my father's pain.

"When my father asked what he might do for the monk in return, the monk merely said, 'Say a prayer to God for us, my son, that He might one day send us a benefactor upon whose land we may build a small abbey.' "

Mara smiled. "And your father gave him the land?"

"Not right away. But he did bring the monks to the castle to fill their stomachs. It was my mother who, after meeting them, actually persuaded my father to give them the plot."

"And they built their abbey."

"Well . . ." Stephen shook his head. "They were a poor order. They built little more than hovels. Until. . . ." He sighed. "You know my mother died following my birth. When my father knew she was . . . was not going to survive, he sent for Gregory. Over the years the monk had brought great comfort to my mother. He . . . he offered solace at her death. She died with my father holding one hand; Gregory the other."

"I'm so sorry, Stephen," Mara said softly.

"He became a great friend of my father's during the succeeding years. He befriended me as well. I adored him," Stephen said simply. "When my father died, he kept watch over me until I-I became a man."

"And now you keep watch over him."

Stephen glanced at Mara and smiled. "Exactly. But I have been remiss in my duties lately."

"You've had other things to think about."

"That's putting it mildly." They exchanged looks. "Still, I should have remembered to bring something with me today. Especially since I'm going to ask him a special favor."

"A *very* special favor," Mara echoed. Her eyes sparkled. "And I think I know a way we might be able to repay him."

The woods through which they passed, on Ullswater's far northern boundary, had once been her father's favorite place to hunt. "In the last few years, however," she explained, "my father hunted closer to home. The deer population in these woods must be significant by now. And we do have Trey with us."

Stephen grinned. "I'm *game* if you are."

Mara groaned. "That was terrible, Stephen."

"Yes, it was," he agreed cheerfully. "But you, my love, had a very good idea." He turned and called to the men behind him. "We're going into the woods to try and take a deer. Walter and Albert, stay here and watch the road. Jack, lend me your bow."

The small man rode forward, unslung his bow and quiver, and handed them to his lord. He shook his head in mock sadness. "I don't know about this. It's usually me what brings down the game in a hunt, y' know."

"Keep your thoughts to yourself, where they belong," Stephen retorted good-naturedly. "Come along, Mara. Trey!"

The big dog's ears perked up. Mara slapped her thigh. "Come, Trey. Hunt!"

The hound bounded off into the wood.

It was slow going at first in the dense forest. Trey loped ahead, zigging and zagging. Small animals skittered away through the undergrowth. A jay scolded from the tree-tops. Trey eventually drew ahead as Mara and Stephen wended their way deeper and deeper into the forest, and soon the dog was out of sight.

Mara and Stephen jogged their mounts, making their way carefully around the trees, and waited to hear the hound's braying bark that told them he had sighted prey. As Mara had supposed, it was not long in coming.

Stephen and Mara reined in sharply. Mara pointed. "It came from over there."

The pair exchanged a slow smile. "After you, my lady." Stephen made a sweeping, courtly gesture.

Mara did not hesitate. She put her heels to her mount and urged him into a lope. It was the first time in a long time she had felt the blood sing through her veins. This was what she loved.

Accustomed to the woods on her father's estate, she was adept at guiding her stallion through the dangerous obstacle course. Stephen quickly fell behind.

But he did not trail far in her wake, and the blood thundered in his ears as well. *God, but she is magnificent,* he thought as he rode. Then he threw caution to the winds and urged his chestnut to greater speed.

On through the forest they pounded, faster and faster, until at last they caught sight of Mara's sleek gray hound. He was just ahead, running flat out. A stag and three does leapt ahead of him. They were headed toward a small glade, a clearing of light and space in the shadowed gloom.

Mara leaned low on Hero's neck. The glen approached swiftly. At the last moment she saw the fallen tree at the clearing's perimeter, barring the way before them.

Mara gripped her reins a little more tightly and directed Hero's head, making sure he saw the obstacle before them.

Trey and the deer disappeared on the far side of the glade. Alert to his mistress's hand on the reins, Hero eyed the fallen trunk and gathered his great body. He took the tree in a graceful bound. Stephen was not as lucky.

He did not see the trunk until he saw Mara's stallion rise into the air. He was off balance, unable to properly guide his mount by the time they reached it. The stallion coiled his muscles to spring, but too late. His front feet grazed the mossy bark, and his left front leg tangled in an outcropping branch. He came down in the glade upon his knees.

Stephen was thrown forward. He clutched at the saddle, then at the stallion's streaming mane. He was unable to save himself.

Mara heard the horse's *whuumpphh* as its massive weight connected with the earth. She wheeled Hero in time to see Stephen tumble to the ground. "Stephen!"

The wind had been knocked out of him. He couldn't move, couldn't speak. His charger regained its feet, shook its head, then its body. It was unhurt.

But Stephen was still unable to move. Mara flung herself from Hero's back and returned to Stephen's side. She knelt beside him and gently took his face in her hands. "Stephen . . . Stephen, are you all right?"

He thought he was. Embarrassed perhaps. Humiliated. But physically unharmed. But he was also, he realized, in an extremely advantageous position.

"Stephen, please talk to me! Are you all right?"

He merely groaned. He kept his eyes shut.

"Oh, Stephen . . . Please, my love, say something! Speak to me!"

He allowed his eyelids to flutter open weakly. "Mara?" he croaked.

"Stephen, oh, Stephen! Tell me you're all right! Where are you hurt?"

Slowly, Stephen raised a limp hand and touched his mouth. "Here," he breathed.

"What? Your mouth?"

"Mmmmmm." Stephen moaned again. "Here. Right here." He tapped a finger to his lips.

Mara sat back on her heels, hands on her hips. "Stephen! Are you—"

"Ohhhh." He rolled his head to the side.

"Stephen!" Mara again captured his face in her hands.

It was the moment he had waited for. Before she could react and draw away, Stephen reached up and tangled his fingers in Mara's hair. He drew her head down to his.

"Yes. Here," Stephen sighed, and flicked his tongue across her lips. "Kiss me, Mara. Kiss away the hurt."

Both stallions stood together quietly. Then Hero shook his head, walked to where the fallen humans lay, and chuffed his warm breath over them.

They didn't notice. They didn't move. They were lost in each other, and very, *very* far away.

Chapter Twenty-nine

The Cistercian Abbey was as secluded as Stephen had said.

It was midafternoon when they left the road and entered a small woodland. To Trey's delight, another two does and a buck bounded away before them. They leapt lightly through the undergrowth, disturbing all manner of animals that darted in every direction. Birds scolded warnings, fluttered into the sky, and returned to their leafy bowers to observe. The band rode on for several more miles on a faint track before they saw signs of life other than animal.

Mara rode at Stephen's side, and was delightfully surprised when she saw the clearing. They went from mottled shadow to brilliant sunlight into an area that had been cleared and cultivated. Brown-robed monks toiled among the neat furrows, their backs bent and brows moist. They all ceased their labors when they noticed the band of riders, and stared at them curiously.

Stephen bent from his horse to speak to the nearest

robed figure. "I am Stephen, Baron of Bellingham. Father Gregory is an old friend, and I've come to ask a favor of him. Can you take us to him?"

The monk nodded and gestured for them to follow. Mara felt self-conscious with so many pairs of eyes upon her. She knew the Cistercians were an isolated order, and wondered how long it had been since they had seen any outsider, much less a woman. She disliked disturbing the peace of their sunny glade and solitary existence, but at the same time was glad she had come. The solitude and peace of the place were a balm. There could not be, Mara thought, a more perfect spot on earth for her and Stephen to be wed.

"Abbey," however, seemed a misleading description of the lovely, quiet place. There was no imposing church, merely several small buildings, simply, sturdily built of wood and local stone. The monk who led them disappeared into one modest edifice and, a few moments later, Father Gregory appeared.

"Stephen, my son, how good to see you. It's been a long time. Too long." The narrow, gray face was changed dramatically by a smile. The monk glanced briefly at the rest of the party, the knights and servant. "But you must have come on important business. Please, please, come inside. Brother Roald," he said to their guide, "please see to the horses. This way, this way!"

Such joviality did not seem to go with the tall, thin monk, but it didn't matter; Mara liked him at once.

Father Gregory led them into the small wooden building that served as their chapel. Summer sunlight streamed onto the wood-planked floor and turned it to the color of warm honey. The father gestured at one of the hard wooden benches pushed against the wall. "Sit, please. You've been journeying. You must be weary. May I offer refreshment?"

Stephen laughed softly and took both the monk's hands in his. "Slow down, Father. Please. First let me introduce you to my betrothed—Amarantha, Ranulf's daughter."

"Oh, my. I'm so sorry. Forgive me." The thin, nervous man released himself from Stephen's grasp and took Mara's hands. "My daughter. I am so pleased to meet you." He glanced at Stephen, brows arched. "Your betrothed, you say?"

"Yes, Father. It's why we've come today."

"My son," Gregory said quietly, mouth quirked in a half smile. "You have come for my blessing?"

"Most assuredly," Stephen replied. "But for something else as well." His expression abruptly sobered. With concise, measured words, he told Father Gregory of the tragic events recently come to pass.

When he had done, the good father slowly shook his head. He laid a hand on Stephen's shoulder. "Oh, my son," he said. "I am so terribly sorry to hear of this. And you, my daughter . . . God's mercy on you, and His healing love." He shook his head again, then brightened. "But you said you had something to ask of me. Tell me, what can I do for you? How can I help?"

Stephen glanced quickly at Mara. "Based on what I've told you, Father, we must needs be married in haste. I want Mara safely my wife."

A slow smile spread across the father's lined and weathered face. "And you wish for me to join you! I am honored." He turned his kindhearted smile first on Mara, then Stephen. "I am more delighted than I can tell you, Stephen, that you have come here, to our modest abbey, to sanctify the union. Your father would be glad, you know. He would have been happy."

"I am glad as well," Stephen murmured in reply. "Certainly there is no one else I would have marry us. Nor could I envision a grander cathedral."

The monk laughed softly. "It is not the *place*, is it, my children, but the occasion, the moment." He looked at them each again. "And I can see this is a very special moment, indeed, for both of you."

Mara felt the monk's warm, brown, callused hand take her own. He reached for Stephen's. "I also see," he continued, "that Almighty God has already blessed this union. He has seen the love in your hearts, and the miracle of His own love will shine upon you. Now, and for all time."

A shiver ran through Mara's breast. The words he had spoken were true. He could see into their souls.

A short time later, without further ado, Mara found herself standing in front of Father Gregory, Stephen at her side. She had changed from her riding costume into the rose tunic and embroidered chemise her mother had made. In her faintly trembling hands she carried a bouquet of wildflowers Jack had handed her at the last moment. Thomas, who would return to Ullswater, and Walter, who would go on to Bellingham, stood near with Jack. Sunlight poured through the windows, mingled with birdsong and the steady, distant sounds of the monks at their labors in the surrounding fields. Father Gregory intoned the words of the ceremony, and Mara felt as if she was floating. She closed her eyes.

None of it seemed quite real. The horrifying events that had changed her life became as a nightmare banished by sunlight. There was only now. The warmth of the day against her skin. The scent of wildflowers, the song of a lark, the rustle of leaves in a breeze. And Stephen. Her husband.

Mara opened her eyes. They were one now. Bound together, truly.

For eternity.

Chapter Thirty

Stephen felt positively mellow. He had rested, showered and shaved, and put on clean clothes. He was a happy man. Now all he needed was a decent meal. He stood before the mirror and ran his hands through his long, black hair. Something strange caught his eye and he froze, hands poised in midair.

His hair had seemed to move as if of its own will. Though he knew he had smoothed it with his fingers, had felt the strands, for a moment he had not actually been able to see his hands. They had just appeared to become . . . transparent.

Stephen shook his head. Ridiculous. A trick of light. He slicked his hair back one more time and stepped away from the mirror.

Much better. He looked like a regular guy, not some raving madman. He wouldn't stand out in the crowd. No one would remember him if went next door to the diner. Stephen smiled at his reflection.

The fresh air outside felt good, even if the smells were

a little funky: motor oil and exhaust fumes. Cars whizzed by him on the interstate. He started to feel vulnerable.

Amanda would be frantic. He'd have a few days' grace, he was sure. She was a very private person, very discreet. She wouldn't go straight to the police. She'd give it a while. But only a while.

There was a drugstore in the strip mall that boasted the Fifties Diner. Stephen bought a pair of cheap shades and a baseball cap. In the diner, he sat at the counter with his back to the windows.

His appetite wasn't as hearty as when he had first started out, but he forced himself to eat—good, solid American food. Meat loaf and mashed potatoes, creamed spinach. He felt a little better when he was done, but anxious. Anxious to return to her.

He broke into a jog once on the way back to the motel, and had to force himself to walk. He didn't want to stand out in any way, give anyone cause to remember a tall, dark, broad-shouldered man. In case anyone came asking around. He stuck his hands in his pockets.

Stephen felt some change and a modest wad of bills. The money wasn't going to last too much longer. Long enough, he hoped. But . . . long enough for what?

He wasn't sure yet. Not yet. He was moving through his past, moving toward something. He always had the sense of a task he must complete. He had to keep going, and make resolution with his dream. He hadn't had it since he had been going back. If he didn't complete his task, however, whatever it was, he knew the dream would return to haunt him to his grave.

The motel room smelled faintly of the soap he had used in the shower. He locked the door behind him and put out the DO NOT DISTURB sign. He sat down in the small chair by the window.

He could now go back easily, quickly. Yet he delayed. He had to think for a minute, concentrate.

He remembered the past clearly now when he returned to the present. He was in love with the most beautiful, amazing woman God had ever created. He was as much in love with her at this moment as he had been in his former life. It was torture to have to leave her in the past and return to the present, however briefly. It was joy, ecstasy to return to her. There was only one problem.

Although, at need, he had developed the ability to return to the present from the past, he had no awareness of the present while he lived his former life. When hunger or thirst summoned, he simply faded out of northern England and into upstate New York. It was a problem he knew, instinctively, he had to solve. There was something he had to carry back with him to the past, some knowledge, some *knowingness*, in order to complete his task. He hadn't figured out how to do it yet, how to pierce the veil from both sides. But it was crucial.

And he didn't have forever.

Chapter Thirty-one

Elizabeth had lived all her life in the village of Bellingham. She was petite and considered pretty, with her piquant features, reddish brown hair, and sprinkling of freckles. People also told her she was a bright little thing, and she had certainly always been curious and eager to learn everything she could. Her father was the town brewer, and she had long known how to make the very best ale. As a small child she had haunted the baker and learned all she could about baking. She loved clothes and had learned to sew, and had even visited the fuller on the river to see how bales of sheep's wool became cloth. She was meticulous in her personal habits, careful of her few belongings, and as neat as a pin. Her mother had always said she would make someone a fine wife, but Elizabeth wanted something more. She wanted to do something—she simply didn't know what it was yet.

It was a bright, warm afternoon in early summer when Elizabeth left her labors, along with everyone else in Bellingham, to stand by the side of the road and watch the baron return to his castle with the woman who would be their baroness. It was that day which changed her life. That day, Elizabeth finally knew what she wanted to do.

There were only five riders and six horses, the extra a pack animal to carry the few items Mara had chosen to bring with her from Ullswater. But the group could have been an army, so powerful was the impression they made.

There was the baron, handsome and strong like a hero prince from one of the tales Elizabeth's grandmother used to tell her. He rode his prancing charger, whose chestnut coat gleamed like polished copper in the sun. His ever-present servant, Jack, followed with his ready smile and plumed hat. Next were two of the baron's knights, heavily armed, lances couched in their tall saddles, stallions draped in colorful trappings; and last came the woman who would be baroness.

Elizabeth caught her breath.

The baroness-to-be did not ride a palfrey, like other ladies, but sat astride a warhorse like her betrothed and his knights. She wore fawn-colored leggings beneath a midnight-blue tunic, and leather boots to the knees. A silver girdle encircled her slender waist, but not merely for effect. She wore a dagger on the right, a short-sword on the left. A huge and shaggy gray hound trotted at the heels of her high-stepping gray stallion, whose dappled coat was like sunlight and shadow in a wooded grove.

Elizabeth knew she would never see anyone as imposing or breathtakingly regal as the woman astride that charger. Or anyone as beautiful.

The hair wound tightly atop the woman's shapely head was as pale as spun silver, and seemed to shine with a light of its own. Her skin was flawless, her perfect features sculpted from marble, her eyes brilliant gems. She was larger than life, unreal, a goddess.

Elizabeth stood spellbound as the troop moved through town and on up the hill to the castle. She did not come to life again until she saw them cross the moat and pass beneath the castle's iron studded gate. Then she picked up her skirt and ran after them as fast as her young, slim legs could carry her.

The day was one of the happiest of Mara's life: first the quiet, magical wedding at the monks' clearing in the wood, then a ride through countryside she had never seen before, but had loved almost at once.

She had felt exposed initially, as they neared Bellingham and left the more heavily forested land behind them. But the hillsides were grand and green, quilted with patches of purple heather, or white.

The town of Bellingham itself was small, quaint, and tidy, with its thatched and timbered cottages and tiny market square. The people of the village lined the main street, smiling and waving and craning their necks for a better view of the baron and his lady. Then the town was behind them, the castle ahead.

"What do you think?" Stephen inquired anxiously. He had pulled his horse alongside Hero, and Mara was touched by the worried expression that furrowed his normally smooth brow. She gazed up at the stone castle clinging to the hilltop, so different from the sprawling and shady Ullswater. But it looked sturdy. Secure and impressive. It was Stephen's castle. Her home.

Mara smiled. "I think it's wonderful."

The lines on Stephen's face relaxed, and they rode together across the wooden bridge and under the gate.

Alfred and the remaining contingent of Stephen's guard stood awaiting them in the bailey. Horses' hooves echoed on the cobbled surface.

"Welcome, my lord baron," the older man said formally. He made a slight bow. "My lady."

"It's good to be home, Alfred."

Boys appeared to hold the horses, and Stephen dismounted to assist Mara. A scattering of servants stood shyly in the shadows of the high walls. They smiled at their master and eyed their new mistress. With a gracious smile, Mara took her husband's arm and they all entered the great hall.

The Norman hall was unlike anything to which she was accustomed. It was a *palais,* built in the French style with no undercroft. The long, wide room was at ground level at the opposite end of the courtyard from the gate and donjon tower. And it was lovely. Mara caught her breath as they entered the wide and heavy double doors.

Many tall windows lined the hall, which was not as long as Ullswater's, but wider. The ceiling was higher as well, the roof raised to nearly twice the height of Mara's home. She looked up and saw a narrow gallery that ran all the way around the perimeter of the room. Opposite the door and beyond a massive Norman arch was a large hearth with an intricately carved mantel, flanked by two colorfully painted screens.

"Entry to the pantry and buttery," Stephen said, and indicated the screen to the left. "And to the right . . ."

Their eyes met, and Mara felt some of her newly found serenity drain away. It had been a long day, the most important of her life. She had ridden many miles, to a new home. Stephen's entire household looked to her either for instruction, or to see how she would acquit herself. On top of it all, she was about to embark on a new, and intimate, relationship—one she had longed for, desired with every fiber of her being.

The days had passed and the bond between them had become a strong and binding chain, but the consummation of the relationship—the physical reality—had always been in the future. Now the future had arrived. Mara's knees were weak.

Stephen, unaccustomed to the ways of women as he was, was nonetheless attuned to the woman at his side. He lent her an arm for support, and guided her to the head of the hall where he turned to face the small crowd gathered behind them.

"The baroness and I thank you for your welcome," Stephen began. There were murmurs as the meaning of his words sank in. Stephen smiled and held up his hands as the volume slowly increased. "I know it's a surprise. We had planned for the festivities to take place here, in Bellingham. And they shall. We will celebrate this marriage, and your new lady, in grand style."

Stephen turned his smile on Mara, then purposely sobered his expression. "But give us one week's time. My wife, as you have surely heard by now, is in mourning for her family. And she needs time to feel at home here. I'm sure you will all do your best to assure her happiness and comfort."

The tone of his voice dismissed them, and his order, politely phrased though it was, was obeyed as if law. Mara was impressed by her husband's easy ability to command—as she had been by his gentleness and kindness, his courage, daring, prowess with a sword. And now . . .

The light was failing fast. Day had reached its end. Servants laid the tables for the evening's meal, and Mara's hands trembled in accompaniment to the weakness in her knees. Gentle pressure on her elbow moved her toward the screen to the right of the fireplace.

"After you, my lady."

Mara entered the apartment she would share with her husband.

"My lady." Elizabeth appeared from nowhere and dropped like a stone into a deep curtsy. Then the girl remembered herself and added: "My lord baron."

Stephen's hand went instinctively to the hilt of his sword. "Who are you? And how did you get in here?"

Elizabeth remained in the curtsy, eyes fixed to the floor. "My name's Elizabeth, lord," she answered swiftly. "Forgive me, I . . . I just slipped in when no one was looking."

Mara and Stephen exchanged a swift glance. A smile

twitched at the corner of Stephen's mouth, but his words remained stern.

"And why have you 'just slipped in'?"

Elizabeth looked up at last. Her light brown eyes were wide and shining. "Oh, to serve the lady, of course. Please, my lord, don't be angry. I couldn't help myself, I couldn't. As soon as I saw her, riding through the village, I knew I had to come. There's never been anyone so perfect, so beautiful. I can do most anything, and I'll take good care of her, I will. I . . ."

Elizabeth stopped abruptly. Her cheeks flushed hotly and both of her small hands rose to cover her mouth. "Oooh, I'm sorry. I didn't mean to go on like that. But, oh, my lady."

The look of adoration in the girl's eyes went straight to Mara's heart. She could not possibly turn the child away. Furthermore, she needed someone like Elizabeth, not only to assist in her personal care, but to help her learn the ins and outs of Bellingham Castle. When Trey left his place at Mara's side and quietly padded over to lick Elizabeth's face, the matter was settled.

At Stephen's almost imperceptible nod, Mara said, "Very well, Elizabeth. I should be happy to have you look after me."

"Oh, thank you . . . Thank you, my lady!"

"Perhaps you could begin," Stephen said smoothly, "by bringing your mistress something to eat."

When the girl had left, hurrying eagerly to her first task, he turned to Mara. "I hope that's all right with you. I didn't think you should have to preside over the hall on your very first night here."

Once again his thoughtfulness surprised and touched her. "No. Thank you, Stephen," Mara said softly. "You've been kind, so kind to me in everything. I don't know that I can ever, ever thank you properly."

As soon as the words left her lips, however, Mara knew she could, indeed, thank him properly. He was her husband now. She loved him, belonged to him. And she would give herself to him.

True to the bond between them, Stephen easily read the message in her eyes. He had desired many women before, but none had ever made him tremble. He glanced at the wide bed that he had ordered covered with peacock blue silk to match her eyes, and tenderly cupped his wife's face in his hands.

The breath left Mara's body in a single, long sigh. Her heart hammered, and her vision blurred as Stephen's face bent closer. She felt his lashes flutter against her cheek, felt his warm breath, the first, faint touch of his lips on hers.

"Oh, my lady, my lord baron—excuse me!"

If the girl had not been so earnest, Stephen would have been angry. As it was, he had to laugh and reluctantly stepped away from his bride. "You will have to learn to knock, girl."

"Yes, my lord."

The delicious aroma of some kind of baked meat came to Mara's nostrils, but she paid it no heed. She had eyes only for her husband. "I'm sorry," she murmured.

"No sorrier than I," he replied under his breath. "I'll leave you. For now."

Mara wanted to tell him she'd be waiting, aching, until he returned. But they were no longer alone. And even were she free to speak, she feared she could not trust her voice. Instead, she pressed a finger to her lips, then to his. He caught her hand briefly and held it, then was gone.

Elizabeth had known she would be good at this new job, and she was. The moment the baron left, she went into motion. As the beautiful lady stood staring wistfully at the door, Elizabeth arranged her dinner on the table by the window. Someone had placed a jug of wildflowers there, and Elizabeth moved them twice before everything was to her liking.

She called to her mistress, "It's ready, my lady. If you'd like to eat."

The lady looked surprised. And pleased. Elizabeth hovered by her chair for a moment, then turned her attention to the parcel the baron's man, Jack, had delivered. It contained her mistress's few belongings, and Elizabeth fussed over each one.

Besides the large bed, table, and chairs and the marvelously soft, but foreign-looking covering on the floor, there were two sturdy chests. One, Elizabeth discovered, contained the baron's personal possessions; the other was empty.

She folded away her lady's few items of clothing, an ivory comb and a few kerchiefs, a lovely embroidered chemise and matching tunic. It seemed so little for such a fine and important lady. But she had probably lost almost everything when that Cumbrian earl had attacked her father's estate, Elizabeth surmised. She sent a sympathetic glance in her mistress's direction.

"Oh, my lady. My poor lady!"

Mara's head rested against the back of the chair. Her long, light brown lashes lay softly on her cheeks, and her breathing was slow and even.

Elizabeth hated to wake her. Young as she was, however, the mothering instinct was strong within her. She couldn't allow her mistress to simply fall asleep fully clothed and sit upright in a chair all night.

Mara roused when she felt gentle hands unfasten the girdle at her waist, and remove her weapons and boots. When she was down to her chemise, she closed her eyes again and reveled in the luxury of having someone brush her hair. She was half asleep, unable to fully waken, when Elizabeth finally led her to the bed.

Mara stirred only once. She turned on her side and reached out. "Stephen," she murmured.

Then she slept soundly.

* * *

Several candles had been lit, and their slim, fragile flames danced in the darkness. By their light Stephen was able to see Mara's form on the bed, blue coverlet drawn to her waist, and two figures curled together on the imported carpet. The great hound lay on his side, Elizabeth's arm thrown loosely across its shoulders. The only sounds in the room were the girl's soft and childish snores.

Stephen's sigh was long and heartfelt. But he and Mara had a lifetime ahead of them. The union of their souls had been made—the union of their bodies could wait a little longer.

He closed the door quietly behind him. Undressing, he blew out the candles, then lay down at Mara's side.

The coverlet was pulled down to her waist. Mara lay clad only in her chemise. Her breath rose and fell evenly, her breasts' pale pink nipples poking at the thin fabric.

Stephen turned on his side away from her. Her nearness tormented him. He turned on his other side, touched her cheek.

She did not stir, not even faintly. His fingers drifted from her cheek to the line of her jaw, the hollow of her throat.

Mara's breathing did not alter. Her eyes remained tightly closed.

Stephen groaned and turned away from her again. It was the hardest thing he had done in his life.

Chapter Thirty-two

Mara couldn't believe it.

When first she opened her eyes, she was disoriented—a strange room, a strange bed. But clarity and memory returned swiftly.

"Oh, no." She sat bolt upright.

" 'Oh, no,' what?"

Mara turned her head so quickly she suffered a twinge in her neck. Stephen sat in a chair by the window. On the table beside him were two cups of ale, a loaf of fresh-baked bread, and a pot of honey. Trey sat at Stephen's feet, tail slowly wagging.

"Oh, no, I fell asleep. Before I . . . Before we . . ."

Despite the fact that she blushed very prettily, Stephen felt honor bound to rescue his wife. "You fell asleep before you ate your dinner," he finished. "Which is why I've brought you some breakfast. Will you join me?"

Trey gave a short, sharp bark to underscore the invitation, and Mara climbed from the bed. She took the chair opposite her husband and glanced about the room. "Are we alone?"

"I sent the girl home, if that's what you mean. She spent the night at the foot of your bed, you know." Stephen tore two hunks of bread from the loaf. "I told her she could stay with her parents at night, or in the hall. But not here. Not again."

Mara felt the hectic blush return to her cheeks. But when she dared to look up, she saw Stephen was smiling. "I'm so sorry," she said anyway.

"There's nothing to apologize for, my love. I'm glad you're rested. We have a long, busy day ahead of us."

Mara arched her brow, but Stephen said no more. He downed his ale and pushed to his feet, chair scraping the floor. "Meet me in the courtyard when you're ready. Dress for a ride."

"Stephen . . ."

But he had gone.

Although she had taken care of herself all her life and had never had a personal servant, Mara found she missed Elizabeth already. As she pulled the blue tunic over her shift and leggings, she recalled the girl's gentle ministrations, and as she laboriously plaited her hair, she remembered how deft Elizabeth had been with a brush. Had she become spoiled so quickly?

No, Mara realized almost at once. She had, however, been lonely. Terribly lonely. In her whole life she had never had a female friend or confidante other than her mother.

Life was going to be different now, it seemed. It had changed suddenly, violently. But the change was done. The past was over, and the future beckoned.

Every eye in the hall, knight and servant alike, turned in Mara's direction when she emerged from behind the screen. No one remained unimpressed.

Mara's beauty and physical stature alone commanded respect. The short-sword and dagger she wore at her waist compounded it. The tale of her bravery, standing to fight at their baron's side, lent her the aura of legend. Not a man among those who had remained at Bellingham failed to see why their lord had chosen at last to wed.

Mara acknowledged the polite greetings of her husband's knights as she moved through the hall. More than one, she noted, kept a wary eye on Trey. She laid a hand atop his head as they moved through the wide doors into the summer sunshine.

Hero and Stephen's chestnut stallion stood saddled and ready in the courtyard. Stephen helped her mount as Jack held the horses.

"Are you sure you want to do this?" Jack asked.

"Do what?" Stephen took the reins from his disconsolate servant and climbed into the saddle. "You mean go somewhere without you?"

Jack nodded, but Stephen cut him off before he could speak.

"Absolutely sure. If we're not safe here, we're not safe anywhere." Stephen saw Walter and Alfred standing together by the doors to the hall, looking equally doubtful. He ignored them. Castle life afforded little privacy, and he intended to create some. He turned to Mara. "Are you ready?"

Mara had the feeling she answered more than one question when she nodded, and now-familiar butterfly wings stirred in her stomach. She put her heels lightly to Hero's sides and he kept pace with Stephen's chestnut. They rode beneath the castle gate and down the road.

For the first several miles the only living thing they saw was a herd of sheep, scattered carelessly over the brow of a greening hill. The only sound they heard was the frightened bleat of a ewe who took offense at their presence and trotted away, lamb at her side. Even the slow, steady *clop* of their horses' hooves seemed muffled by the green and warming sod. So companionable was their mutual silence, Mara did not feel the need to ask where they were going, or why.

The peace of the countryside was irresistible, and it filled her as Stephen had known it would. He watched her grow more and more relaxed as they covered the lands that belonged to him. Gradually, as they headed east, the hills flattened and woodlands reappeared. Trey left them for a while, concerned with his own pursuits, and the horses idly pricked their ears at occasional squeaks and rustlings from the undergrowth.

After a time, Mara closed her eyes to savor the subtle sensations of the warmth and shadow against her skin. A long, deep sigh escaped her, and it was as if, with the exhalation of that breath, the last, tattered remnants of grief and fear that clung to her soul were released, and they blew away on the soft summer wind.

Mara was not surprised when she felt Stephen grasp her hand. She returned the steady pressure of his fingers. Then he reined in his horse and her heart fluttered. Their fingers remained entwined.

"I know how unhappy you've been," Stephen said. The deep and seductive rumble of his voice did not disturb the stillness of the wood but, rather, seemed a part of it. "I know what you've suffered and, had I been able, I would have done anything in my power to prevent it. But it happened, and now it's over. All I can give you is a new beginning, a new life—mine. I give it willingly, and with all my heart."

Mara sought for words, but there were none. There were no thanks to offer for a gift so great. She pulled her hand from Stephen's and placed her palm against his cheek. Slowly, slowly, she bent toward him. Her eyelids fluttered closed.

Stephen met her kiss, answered it, felt his passion rise, filling him. He pulled away. "Not yet," he breathed. "Not here."

It took Mara a moment to regain her dizzied senses.

215

Then she followed Stephen's lead, gathered Hero's reins, and kicked him into a lope. Her pulse thundered along with every pound of her horse's hooves.

In another mile the woods thinned. Grass grew in patches of lush carpet on the forest floor. Ferns waved lazily in the shadows. Mara looked up and saw from the sun they now traveled in a southwesterly direction. She realized they had ridden roughly in a large circle. Soon, she thought, they would come upon the castle.

But Stephen was not headed to Bellingham. He held his mount to a collected canter as the land began to gently rise and fall again. At the crest of a yew-studded hill, he pulled the stallion to a halt. Mara drew alongside, and Stephen smiled when she caught her breath.

"Kielder Water," he said by way of explanation. He gazed down on the long, dark lake below them, and pointed to the south where a river left to flow to the sea. "The Tyne," he continued. "It runs behind Bellingham, thirty miles or better, to Tynemouth. And the great ocean. Someday I'll take you there."

Mara held Stephen's gaze for a long, breathless moment. "I only care about now," she whispered.

Without another word, Stephen turned his horse and headed down the slope of the hill. In minutes they had reached the water's edge, where they dismounted in unison. Stephen loosened the saddle girths and tied the animals' reins to the low-hanging branches of an evergreen.

Mara stared out over the water. It reminded her a little of the Ullsmere. Wavelets lapped at the uneven, pebble-strewn shoreline. A jay scolded, perched for a heartbeat atop a nearby boulder, and was gone again in a flash of blue. A fish jumped with a splash and a swirl. Trees that crowded water's edge mottled the shadows.

Mara did not look at her husband. She did not need to. She knew his gaze devoured her; she could feel it, like a warm wave of blood thrilling through her veins. She turned her back to him.

All her life, everything that had come before, became concentrated in this single moment. There was no past, no future. Only now. Her entire body tingled, from the top of her head to the tips of her toes. She had never been so alive, so totally aware of every inch of her flesh. She had never before taken such pride in her lean, hard tone; her heavy breasts; the narrowness of her waist; the sleekness of her legs. She wanted to touch herself, to run her hand from the sharp bones at the base of her throat over her smooth belly and the mound of her womanhood. She wanted to reveal herself to him. Intimately, slowly, sensually.

The moment had finally arrived. The moment that had been destined since those frozen seconds in time when she had risen from the lake and had stood before him, innocent, naked, dripping.

This time she would not run. This time she would know truly what it was to be a woman.

Slowly, Mara dropped short-sword and dagger, her silver girdle, and pulled the tunic up over her head. She removed her leggings and dropped them atop her weapons. She unwound the plait from her head and, with nimble fingers, separated the long tresses until they fell free, over her shoulders and down her naked back.

Still, she did not look at her husband, and no word passed between them. None was needed. The scene had been written long before, and they needed only to play it.

The water was cold. So cold. It licked Mara's toes, her ankles, her knees. She drew in her breath sharply, held it, clenched her teeth, and walked in up to the level of her breasts. When the ground fell away abruptly to the depths, she struck out and swam.

Water flowed over her shoulders and back, and it mingled with the streams of her long, long moonlight hair. A small wake followed the kick of her slender ankles. She swam back toward the shore.

217

Sand and stone gritted once more beneath Mara's feet. She let her fingertips trail in the water as she waded onto a small spit of beach. A breeze breathed into momentary life, and the branches of a great fir tree swayed gracefully. Stephen stepped from its shadows.

It was as it had been in the beginning, in that first moment. Her vision was filled with him. It savored him, licked him, learned every line of him. Immobile, her eyes took him inside her, absorbed him into her soul, from the handsome and angular planes of his face, to the dark hair breaking at the tops of his muscular shoulders, down the broad, smooth expanse of his chest to the indented waist and firm, flat belly, to the masculine part of him.

That part of him, however, was not as she had seen it before. This time it was swollen with passion and need. It throbbed and pulsed with the life force it longed to give to her. Her entire being was drawn to it, yearned for it.

Hers and Stephen's lips parted as they met. Their flesh tingled where it touched, thigh to thigh, belly to belly, breast to breast; she cold, he burning. Hands sought and met, palm to palm. Then Stephen caressed her lightly with his fingertips, feather-soft across the insides of her elbows and upper arms, down over her ribs and the swell of her hips.

A force greater than her conscious will forced Mara's head back, pulling her mouth from Stephen's. A cry escaped her throat as her arms encircled his neck. She felt his hands grip her waist tightly, pulling her closer, closer.

She was aware of every inch of him, every searing inch. She was acutely aware of her nipples pressed to his hard, smooth chest. The jut of their hipbones ground together. His hard, tense manhood pressed closer.

She wanted, ached, needed to surrender to him. Like wax against the candle's flame, she melted. Her arms loosed from his neck. Her hands slid down his sides, over and down the valleys and canyons of his rib cage, across the rise of his tight-muscled flanks. As her knees buckled, her fingers caressed the bulge of his manhood and crisp, curling hairs on his thighs.

Panting now, her lips parted, Mara's hands briefly cupped the base of his shaft. She laid her cheek against it, inhaled the musky fragrance of him.

All strength left her body. She leaned back on her elbows. Lay back upon the ground. Her knees parted.

Stephen dropped down in front of her. One hand reached to touch her face. She gripped his hand, kissed his palm.

He lowered himself onto her.

Mara closed her eyes. The feel of him was exactly as she had imagined. His smooth, hard chest crushed her breasts, his flat belly strained against her own; his muscular thighs pushed her legs farther apart. His lips captured her mouth.

It was the probe of his tongue she felt first. She felt the thrust of him in her mouth and met him joyously, exuberantly, even as her hips rose to welcome the rest.

The pain was searing for a moment, only a moment. Then she was aware only of the size and length and stroke of him—in her, filling her, completing her being, the reason for her existence. Rocking with him, moving to the ecstasy of her body, they continued on a journey that had begun long before. Its end was shattering in its intensity, and their cries intermingled.

A soaring hawk moved lazily away. A cloud momentarily covered the sun. Inexplicably, the world continued to turn.

Chapter Thirty-three

A breeze chased a band of ripples across the lake. Mara felt it hurry over her skin, and she leaned up on one elbow. Stephen's eyes were closed, but she doubted he slept. She felt him awake, as surely as she felt his flesh pressed to hers, from hip to ankle. She lightly touched her lips to his smooth, pale chest.

Stephen wound his fingers in her hair, still damp, and gently turned her head so he could look into her eyes. "I love you."

"I know. As I love you."

His fingers relaxed and Mara laid her head on his chest. A familiar heat sparked in her belly, then faded to a warm glow. She was exhausted.

At first they had thought the fire ignited between them might never be quenched. They had made love again and again, as if they had only days ahead of them, not a lifetime.

Yet while desire was infinite, strength and endurance were not. Sated, amazed, and delighted, giggling like children, they had eventually collapsed in each other's arms. They still had not found the energy to move.

Mara lazily shifted her gaze to her hound, who had reappeared only recently, also exhausted. He lay stretched on his side, feet twitching, dreaming of the hare that got away.

Stephen's chestnut stallion drowsed, one hind leg cocked, head low. Hero, however, stood at attention, ears pricked, and gazed into the distance over the lake at something only he could see. Of a sudden he snorted, shook his head, and freed his reins from the branch where they had been loosely tied.

Mara sighed and attempted to gather her strength. The horse would have to be retied. But before she could move, Hero walked to her side, reins dragging. He dropped his head and blew his warm breath over both her and Stephen.

Though the charger had been trained to trample an enemy on the field of battle, Stephen knew neither he nor Mara had anything to fear from the horse. The huge animal had developed such an attachment to Mara, Stephen did not even worry he might run away. He closed his eyes again, dozing pleasantly, until he felt a scalding teardrop on his chest.

"Mara!" Stephen sat up and took his wife in his arms. "What is it? What's wrong?"

Mara shook her head. "Nothing. Truly." She swiped at her tears and tried to smile, but memory was upon her and she could not loosen its grip.

"Tell me, Mara. Please," Stephen persisted.

"It's . . . Remember that night?" Mara looked into her husband's eyes, and once again tried to smile. "The night you rescued me from Baldwin, and we found that . . . that falling-down cottage? You built a fire, I'll never know how, and . . . and held me. Hero came over and blew on me, like he did just now, and it . . . it all came back to me."

221

A shadow suddenly fell across Stephen's day. Until this moment, Mara had not said a word to him about her time as the earl's captive. He had pushed it from his mind. He could do so no longer.

"Mara, did Baldwin . . . Did he hurt you?" he inquired gently. "You've never talked to me about it. You may not wish to now."

Mara shook her head. "No, I don't mind talking to you about it. And no, he didn't hurt me—not physically. Although if you hadn't come when you did . . ." She looked off across the lake.

"He's a bad man," she continued presently. "A very bad man, an evil man. And he's sick, I think. In his mind." She looked back at her husband. "That's what scares me the most about him, Stephen. His actions are totally unpredictable. There's only hatred in his heart, and the desire for revenge against anyone he thinks has wronged him. That includes not only me now, but you."

Stephen smoothed a damp strand of hair from her temple. "There's nothing to be afraid of anymore, Mara. He can't harm you. Especially here. These are my lands, well tenanted, far to the north. Baldwin knows well the strength of my men-at-arms. And of my alliances with the Earl of Northumberland and the other northern barons. He would not dare make an overt move against us here."

Mara was not comforted. "I know, Stephen. I know. But what about a *covert* move? If anyone can find a way—"

"Stop." Stephen laid a finger on her lips. "I want you to put that man out of your mind. For good. And think about something else, something pleasant."

Stephen's mood was irresistible, and it infected her. "Something pleasant? Like what?"

"Like a grand celebration. Particularly now that we have something to celebrate."

Mara had to laugh at the twinkle in her husband's eye. "So tell me about this 'grand celebration.' "

Stephen hugged his knees and grinned. "I dispatched

messengers this morning. Even as we speak, they ride far and wide to invite local gentry, townsfolk, one and all, to a feast and festivities at Bellingham Castle, week's end."

Mara felt her stomach sink. "But, Stephen, I . . . I haven't even anything to wear!"

"So I see."

"Don't tease, I'm serious!" She was also frightened. An armed and mounted knight charging down on her did not scare her half as much as a crowd of people—strangers in particular, all come to eye the new baroness. "Stephen, I . . . I'm not sure this is such a good idea."

He sensed her discomfort at once, as well as the reason for it, and took her hand. "Mara, you are not only the most beautiful, but the bravest woman I've ever known. You'll do just fine," he said gently. "Furthermore, you will definitely have the finest gown of anyone attending. Perhaps even a silver comb for your hair. Or an amber necklace. Who knows?" Stephen shrugged and rose lightly to his feet before Mara could question him further.

"Stephen—"

"One surprise at a time," he replied enigmatically, and picked up the clothes he had scattered carelessly on the ground. "You'd better get dressed, my love. The day wanes."

Mara obeyed, a smile at the corners of her mouth. Life with Stephen, it seemed, was going to be full of surprises.

The end of the warm and mellow summer day swiftly approached. Streams of fading light fell through the high windows onto the heavy tapestries that had once graced Ullswater Castle, wrought by Beatrice's own hand. The yellow, green, blue, and pink silken threads shone as if with an inner light. The scenes were merry: picnics in the countryside with beautifully dressed ladies and fine lords; hunting scenes with prancing horses, leaping hounds, and laughing gentlemen. But they did not lighten the heavy atmosphere that had fallen upon Baldwin's hall.

Not even the gay banners of blue and yellow silk brightened the pall on the room. Nor any of the other great treasures stolen from Ranulf's castle.

Maggie rubbed at the place where her eye should have been. Though she could not remember a time when there had been anything there but an empty socket, still it seemed sometimes she would swipe at that spot and there would be an eye, as if she had forgotten all about her disfigurement. It happened most often when she daydreamed and forgot herself. Or was under extreme stress.

The hall was deserted now, but for the two guards who stood nervously by the door. A third man, who had been unfortunate enough to mention to his earl the rumor that buzzed about the countryside, had fled minutes earlier. The cut over his cheek, where he had caught the pewter mug, would bleed for a good while to come.

"Spiderwebs," Maggie muttered. "Should pack it with spiderwebs. Maybe a bit o' wool."

"What?"

Baldwin spun so quickly Maggie jumped. She moved a little closer to the back of his chair—where it was more difficult for him to reach her, should he be so inclined.

"What did you say?" the earl demanded again.

"Nothin'. Was just talkin' to m'self."

"Leave me. Go on, get out of here!"

Maggie scurried for the door.

"Stop! Wait! Where are you going?"

Maggie didn't bother to answer this time. Periods when her master was almost totally irrational had become more and more frequent. She was learning how to react to them, however—as she had learned many other hard lessons over the years. Silently, she slunk back to her place behind his elaborately ornamented chair. He began to chatter to her—or to the walls; she was never quite sure which—almost at once.

"Festivities? Festivities? A celebration? To celebrate what? The coupling of those two overgrown and muscle-bound imbeciles? Imagine! If you care to. How revolting. Like beasts in a field. Maggie. Maggie! Where are you?"

Maggie sidled around the arm of his chair. "Here, m'lord. Here."

"Ah, good." The mad light momentarily died from his eyes. Baldwin steepled his fingers and rested his chin on his fingertips. "I'm not invited, you know. But that's all right," he continued when she remained silent. "I'm a bigger person than they imagine. Much bigger. My generosity is unbounded. Isn't it, Maggie? You should know."

Wisely, Maggie nodded. A forced and stiff smile revealed her small, white teeth.

"I am so generous, in fact, that I am going to overlook the injury the . . . happy couple has done me. I am going to forget that I am not invited to their little celebration. And I am going to send a gift anyway." Baldwin chuckled. "Oh, yes, it will be a nice little gift. A lovely gift. Totally appropriate. I shall have to give it some additional thought, although I have the basic idea in mind. It will be a surprise. Such a surprise!"

Baldwin clapped his hands like a child, startling Maggie again. When he rose from his chair, giggling, she followed, knowing what she would see if she could look into his eyes. Once more, lucidity had slipped away. He probably wouldn't even notice if she disappeared, hid away from him during the tortured hours she knew were to come.

But she couldn't leave him. Wouldn't. Pathetic as it was, he was all she had. And she loved him.

Elizabeth had everything in order for her lord and lady's return. Their apartment was neat; the cover on the big bed was smooth; clothes were neatly folded away in the

225

chests; wedding gifts were artfully arranged on the table by the window. Elizabeth stepped back to admire her handiwork.

There was a bouquet of flowers in a jug on the table. The widow Morpeth from the village had picked them herself, despite the terrible stiffness in her joints, and had sent them over as a token of welcome for the new baroness.

Elizabeth patted the wild yellow rose she had tucked into her bodice, purloined from the lady's bouquet. No one would notice, or care. The mistress was so generous and kind! She certainly would not mind, either, if Elizabeth took just one of those buns. She tiptoed over to the basket.

The baker and his wife had baked them specially for the lady. They were filled with raisins, a rare treat, and a bit of sugar was melted atop each one. Elizabeth popped one of the delicacies into her mouth before she might have second thoughts.

"Aha! Caught you!"

Elizabeth whirled, cheeks stuffed and flaming, to see the baron and his wife standing in the doorway. Hands pressed to her mouth, she swallowed.

"Oh, I'm sorry . . . I'm sorry! I didn't mean—"

"It's all right!" Mara laughed. "The baron is only teasing you. You take such good care of me, Elizabeth, you may help yourself to anything you want."

Embarrassed nonetheless, Elizabeth bustled about the room rearranging everything she had already set to rights. Stephen watched until his amusement at her officiousness frayed at the edges. Mara had seated herself in a chair by the window, the day's last light laying sheets of silver atop her yet unbound hair, and he wanted to stroke it, take her into his arms again, and run his fingers through its silken masses.

"You may go, Elizabeth," he said, more sharply than

he intended. When he heard the door close behind him, he crossed to Mara's side.

His nearness made something within his wife tighten, coil like a spring, demanding release. She rose and moved into his arms in one fluid motion. Her lips parted and a gasp of pleasure escaped her when he twined his fingers in her hair and gently pulled her head back. His mouth found the hollow of her throat.

Playfulness mingled with desire. Mara shook her head free of Stephen's fingers and nipped at the lobe of his ear. "My surprise," she coaxed in a husky voice. "Tell me what my surprise is."

"Who needs to talk? I'll show you."

In one deft movement, Stephen raised both her tunic and shift and lifted Mara up against him. Her legs wrapped around his waist, and she moaned softly with the passion excited in her. Surprising herself, she groped unashamedly at his breeches.

"I love you, Stephen," she breathed, the words thick in her throat. They were the last words spoken for a very long time.

Chapter Thirty-four

Mara was as deeply asleep as she had ever been, body relaxed, mind at peace. Her lips were slightly parted, hair in magnificent disarray, head pillowed on her husband's shoulder. She did not rouse when Stephen moved from beneath her and softly called her name. He had to shake her gently, several times, before her eyelids fluttered open.

"Mara . . . are you awake?"

The room was still dark. "No." She smiled up at the place where her husband's voice seemed to be coming from, turned over, and drifted away at once.

"Mara, come on. You have to get up."

She wanted to. She wanted to do anything, and everything, he asked of her. But she was so tired. She couldn't seem to move.

Stephen rolled Mara onto her back, leaned over, and planted a kiss on her lips. Slowly, languidly, her arms went around his neck. He kissed her again and felt her response grow stronger, more demanding. Her lips moved against his; her arms tightened across his shoulders. Quickly, before she could react, he slid his hands under her legs, lifted her from the bed, and set her on her feet.

"Stephen!"

"Get dressed, Mara. Hurry up."

Objects in the room began to take on definition as a sliver of the red sun appeared over the horizon. Soon its light would warm the castle walls, rouse the courtyard dogs from their slumber, and set the horses astir in their stalls.

But it was not yet true day, and Mara was not yet fully awake. She watched her husband pull on his clothes.

"Here." Stephen handed Mara the things she had discarded, hastily, the night before. "Now, please, get dressed. It's almost dawn, and I want to be away by the time the sun's up."

"But wh—?"

"Don't ask. Just hurry up."

When he was certain her morning toilette was finally under way, Stephen left to saddle their horses.

Most of the people in Bellingham Castle were privy to Stephen's secret. Rumor-mongering being what it was, even most of the villagers knew. No one was surprised, therefore, when the first of the gaily colored wagons, which had been camped for the night beyond a distant hill, rolled through town.

As dawn broke, the crowd gathered and the procession continued, cart after cart. Some were pulled by plumed horses; all were filled with wonderful and mysterious items. To the delight of all the onlookers, a juggler appeared and paused for a moment to display his skill with three bright red balls. Then he moved on, the rest of the impromptu parade with him. At its end came the villagers, all headed for the castle, gates wide and welcoming.

*   *   *

Mara could not help wondering if Stephen was going to lead her once again to the Kielder Water. They were headed roughly in that direction, and her pulse throbbed a little faster in her veins. She wondered, with a private blush, if she would ever have enough of her husband. Probably not, she decided, and smiled to herself. At almost the same instant, they crested the hill that overlooked the lake.

Stephen reined in his stallion, turned to his wife, saw her rosy-cheeked smile, and chuckled. "Now, now, wife," he chided. "There's much to do today. We haven't time for dalliance."

Mara's blush deepened, and her curiosity mounted. What was Stephen up to? A question formed on her lips, but he put his heels to his mount before she could give it voice. She followed him down the hill, Trey at her heels.

They loped by the side of the Kielder Water, horses' hooves occasionally splashing in the shallows. Pleasant memories blew softly across Mara's cheeks with the warm morning wind. Then they headed back in the direction of the castle.

Mara couldn't imagine what Stephen had in mind. Simply a morning's ride? But why the urgency? And why had he mentioned a surprise yesterday? A few minutes later, Mara found out.

The castle came into view. But there was something different about it. It took a second for the difference to penetrate her consciousness. Mara halted Hero sharply.

"Stephen!"

"Mara!" he mocked gently.

She lifted her arm and pointed at the streams of people still crossing the castle bridge. "L-look at that. What's going on?"

"I don't know. Perhaps we should find out."

Mara gave her husband a tight-lipped glance, but it hid a smile. She urged Hero into a lope.

The people made way for their baron and baroness, and the pair trotted through the bailey and on into the courtyard unimpeded. Startled and uneasy, Hero halted of his own accord. Trey uttered a low, uncertain growl. Mara's jaw dropped.

The courtyard had been transformed. The colored wagons had been set up in neat rows, pennants billowed in the breeze, and performers vied for attention. Three small dogs jumped through a hoop; the juggler reappeared with his red balls; and off in a corner a dancing bear reared on its hind legs and took a few tentative steps. Gaily dressed merchants waved and pointed at their wares.

Mara's hands went to her mouth, and she slowly shook her head. When Hero sidestepped nervously, her hands returned to his reins.

"Oh, Stephen, what is this? What have you done?"

"Do you, by chance, recall telling me you hadn't anything to wear?"

Mara nodded dumbly.

"Well, I think you'll be able to pick out some suitable material for a new dress now."

"And I know how to sew!" came the sound of a bright, familiar voice.

Mara glanced down and saw Elizabeth, eyes twinkling as she stood near Hero's shoulder.

"I'm quick, too," the girl continued. "You shall have the finest gown in all of England. But come. Come, lady. We must hurry and look!"

"Go on," Stephen urged with a laugh. He gestured, and a boy appeared to hold Mara's horse and the increasingly agitated Trey. "Look at everything. Pick out anything you want, as much as you want. And don't forget to choose the entertainment you'd like for a performance in the hall."

Mara looked up at her husband. "But, Stephen, I . . . I hardly . . . I don't know what to—"

231

Stephen leaned down from his horse and cupped his wife's delicate chin in his hand. "Go on, my love," he said quietly. "Fulfill your heart's every desire. It's my gift to you. And the celebration of our marriage." He kissed her lightly on the lips. "Now go on. Off with you."

Mara had no choice with Elizabeth tugging at her tunic. She cast Stephen a parting smile and was lost at once amidst the throng.

The variety of wares was dizzying, almost unbelievable. Stephen had bid the best merchants, with the widest selections from all over the world, come to Bellingham Castle. Mara was thunderstruck and hardly knew where to begin. Elizabeth, however, seemed to be in charge for the moment, and the girl dragged her to the aisle where the materials were displayed.

There was English wool dyed in Flanders; rare silks; robes lined with sable, marten, ermine, and squirrel from the continent; gold cloth, purple cloth, linen, and muslin. Mara made several selections that Elizabeth gathered in her arms and carried as if she bore a wonderful prize. The castle steward followed at a discreet distance bearing a purse heavy with coins.

In the next aisle was a merchant with wares from Spain and neighboring countries. He gestured with fat, beringed hands at his merchandise, and Mara drew in her breath. There was olive oil, fragrant soap, incredibly soft Cordovan leather, and foods Mara had never seen before: figs, dates, almonds, oranges, lemons. At the merchant's insistence, she sampled a fig and a handful of raisins mixed with almonds.

"How amazing!" Mara exclaimed. "I've never tasted anything like it. Oh, please, how much do you have?"

The merchant beamed, his generosity rewarded, and the steward's purse grew lighter.

There was ivory, brass, and precious gems; sweet wine from Italy; hunting dogs; silver; pepper, cinnamon, cloves; even a parrot in a cage. The steward's purse grew smaller still.

The sun had reached its zenith; the air was still and the day grew hot. Stephen, on a mission of his own, purchased some oranges, had someone squeeze them, and had a frothy, brimming mug of the juice delivered to his wife. Mara was as delighted as a child, and as full of wonder. Elizabeth tugged at her sleeve.

"Oh, please, lady," she begged. "Save a bit for me!"

Mara laughed and handed the pewter cup to the girl. Since one of the other servants had taken the armload of materials into the castle, Elizabeth's nimble fingers had been busy helping Mara to sample everything— whether she was invited or not.

It was midafternoon by the time Mara had eventually seen everything, nearly exhausting herself in the process. Underlinens damp with sweat, she returned to the cool and welcome shade of her apartment. She was sure she had seen everything at least once, most things twice. And although not extravagant, she had taken Stephen at his word and purchased everything she had thought she might need—and a few things that had merely attracted her fancy.

"Oh, look, lady . . . just look!" Elizabeth crowed proudly as she spread the treasures on the wide bed, fingering each one.

Mara herself smoothed the materials for new shirts and a pair of breeches she had selected for her husband, and laid them aside. "Put this all away, will you, Elizabeth? Everything but *this*. I've something to see to in the hall. Then you may go home for the rest of the day."

Mara smiled to herself. She had plans. She lifted the filmy, gauzy amber silk and let it slither through her fingers. Yes, it would be perfect.

It and nothing else.

* * *

Stephen's day lasted a little longer than his wife's. Accompanied by Jack and Alfred, he visited each wagon and gave its owner instructions.

Most of those who had come had traveled far and done so only on the promise of many customers. Everyone for miles around had heard of the impromptu fair and would be coming to see the vast array of merchandise, and buy. Guests invited to the wedding celebration would also undoubtedly be customers, and Stephen therefore had arranged for the troop to camp for several days. He directed them to a large field just northwest of the castle. As the sun sank toward its rendezvous with the horizon, Stephen watched the last of the wagons rumble across the wooden bridge.

He sighed, hands on his narrow hips. "A long day," he commented. "And a successful one, I vow."

"Aye," Jack agreed. "The lady was happy."

Stephen grinned.

"I just hope she has reason to stay that way," Jack added.

"What do you mean?" Stephen asked.

"I mean there was a lot of people in an' out of here today. There was one or two of 'em I didn't like the looks of. It'd be a mistake, I think, to forget how long Baldwin's reach is, m'lord."

Alfred nodded enthusiastically, in support of Jack, but Stephen ignored him.

"People came from everywhere. There were several, I'm sure, we've never seen before. Don't be such an old woman, Jack." With that, Stephen strode away. Even as he crossed the yard, however, a film seemed to blur his vision, and he momentarily lost his concentration.

Something suddenly nagged at him. Something deeply disturbing.

Mara was in danger. Her very life. Only he could save her. And he could save her only with a very special knowledge. Panic-stricken, Stephen groped for it.

Then it was gone, as abruptly as it had fallen upon him, and he returned to his senses. He shook his head, as if emerging from an unremembered dream. The moment might never have occurred.

What had he been thinking? He was unwilling to hear any more pessimistic opinions, particularly from doom-and-gloom Jack. Mara, that last time he had seen her, had been as bubbly and gay as a young girl. He intended to take advantage of her mood, and resumed his march across the yard.

Stephen was not disappointed.

Darkness had blanketed the land for several hours before the messenger was ushered into the earl's great hall. He hurried to the chair at the end of the long room and quickly knelt before his lord.

"Tell me," Baldwin's voice commanded. "Stand up and tell me what you've learned."

The man pushed to his feet with effort. He had ridden long and hard, and had nearly killed the horse under him to bring the information to his earl in a timely fashion. "The baroness's fancy was caught by many things," the man began. "She purchased much. But—"

"But what?" Baldwin interrupted shrilly. "What is the one thing you were sent to learn?"

"That she favors the treasures of Spain and Portugal," the man blurted. "Particularly the foods. Figs, dates—"

Baldwin clapped his hands with delight, startling Maggie, who stood behind his chair as usual. "Good, wonderful! You've done well." Baldwin beamed. "But you are not done yet, I'm afraid. The merchants are camped outside Bellingham Castle, I understand?"

The man nodded.

"Go to the stable. Get a new mount. You will ride to Bellingham through the night." Baldwin rose, took Maggie's arm, and hooked it through his own. He felt good. Very fine, indeed.

"You are going to make a purchase for me," Baldwin continued, and handed the man a bag of coins. "Those tidbits the lady seemed to favor. I want an impressive array of the goodies. Bring them back here to me. With haste!"

Exhausted as he was, the messenger lost no time fleeing the hall. The sound of his lord's laughter rang in the air behind him.

Chapter Thirty-five

Stephen sat up and got out of bed very carefully. He walked across the floor to the dresser as if he trod on eggshells, then stared into the mirror intently.

"Remember," he chanted. "Remember, Steve. Remember."

It was the tail of the kite, just out of reach. He reached, leapt for it. But it dangled tantalizingly above him, beyond him. He squeezed his eyes shut and pressed his fingers to his temples.

"Rememberrrrrr."

The memory tickled at the back of his mind. He held on tightly to the feeling. It firmed, and moved within his grasp. He hung on to it for dear life.

The veil had been pierced. As Stephen of centuries before, he had experienced a moment of knowledge of the present. He had done it!

Stephen turned from the mirror and paced the small aisleway between his bed and the window, curtains securely drawn. He had finally managed to do it! If he did it once, he could do it again—if he concentrated harder he would remember longer, recall more. He was fairly sure he could bring his present knowledge back into the past. But what? What did he know?

With a grunt of frustration, Stephen sat down, hard, on the edge of his bed. It was connected to the dream. That much he knew. But how? It had been so long since he'd had the dream. Ever since he'd begun regressing, as a matter of fact. What, exactly, had been in that terrible nightmare?

He had become very good at achieving the state where his mind relaxed, and went freely, surely, to the place Stephen wished it to be. He willed his thoughts to wrap themselves around the nightmare he had tried so hard to banish forever. In moments, he revisited the scene of the battle.

The smell of blood was cloying. Dust hung in the air. Groans of the dying, and the squeals of injured horses came to his ears. He felt keenly his exhaustion. And fear.

The time and place were strange to him no longer. The nightmare had not come from nowhere and nothing to randomly plague him; he had *lived* it. He was Stephen, the baron. He was victorious. He had defeated the earl. He had been reliving his past in the dream. He had been reliving the most horrible moment in his life . . . in any of his lifetimes.

"Mara!"

Stephen leapt from the bed. His breath came in ragged gasps. Terror froze the blood in his veins.

She had died in his arms, an arrow through her throat. He had won the battle but lost his life, his heart. He had not yet regained it. His grief had lasted the centuries and haunted him still. He had promised to protect her. He had vowed she would always be safe with him. He had failed.

Tears he did not notice streamed down Stephen's face. The full force of the knowledge stunned him. He even knew why the dream, and his depression, had started near his twenty-second birthday. That's how old he had been, as the baron, when he'd lost the only woman he would ever love.

His knees felt weak. All the strength seemed to have drained from his body.

There was going to be a battle. He was going to lose Mara. Again.

Pulling together every resource available to him, Stephen attempted to regain control of himself and his emotions. He had to think, clearly.

Contrary to everything he had ever believed, Stephen had accessed a past life. He had learned to revisit, relive it, at will. He was a skeptic no longer. He had lived before, loved before. And Amanda had been right: An event in a previous existence affected his current one.

He had broken a promise, the most important promise he had ever made. His grief would be eternal, life after life after life. Unless . . .

The hope was so fragile, Stephen dared not let it out of the dark and into his heart for fear it might disintegrate in the light of day.

And yet he *had* broken through to the other side. As the baron he had, for an instant, recalled the present. If he could just do that again, as readily as he accessed the past from the here and now, he might be able to do something.

But could he alter history? Was it possible? *Could he save her?*

Stephen glanced at the telephone. It appeared to throb and pulse with a life of its own, beckoning to him. Just one call. He could make just one call. Millie might know. Millie might be able to help him.

Stephen found himself reaching for the phone. He watched his arm snake out, fingers stretch. His blood turned to ice.

He could see right through his hand, his arm, to the

telephone beneath. The strength left his legs and he sat down, hard, on the bed. He clasped his hands—and was whole again.

What was happening? Gooseflesh covered Stephen's entire body. Was he losing himself, spending a part of him each time he visited the past?

His need to call Millie was more urgent than ever, though Stephen knew that to connect with someone, anyone, would be to end his freedom. He could try "callblocking," but it probably wouldn't be available on a motel room phone. He couldn't take the chance. To lose his freedom would be to lose his chance to save Mara . . . If there *was* a chance.

Slowly, gently, Stephen eased back down on the bed. He had to go back again, to try to remember his present while he was there. It was the only faint flicker of hope he had.

Chapter Thirty-six

Mara was exhausted and as nervous as she had ever been in her young life. For three days she had worked ceaselessly to ready the castle and its grounds for the upcoming fete. All the while, guests had been arriving in a seemingly ceaseless stream. The farther away they lived, evidently, the earlier they thought they should arrive. Mara had been pressed into the unaccustomed role of hostess, in addition to her many other duties. With Elizabeth's aid, however, and Stephen's, all went smoothly.

It was Stephen, accompanied by Jack, who went to the bailey to greet the latest arrivals, fulfilling his role as host and lord of the manor. "Welcome to Bellingham. Please enter and accept the hospitality of my wife, the baroness, and myself," was heard over and over again as the day of the grand celebration drew nearer.

Lords and their ladies from all over the north arrived, accepted the castle's welcome, and proceeded on to the courtyard. There they were greeted by a host of servants who held the reins of their gaily bedecked chargers and palfreys, dappled grays, blacks, chestnuts, and bays; the animals' trappings boasting the colors of their noble riders. Bedazzled servants assisted the grand ladies and gentlemen from their high and elaborate saddles to the cobbled ground. From there the castle steward escorted them to the hall—and to the sight they all, in truth, had come to see.

"Lady Agnes. Lord William." Mara inclined her head graciously, a soft smile on her mouth. She gestured gracefully from her seat at the center of the head table to a bench on her right. "Please join me for a cup of wine. Or would you prefer ale, Lord William? You must be thirsty after your long journey."

Almost everyone greeted by the already fabled Baroness of Bellingham joined her at the table, thirsty or not. Those who had heard of her ferocity as a warrior were struck by her gentleness and beauty. Those who'd been told of her beauty were awed by the reality. Mara herself had almost begun to enjoy her role as hostess.

Elizabeth's nimble fingers had been as busy as she had promised they would be, and Mara wore clothes she had never even dreamed might exist. The wealth of fabrics she had selected from the merchants had been magically transformed into chemises, tunics, mantles, and scarves in every conceivable color. She had new silver combs for her hair, a golden circlet for her brow, the amber beads Stephen had promised, rings and brooches set with precious stones. She felt like a queen, and her self-assurance was reflected in every word and gesture. Not a man or woman greeted by the baroness left the hall without being deeply impressed.

Yet in spite of her increased self-esteem, Mara could not help breathing a sigh of relief each time another noble couple was ushered from the hall to their quarters in the newly refurbished tower. As prominent as her father had been, he had also been reclusive, content to pass the time with his family and the men-at-arms who had long been his friends. Mara had known little contact with the outside world. To meet so many people at once and to be, moreover, the one they had come primarily to see, was daunting. She kept Trey almost constantly at her side; Elizabeth as well, when she was not busy elsewhere.

Just before noon on the day of the celebration, Mara greeted the last of the guests. Stephen led the courtly gentleman into the hall.

"Mara," he began, "I'd like you to meet our very good friend and ally, Henry, Earl of Northumberland. Henry, may I present my wife, Amarantha, Baroness of Bellingham?"

The elegant, velvet-clad gentleman, jowls heavy but expression benign, bent low over Mara's hand. "I'm so pleased to meet you, lady," he said. Mara liked him immediately. She could tell by the mere sound of his voice that he meant whatever he said. She had no doubt whatsoever that he was indeed happy to meet her.

"And I you, my lord," she replied with a smile. "I'm so glad you arrived in time for the festivities this evening."

"As am I. Word is this celebration will be the talk of the district for years to come. And now I see for myself why such a celebration was planned." The white-haired earl turned to his host. "May I offer my congratulations? Your baroness is stunning."

Mara blushed and excused herself with reluctance. Of everyone she had met so far, she liked Henry the best and looked forward to conversation with him. But she knew Stephen also had looked forward to having the earl's ear in private for a time. As the two most powerful lords of the north, they had much to discuss. With a slight and graceful curtsy, she withdrew from the room.

Elizabeth was all atwitter. "Oh, my lady," she sighed. "Did you ever see material lovelier than this?"

"Don't touch it!"

Elizabeth froze, hand poised over the shining silver fabric, a look of distressed surprise on her face.

"I'm sorry, Elizabeth," Mara said from the cramped metal tub where she sat soaking in warm, soapy water. "But you've been eating oranges again, haven't you? And you were going to put your sticky fingers on that chemise."

Elizabeth's features were transformed into a mask of guilt. She clasped her hands behind her back. "Oh, my lady, I'm so sorry. I . . . I just can't seem to keep my hands off them. I've never seen their like before, and they're so good—"

"It's all right," Mara interrupted. "Just help me dry off, will you?" She rose from the water, her tall, sleekly muscled form dripping, and stepped into the linen cloth the girl held for her.

As she toweled the water from her limbs, Mara glanced at the once overflowing bowl of fruit and shook her head. Having Elizabeth around was like having a mouse in the pantry. But she didn't begrudge the girl a single bite. Her help was invaluable.

Dry at last, Mara donned the ensemble Elizabeth had created for her: chemise of the finest, softest silver fabric with long, flowing sleeves; over-tunic of sapphire-blue silk; a silver girdle studded with amethyst to define her slender waist. Her moonlight hair was wound atop her head like a crown, bound with a silver circlet adorned by a single, large amethyst that lay upon her brow. The effect was breathtaking and Elizabeth, surveying her handiwork, pressed her hands to her mouth.

"Oh, Baroness," she breathed.

Mara blushed. She felt beautiful. "Thank you, Elizabeth," she said simply. "Thank you for everything." Then she turned toward her chamber door. It was time to celebrate—officially, and at long last—her marriage to the Baron of Bellingham.

* * *

Each of the long tables had been filled to capacity. Wine and ale had been poured into the new silver goblets Mara had acquired, and a dozen or more servants scurried to keep the cups filled. Discussion was lively, laughter frequent. Silence fell when she entered the room.

Several indrawn breaths were audible, but Mara did not see who her most ardent admirers might be. She had eyes only for her husband.

Stephen loved Mara with all his heart. But he had lived with her now for a time and thought he had surely seen her at her most lovely; rising, naked and dripping, from the lake; asleep with lips slightly parted; or astride her stallion perhaps, hair whipping in the wind.

But he was wrong. He had had no idea the full extent of her astounding beauty until this moment. It left him stunned and speechless. Slowly, as if stiff with age, Stephen rose from his chair and extended his hand.

It was as if some secret signal had been given to each and every guest. As one, they all lifted their cups.

"To our lady, Baroness of Bellingham," the Earl of Northumberland's voice rang out.

"The Baroness of Bellingham," came the chorus—and then a cheer, and another, and then gay pandemonium.

Mara laughed as she took the seat at her husband's side, amazed and delighted. "They like me, don't they, Stephen?" she whispered.

"Yes, they like you, Mara. And I adore you."

They had one long moment to gaze into each other's eyes; then the evening belonged to their guests.

Mara was besieged almost at once, despite the impressive array of dishes brought in grand procession from the kitchen. Lords and their ladies crowded one another in an attempt to get nearer the fascinating new baroness, speak with her a moment, touch her hand. Fortunately, so many wished to say so much at once, Mara didn't have to worry about making polite or witty conversation; she merely had to smile and nod occasionally.

After a while the crowd around her thinned. Wine and ale were consumed more freely. More attention was paid to the ample and elaborate fare, the roasted meats and boiled fish, herbed vegetables, crusty game pies, and loaves of bread twisted into cunning and fanciful shapes. Mara felt herself relax.

As the evening progressed, cliques formed. Neighbors and old friends moved together to catch up on one another's lives. Mara found herself blessedly isolated for the first time since she had entered the hall. She was free to make her own conversation, or listen in on one that interested her. Sipping her favorite wine, one Stephen had gone to much trouble to provide, she leaned nearer her husband to try and catch the words he exchanged with the Earl of Northumberland.

Despite the warmth of the crowded hall, and the wine singing in her veins, Mara's blood turned to ice.

"—and Beatrice were well liked," the earl was saying. He had not yet noticed Mara's attention fixed upon him. "And not only by their neighbors and friends. Rumor has it that the king is most distressed—"

"Livid would be a better word," Lord William interrupted. His round, florid face was redder than usual. "I happened to be there, at court, when Henry received word of Earl Baldwin's perfidy. He grieved, genuinely grieved. Then he lost his temper. Mightily."

Stephen smiled grimly. "So, you think he'll take action?"

"I'm certain of it," William replied quickly. "It's only a matter of time now. Baldwin will answer for his actions. Henry is as proud of this 'common law' of his as anything he has accomplished in his reign so far."

"Good! Praise God and the King of England."

Startled by her words, the three men turned to Mara.

"I most humbly beg your pardon, lady," Henry began. "Had I known you attended our words, I—"

"Please do not apologize, my lord," Mara said firmly.

246

"I *welcome* your words. And your opinion. Do you truly think, Lord William, the king will be able to exact justice?"

"Well, I, I . . ." The portly gentleman's flush deepened and he glanced uncomfortably at his host. But Stephen gave him an almost imperceptible nod.

"Go ahead," he urged. "You, like everyone else, must have heard that my lady wife is not only my mate, but my partner and my equal in all things. Please proceed."

William cleared his throat. "Very well then, yes. Yes, I think the king will most certainly hold Baldwin accountable for his actions."

"It is one thing, however, to hold the earl accountable," Mara continued. "Quite another to bring him to justice. Think you the king has the power to bring Baldwin down?"

William looked shocked. Henry's bushy gray eyebrows shot upward, and Stephen smiled.

"Obviously, you do not think he can," Northumberland said at length.

"I confess I have my doubts, my lord. I've been Baldwin's victim, remember, as well as his . . . guest. I've seen his madness firsthand. I should not underestimate him, if I were you. Nor should the King of England."

The three men exchanged glances, her husband still with a small smile at the corners of his mouth. He seemed about to speak, but a minor interruption stayed them all. He looked with irritation at the girl who tugged at Mara's sleeve.

"Excuse me, please, Baroness. I'm so sorry," Elizabeth said excitedly. "But look, look what's just arrived! Another gift! And such a fine one."

Mara glanced at the large basket Elizabeth now lifted with difficulty. It was filled to overflowing with all her most recently discovered favorites; dates, raisins, dried figs, almonds both plain and candied, aromatic sticks of cinnamon, and a scattering of lemons and oranges. It was indeed a grand offering. But an untimely interruption nonetheless.

"Take it away, Elizabeth, please," Mara said in a soft but firm voice. "This is not the time for such things. Take it to our apartment. Help yourself, if you like," she added, although she knew it was not necessary. As Elizabeth moved obediently away, Mara returned her attention to the three noblemen.

"My lady has a point," Stephen put in smoothly, skillfully reweaving the threads of the conversation. "The Earl of Cumbria is not a man to be taken lightly."

"Indeed not, I agree," Henry affirmed. "But peaceable though our sovereign may be, he is not also timid. He will not simply ask the earl to answer to him. He will see that his wishes are enforced. I should expect a full deputation to be calling upon our friend Baldwin sometime soon. A well-armed deputation."

"I hope so," Mara said. "And they should not only be well armed, but wary as we—"

Her words were cut off by a short, sharp scream. Glancing down the table, Mara saw the Lady Milford push to her feet, one hand clutched to her breast. Her other arm was pointed rigidly to a spot somewhere over Mara's left shoulder. Before she could even turn her head, several other ladies gasped, and a few of the gentlemen uttered sounds of distress. One of the female servants shrieked.

Stephen was the first away from the table. In his haste he knocked over his chair, and it clattered loudly to the floor. Mara nearly tripped over it as she followed her husband toward the screen that shielded the door to their rooms.

A figure lay sprawled beside it, limbs still twitching. The girl's eyes were rolled up in her head, and bloody foam leaked slowly from between her half-parted lips. The basket of delicacies was upended, its contents strewn across the floor.

"Elizabeth!" Mara knelt at the child's side and took her hand.

But it was too late. The fingers that clutched at her moved merely with a spasm of death. Mara stared, shocked and grieving, at the now motionless figure on the cold, stone floor.

"Poison," someone whispered. "I've seen it before."

"Poison," the Earl of Northumberland repeated grimly, and turned his saddened gaze to his host. "Poison in a gift for the baroness."

Stephen said not a word. The world around him seemed to fade for a moment. The room and its contents, the people, became blurred and indistinct. He had the overpowering feeling that he was suddenly someone else. Someone who was trying to warn him about something. Danger. Danger to Mara.

But of course there was danger. Someone had just tried to poison her.

Stephen shook off the feeling and returned to himself. He went to his wife and wrapped her in his arms.

Mara did not weep or feel afraid. Not right away. She felt nothing, experienced nothing but cold, numbing darkness. Darkness that enveloped her very soul.

The ladies looked away as the child's body was borne solemnly from the hall. They murmured sympathetically as the baron escorted his wife to her chambers. A few of the men gathered in tight groups to speculate on the meaning of the outrage, the perpetrator.

A short time later, as one, the crowd moved toward the great double doors. The sad remains of the elegant feast littered the long tables. A small dog jumped onto a bench and proceeded to gnaw on a leg of roasted hare. No one noticed, or cared. Soon the great hall was empty and silent.

Chapter Thirty-seven

The silence in the great Cumbria hall was tremendous, huge and overwhelming. Two women who had been clearing the long tables froze into immobility. The guards on the doors scarcely dared to breathe, as if the lack of this vital sign of life might render them invisible.

Even Maggie cringed behind her lord's chair, trembling. The unfortunate man who had delivered the message tried to concentrate on the greasy rivulet of sweat that coursed the length of his spine, instead of on the probability of his imminent and undoubtedly painful demise.

The hall itself seemed to hold its breath.

But Baldwin did not explode. He had felt the hot lava of his wrath rumble upward from his bowels to his chest, where it expanded until he could scarce draw breath. He did not give in to it, however. He feared the eruption would consume him, and he could not afford to lose control just now. That had happened all too often of late. Perhaps it helped to explain why he had had so little success in the attainment of the single goal left in his life: to destroy Ranulf's daughter.

The moment stretched as the earl struggled to regain control of his ragged respiration.

"Very well," he said at length, with chilling calm, to the exhausted man who stood before him. "You did what I asked. The outcome was not your fault. You may go."

The earl listened to the man's hastily retreating footsteps, but did not look up. If he did, he knew the hot and horrible anger that writhed behind his eyes would flare out and engulf the hapless messenger, burn him to cinders. He had to save the destructive energy within him. Save it and use it against his true enemies. Like the ones who approached his gates even now.

"My . . . my lord?" Maggie reached out and touched her master's sleeve. "May I fetch you somethin'? A cup of ale mebbe?"

Baldwin shook his head slowly, gaze fixed on the toes of his shoes, and Maggie's fear deepened. She had never seen him like this, and she didn't like it. Far better he rant and rave and vent the poison from his system. This new and unusual serenity boded no good at all. Absorbed in her thoughts, she jumped, startled, when her lord suddenly gripped her hand and smiled up at her.

"A deputation from the king arrives, you know," he said evenly. "Even as I speak they approach my gates. Soon they will be here."

Maggie nodded. She knew. She had been present when the message had been brought. The way her lord had received the information had been her first indication that something was terribly wrong. Something out of the ordinary. He had responded with eerie calm, just as he had when he learned that his deadly wedding gift had claimed the wrong victim. Maggie licked her too-dry lips.

"You probably think I don't know why our illustrious monarch sends his deputies," Baldwin continued, no longer talking to Maggie but to some invisible spot in space. "But I do, oh, yes. I know. And I want them to have a wonderful reception. Yes, indeed." The earl's attention returned to Maggie. "We'll greet them together, you and I. You and I. And my men-at-arms. It will be a very special greeting. Won't it, Maggie?"

The gray and drizzly day couldn't have been more appropriate, Mara thought. Only such a day as this was proper to bury a child—a day when God and the angels, the very skies, wept along with the mourners.

She stared down into the dark, sodden hole in the earth at the hastily built casket. So small. She could not bear to lift her eyes to see the grieving parents. To hear the mother's choked and muffled sobs was enough.

So she watched, watched as the first shovel of dirt was loaded upon the too-small coffin. And another. Signaling the end of Elizabeth's short, sweet life.

Mara closed her eyes. Still she heard the earth falling on the wooden box, the mother's heartbroken weeping. She could not weep herself. She was numb, leaden. As if Baldwin had murdered them both.

Then it was over. The village priest moved to comfort the distraught parents. The mourners drifted away, silent. Stephen took Mara's arm.

She trudged up the hill at his side, back to the storm-darkened castle. Her clothes were soaked, her mantle so heavy with moisture it dragged on her, weighted her down. Droplets of water glistened on Walter's and Alfred's mail tunics, and the usually gay plume on Jack's hat drooped in soggy ruin. Even Trey seemed depressed, padding along behind them with his nose nearly touching the damp ground.

The castle gates were open. Only a skeleton guard stood watch, for almost everyone had attended the somber funeral. No one who had known Elizabeth was unaffected by her horrible death.

Besides the girl's parents, however, Mara's grief was the deepest, and Stephen ached for her. The girl had touched their lives only briefly, but brightly. Her loss left a terrible void. And Mara had already known so much loss in her life. Stephen feared for her.

The fear seemed to deepen by the hour. It nagged at him, almost as if someone constantly tapped on his shoulder, trying to get his attention. What was wrong?

The feeling dissipated as they were greeted at the doors by an anxious serving woman who relieved Mara of her cloak.

"Lady, lady," she clucked. "Please let me help you into some dry clothes. Here now."

Mara waved her away, but Stephen nodded at the woman and gripped his wife gently by the shoulders. "Go with her, love," he said softly. "You're shivering. Change clothes, then come sit with Henry and me by the fire."

Mara glanced up and saw the Earl of Northumberland regarding her from the other end of the hall. She'd almost forgotten he was here. The other guests had left hurriedly the day following Elizabeth's murder, but the earl had remained. And she knew why.

The forces of the north had to ally and stand together against the treacherous Cumbrian earl. There was no longer any doubt that Baldwin might move against any one of them, at any time. His greed and thirst for revenge were obviously out of control. If he dared to defy Henry, their king, not once but twice, there was no telling what else he might do. They all must be prepared.

The thought of additional aid, however, did not comfort Mara. Since the moment she had seen Elizabeth lying dead on the floor, a dark and heavy pall of depression and dread had descended upon her. Nothing, she feared, could lift it.

She went through the motions of shedding her wet clothes and donned dry ones without thought. She allowed the serving woman to unpin her hair, brush it out, and leave it hanging down her back to dry. Then Mara rejoined her husband and their guest in the great hall.

Both men rose politely, Stephen with an ache in his heart. He was used to seeing his wife stand tall and strong and invincible. Now she looked so young and vulnerable, bowed with a great weight of grief and loss.

Walter, Alfred, and Jack nodded their greetings from where they stood, behind the seated men. They, too, noticed, and mourned, the change in their mistress.

"Please, sit and resume your conversation. I'm sorry I interrupted."

"The interruption is most pleasant," Henry said as he settled back in his chair by the fire. "And the conversation is exactly what you would expect it to be. We scheme to arm ourselves against the faithless and murderous Earl of Cumbria."

"And you believe strength of arms will protect you from the man?"

Stephen shifted in his seat and pointedly avoided exchanging glances with his friend. The conversation was uncomfortably like the one they had had on the evening Elizabeth died. Mara had expressed doubts then, too, about their ability to protect themselves from the rapacious earl. And look what had happened.

The viper had managed to slither into their midst. Mara, his own Mara, might have died. They must never again underestimate the man's capacity for treachery and evil.

"Mara's right," Stephen said heavily. "Mere strength of arms may not be enough to ward off Baldwin's evil. We must guard against deceit and trickery as well."

"I agree." Henry nodded. "But I am still going to bolster my personal forces and advise my neighbors to do the same. You never know but a show of strength might discourage our friend."

"It certainly can't hurt," Stephen concurred.

"I'm going to send some of my men here, to you, as well."

"I'll not turn them away, and I thank you." Stephen looked at Walter and Alfred, who both nodded briefly with approval. "And I will send word to Thomas at Ullswater of all that has transpired. My wife's properties are undoubtedly still a prime target of Baldwin's."

"Undoubtedly," Henry repeated, and glanced uneasily at the lovely baroness. Everyone present knew what Baldwin wanted most: Ranulf's daughter, dead or alive. He donned his most comforting smile and leaned forward to pat the lady's slender hand. "Don't worry, my dear. Your husband is more than capable. You are in good hands, and you have good friends. You will be safe. And Baldwin will be dealt with, one way or another. He will not get away with his murders and deceits. Not much longer anyway."

"But perhaps just long enough," Mara murmured.

"I beg your pardon?"

Mara shook her head and forced a smile to her unwilling mouth. "It's nothing, my lord. Nothing."

But it wasn't nothing. In spite of the brave words and assurances she had heard spoken, the pall of misery that surrounded her had not lifted. Quite the opposite. Mara felt as if she had just stumbled onto a great, long slide, at the bottom of which lay a yawning, black pit.

In the pit was the Earl of Cumbria.

There was something else different about her master, Maggie observed, besides the strangely calm reactions to things that would normally drive him wild. He insisted upon her presence almost constantly now, as if she were his aide, or the head of his army. He even talked to her as if conferring with her, or asking her advice—although she knew he never really wanted or expected a reply. She wasn't sure she liked her new situation.

There were the other servants, even the men-at-arms,

for one thing. They'd always looked at her a little strangely. Now they treated her with outright dislike, even scorn. For another thing, Maggie wasn't certain she wanted to be at the earl's right hand, privy to all that he thought and said and did. As deeply as she cared for him, she realized that he was not a very good or nice man. Now she was witness to just how deeply his madness ran. As in the present situation.

Deputies of the king. Maggie was more than a little awed. And absolutely thunderstruck by the orders the earl had given his own men. Had she been able to find her tongue, she might have voiced an objection, tried to dissuade her lord from such a suicidal path. But she was dumbstruck as well, and followed him silently into the courtyard to greet the king's men.

"Baldwin, Earl of Cumbria?" asked the handsome, mail-clad knight who seemed to be the leader of the half dozen mounted soldiers.

"I am he."

"And I am Norbert, official emissary of Henry, our king."

"Welcome, Norbert. May I extend to you and your men the hospitality of my hall?"

"My thanks, but I must decline." The knight produced a parchment scroll that he unrolled and handed to the earl. "I have been sent, by order of His Majesty, King Henry, to escort you to the court, there to answer for certain crimes. This is the official document, should you wish to examine it."

Baldwin took the proffered scroll and held it daintily between two fingers, as if it were something soiled. He did not look at it but continued to gaze upward, smiling, at the mounted knight.

"Escort me to the court," the earl parroted.

"Yes, sir. By order of the King of England."

"Really." The pleasant smile remained fixed.

"Yes, sir."

"You. And who else?"

The knight looked slightly ill at ease. "My men-at-arms, sir. All deputies of the king."

"I see. Well. How unfortunate."

Now the knight appeared truly puzzled. "Sir?"

"How unfortunate that so many good men have to die," the earl replied conversationally. "Guards!"

Baldwin's men, armed to the teeth, had been waiting in doorways, shadows, and behind wagons. Now they sprang at the unsuspecting riders.

Horses squealed as men jumped from their hiding places and grabbed at the horsemen's reins, preventing the riders from fleeing to the open gates. Swords hissed as they were drawn from their scabbards and men shouted in fear and surprise. The king's knights, to a man, were courageous in the face of overwhelming odds. Only one was cut down in the initial rush. The rest were able to draw their swords in time to meet the attack.

The clanging ring of steel filled the air with raucous sound. The grunts and groans of straining men interwove with the clash of weaponry to create an auditory tapestry of battle. A horse whinnied piteously as an ill-aimed sword stroke opened the artery in its neck. One of Baldwin's guards shrieked as his arm spun away, and bright blood fountained. Two more of the earl's score of knights went down almost simultaneously, tumbling over one another as they fell. But they were the last of his men to die. The battle was quickly over.

The king's knights had been unhorsed, disarmed, and overcome in a matter of minutes. Each was held firmly by one of Baldwin's men. They were arranged in a line before the earl.

"So the king commands my presence, does he?" Baldwin took the time to look into the eyes of each man. His smile never faltered.

"Kill them," he said at last, quietly.

Maggie pressed her hands to her mouth as six daggers

whispered harshly from their sheaths. She closed her eye as the blades were pressed to six throats. She blocked the sight of the deaths, but she could not block the stench. The coppery smell of blood filled her nostrils and she turned away, retching.

"Ah, good. Well done," she heard her lord pronounce. "Now to horse. All of you. We ride at once to Bellingham."

Eye still tightly shut, Maggie listened to the sounds of boots hurrying across the cobbled yard. Shortly she heard the clang of metal-shod hooves, a jumble of confused conversations, and the shouted instructions of those in charge. She wondered what had become of her lord. She opened her eye.

"There you are, Maggie." The sickly grin remained unchanged. "I've been wondering when you were going to rejoin me. I've been waiting for you. Are you ready?"

"Ready?"

"Yes. Ready to ride with me to Bellingham. Didn't you hear my order?"

"Yes, but . . . but—"

"But what, Maggie?" For the first time the smile began to waver. "Don't tell me you're going to disobey me?"

Maggie shook her head vigorously. "But we're . . . we're riding to war, aren't we? A battle?"

"Well, I wouldn't say that, exactly. I'd like to avoid actual combat, if at all possible."

"Then . . . what are y' thinkin' to do?"

Baldwin steepled his fingers. "I'm not quite sure yet, my dear. But it will come to me—it always does. I have more than one trick up my sleeve, as they say. The point is, we must move swiftly now." His eyes slid momentarily to the bodies lying in their spreading pools of blood. "Surprise is always a good thing to have on your side. And a little treachery." The smile bloomed anew. "Don't worry. I'll think of something as we ride. Or something will come up along the way. Now go on, get mounted. Off with you."

"Yes, m'lord," Maggie mumbled. She obediently climbed onto the gentle palfrey someone brought her. Almost immediately, the large mounted band fell in behind the earl and moved as one toward the gates.

"Come, Maggie. Come." Baldwin gestured her forward. "You'll ride at my side. Hurry now."

Maggie kicked her mare into a jog and moved to her master's side. In tandem, they passed beneath the portcullis and over the wooden bridge. Maggie could not help wondering, with a shiver of dark premonition, if she would return this way again, at her lord and lover's side.

Or was she descending with him, at last, into hell?

Chapter Thirty-eight

Father Gregory loved the long summer days. He enjoyed the extra hours he spent working beside his brother monks in the green and fragrant gardens they cultivated. As he bent over to pull a weed, he sent up a little prayer of thankfulness. He took so much pleasure in the life he led he was tempted to feel guilty about it at times.

Gregory had eventually even grown to like the solitude of the Cistercian order, although it was not what had initially attracted him to the sect. He had actually feared he might not be able to adjust to such a quiet and solitary life. But he had found such an existence to his taste after all.

It did not, however, prevent him from taking pleasure in the infrequent visitors who dropped by, or those who accidentally stumbled upon the secluded abbey. Father Gregory smiled, therefore, when he saw a pair of riders, a man and a woman, emerge from the shadows of the surrounding forest. He straightened, one hand pressed to the small of his back, and cast aside the weed already

260

wilting in his hand. Though the riders were yet too far away to call to, the monk raised his hand in a signal of welcome.

"Wulfric," Baldwin called over his shoulder, "accompany us. Have everyone else remain in the shadows. There's no point in causing any alarm. Yet." The earl smiled at his companion. "Come along, Maggie. We'll have a chat with this . . . man of God, and see what we might learn."

Maggie's one good eye regarded her lord dubiously. Dealing with ordinary people was one thing, but fooling with priests and holy men was quite another. Despite a terrible sinking feeling in the pit of her stomach, Maggie kicked her palfrey into motion and followed her earl along the dusty track toward the man who had waved.

So there were three of them, Gregory saw, and one a large and well-armed knight. Well, no harm. He was undoubtedly the bodyguard of these travelers. All three would be shown hospitality.

"Welcome," Father Gregory said when the riders halted in front of him. He noted the woman's deformity at once, and his heart went out to her. "Welcome and God's blessing be upon you."

"Thank you, Father," Baldwin replied smoothly. "Might I beg a cup of water for my lady companion here? I fear the long and dusty road has parched her tongue."

"Of course, my son. Please, come inside. Right this way."

"Secure the horses, Wulfric," the earl said in an undertone as the monk led Maggie into a wooden building. "Then join us. Be alert."

"Aye, m'lord."

The simple and rustic interior of the monk's main hall did not appeal to Baldwin, but he concealed his distaste and seated himself in the chair the man indicated.

"So tell me, my son," Father Gregory began as he

poured three cups of water. "Has your journey been a long one?"

"No, not long," Baldwin answered. "Though I look forward to its end."

"Might I ask where you are bound?"

"For Bellingham Castle. Do you know it?"

"Oh, indeed." Father Gregory smiled broadly. "The baron Stephen is a noble and worthy young man."

"So you know him?" Baldwin asked.

"Ah, yes. I know him well. He is a great friend. As was his father before him." Warming to his subject, glad of the company who apparently knew Stephen as well, Gregory sat back comfortably, palms flat against his knees. "Yes, we are old friends, Baron Stephen and I. His father died when the lad was only eight, you know. I spent as much time as I could with him after that. He's a fine young man. And he was married recently, you know!"

"You don't say," Baldwin remarked.

"I must confess I had the very great honor of joining the baron and his lady myself." Gregory beamed. "They were married right here, in our own humble chapel."

Baldwin's eyes burned like twin fires.

"Yes, I must say," Gregory went on, "Stephen is not only a true friend to myself, but to all the brothers here. His father gave us not only the land for our little abbey, but the funds with which to build it. And although there is no need for such continued generosity, Stephen sends us gifts from time to time of food and ale. Yes, we are truly blessed in his friendship. He, and now his lovely lady."

Baldwin could scarcely conceal his elation. Not daring to speak, he merely raised his brows.

."Oh, I am so sorry. I have completely forgotten to introduce myself. I am Gregory, Father Gregory. And you, my son?"

Baldwin momentarily ignored him. "You would do anything for him, for Stephen, wouldn't you? As he would do anything for you."

"Why . . . why, yes. I imagine so."

Baldwin turned to Maggie. "You see? I told you something would come up along the way."

Father Gregory's smile slipped into an expression of puzzlement.

"You don't understand, do you? But you shall. I am, by the way, Baldwin, Earl of Cumbria." He inclined his head. "And this is my companion, Maggie."

Gregory rose and took the woman's hand. "Most pleased to make your acquaintance," he said smoothly. But the light and warmth seemed to have gone from the day.

Baldwin, Earl of Cumbria. Was that not the name of the man Stephen had told him about? Gregory wondered. The one who had attacked Ullswater Castle and murdered the baroness's parents? The man who had kidnapped the lady herself?

Gregory felt the blood leave his face. He took an involuntary step away from the grinning earl.

"Ah, you recognize my name, I see. Well, no harm done. Wulfric!" Baldwin called.

"My lord?" The tall, burly knight stepped away from the wall against which he had been leaning.

Baldwin rose and strolled to the window. There were quite a few monks toiling in the gardens—but they would be no problem. Especially once he had their leader under his control.

"Wulfric, grab the good father here."

Maggie's startled gasp escaped before she could raise her hands to her mouth. Baldwin ignored her.

"Tie him up," the earl continued. "Then give me your dagger."

Though it was late, the last soft light of the summer evening seeped in through the window and filled the room with a dusty haze. Summer scents lingered as well, and the fading cry of a child being rounded in for a belated bedtime. A melancholy smile touched Mara's lips as the sound struck her, and Stephen reached across the small table where they had taken their dinner to clasp her hand.

"Someday," he whispered, reading her thoughts as clearly as if she had spoken them aloud.

Mara raised her eyes from the half-empty wine cup. "I hope so. With all my heart, I hope so," she murmured. But a dark, premonitory sadness in her heart told her it was not to be so. The future for them was empty, not to be filled with the laughter of children.

The sorrow in her eyes, the tone of his wife's voice, stabbed at Stephen. The quiet joy that had once filled her seemed to have drained away, and it broke his heart. It was almost as if she sensed her own imminent doom and had lost the will to live.

"Time, she needs time," Jack had said to him only earlier that day. The little man mourned for the loss of his baron's happiness as Stephen grieved for his wife. "The girl Elizabeth's not cold in her grave, murdered by the same man who took the lady's family. And he's still a free man, not yet brought to justice. Aye, I know it's not right. But if there's a God in heaven, it soon will be. Just give it some time, let things right themselves, an' the light'll come back to yer lady's eyes."

Stephen prayed for that day, that moment. In the meantime, he would do everything in his power to wrap Mara in the protective and healing blanket of his love.

Even as he rose, however, the feeling of protectiveness toward his wife surged in him so strongly it nearly brought him to his knees. The strange, nagging feeling came to him again, the voice inside his head that seemed to constantly urge him to keep Mara safe.

But of course he would keep her safe. He shook off

the feeling and bent his mind to his purpose of the moment.

Mara's heart beat just a little faster as Stephen rose, still holding her hand, and came around the table to stand in front of her. She offered him her other hand and let him pull her gently to her feet. She raised her lips to his kiss.

The passion between them was not the same. Under the circumstances, it could not be. But it was not less. It simply found different expression.

Stephen kissed Mara lightly, fleetingly; traced the line of her jaw, down her neck to the hollow of her throat, until he felt her arms steal around him. Then he held her and pressed her against his length. He let her feel the hardness of him, his need and love for her. When her warmth mingled with his, he lifted her, carried her to the great bed, and laid her gently on the silken cover. Slowly, languidly, he undressed her.

Mara reveled in every moment, hungry not only for Stephen's touch, his love, but grateful for the respite from the almost constant heartache and fear she had lived with since Elizabeth's poisoning. These were the only times when she seemed able to free herself of the premonition that mantled her. Only in her husband's arms was she able to believe there might be a tomorrow. Children. Happiness. Freedom from the nightmare from which she could no longer seem to wake.

When Mara lay naked in his arms, Stephen slipped quickly from his own clothes. He shivered with pleasure as her cool hands caressed his muscular shoulders and broad, smooth chest. He buried his face in the fragrant, velvet valley between her breasts and felt her fingers twine in his long, thick hair.

The feel of him was exquisite: the satin of his skin; the long, straight silky hair under his arms; the weight of him. His maleness, prodding her gently, begged her to open to him. Tears pricked at Mara's eyes and ran down her cheeks.

"Stephen," she whispered.

He raised his head until their eyes locked.

"I love you, Stephen," Mara whispered. "I love you so deeply that I know what I feel will never die. It transcends everything, all of life. Even death. I love you forever, Stephen. I belong to you forever."

He answered her with his mouth, with his hands, and with his body.

The night had darkened sufficiently that the stars winked faintly in the sky. But day had not yet fully transitioned into night, and shadows pooling and melting into other shadows made visibility difficult. The guard on watch in the tower overlooking the gates was not certain at first what he saw. Then the moving darkness resolved itself into a robed and hooded figure.

"Halt!"

The shout fell oddly flat onto the stillness of the night.

"Halt and identify yourself!" the guard called again.

"My name is Theobald . . . Brother Theobald. I'm— I'm from the abbey, and I've come with a message for the baron."

"Hold. Someone will approach you."

The guard in the tower nocked an arrow and held it pointed at the monk while another man exited through a side door in the great gate to investigate. Moments later he hurried back inside, the brother in tow.

"Fetch the baron! Fetch Lord Stephen!" he cried, and still another guard ran in the direction of the hall.

The air was hot and sultry, and the great doors had been thrown wide to catch any stray breeze that might come their way. Candlelight flickered from the long tables now pushed against the walls and cleared of the remains of the evening meal. Too hot in their own chamber, Mara and Stephen had dressed and returned to the hall to cool their heated bodies before retiring for the night. They held hands and smiled at one another, enjoying the gentle peace of the night.

Then it was abruptly shattered as a guard and another figure burst into the hall.

"What is this disturbance? What's going on?" Stephen asked as he rose and tucked in the shirt he had hastily donned. Then he recognized the brown-clad figure. "Brother Theobald!" he exclaimed. "What on . . . ?"

The question died on Stephen's lips. The monk was pale with shock and fear. He clutched a cloth-wrapped bundle to his breast.

"What is it, brother? What's wrong? How can we help you?"

"A . . . a message," the monk stammered at last. "I was t-told to bring you this m-message. From Baldwin, Earl of Cumbria."

Mara's hammering heart stopped abruptly within her breast. She watched in tense silence as the cleric handed Stephen the bundle. The poor man's hands were shaking violently.

Stephen glanced at her once, and she nodded. She had thought she was prepared for anything. She wasn't.

As Stephen fumbled with the parcel, it fell open. An object tumbled to the ground. It was a ring, a holy ring. Father Gregory's ring.

With the finger still attached.

Chapter Thirty-nine

Stephen walked slowly from the diner. Intellectually, he knew he was hungry. He had to be. He hadn't eaten in over twenty-four hours. But his stomach threatened to rebel. He hadn't even been able to get down any of the thin soup he had ordered. Not that it mattered. It seemed he was almost done.

The wind from a passing car ruffled his hair. Dimly, he smelled the exhaust. He thrust his hands into his pockets and smiled grimly. *Empty.* The soup, a cup of coffee, and a small tip for the waitress had taken the last of his cash. Tomorrow, or the day after, the motel manager would come knocking on his door, wanting his week's payment. Then it would be over for good. Stephen inserted his key in the lock and opened the door.

He was almost past caring anyway. A mental hospital was as good a place as any, he supposed, to spend the rest of his life. Drugs, hopefully, would help him forget. Until he died, reincarnated, and began his next life. Then the broken promise would start coming back to haunt him again. His eternal, undying love for Mara would take him over once more. The cycle was endless. He could not end it. He could not save her.

Stephen sat heavily in a chair by the window. He didn't bother to close the curtains. What difference did it make? He had failed. He might as well give it all up now. He almost wished somebody *would* recognize him. Then it would all be over. Until it started again. Stephen uttered a mirthless chuckle.

Would he have any better luck in the next life? If he could, indeed, pierce the veil again, would he be more successful next time in *remembering* the present when he went back to the past? Maybe. He'd almost done it this time. Almost, but not quite. Baron Stephen was aware of another presence, but could not hear the voice. And if he could not hear the voice, he could not receive the warning.

A familiar nausea churned in Stephen's stomach. He could not bear to think of it anymore. He didn't even think he wanted to return to the past again. Why relive the unspeakable agony of her inevitable death?

He couldn't. Neither could he seem to stay awake any longer.

Stephen stared at the bed, then at his hands. They were definitely becoming transparent. No longer did he think it a trick of light, or of the mind. He was fading away. But why? And where to? The past?

If only it were true. He might have some hope then. If he disappeared from this world to return to the past corporeally, perhaps he might then be able to bring memory with him as well. If only.

But he had very little hope left, merely his endless exhaustion. Stephen looked back at the bed. If he lay down, would he sleep? Or would he slip back into the past?

It didn't matter. His eyelids were so heavy he couldn't keep them open any longer. He tried to resist, but it was useless. He could almost hear her calling him, pleading with him, begging him. . . .

Chapter Forty

Mara stood so straight, so rigid, she felt as if an iron rod had been driven down through her spine. Her flesh felt cold, and her heart had turned to ice. Though her left hand rested on Trey's head, she was unaware even of the dog's presence. "Don't go," she whispered. "Don't go, Stephen. Please don't go."

Stephen stared at his wife, oblivious of everyone else in the room; Walter and Alfred on his right, Jack and Thomas to his left, those of his men who were not standing guard ranged behind them. He looked into her sapphire eyes and knew he did not have to say the words. She had known even when she had begged him that he could not leave Baldwin's challenge unmet. Yet he had to speak the words, just as she had been compelled to utter hers.

"Father Gregory is my friend," he said softly. "Not to mention a peaceable and innocent man of God. You know what will happen to him if I don't go."

Mara didn't bother to nod. She knew full well what would happen. She also knew it was futile to argue further with Stephen, and recalled what had already passed between them, once the horrifying sight of Father's Gregory's severed finger had been revealed.

The monk Theobald had started to cry, the only sound in the terrible silence. "He . . . Baldwin says to come, come right away, or . . ." There had been no need to say more.

Mara had stared straight into her husband's eyes, fighting the sickness that churned in her belly. "Baldwin's planning a trick of some kind. You know he is."

"And I will be on my guard against it. I'll also have most of my knights. I will send for Thomas at once, and he will be here by dawn. I'll meet Baldwin with no small strength."

"Then I'm going with you, too," Mara had stated flatly.

Stephen shook his head slowly but firmly. "No, you're not. You and I both know what Baldwin is really after. I don't intend to let him get anywhere near you."

"But you need every man who can ride at your side!" In spite of her effort to control it, a note of desperation had crept into Mara's voice. "You won't leave me alone here, unprotected. I know you. You'll leave your best and bravest behind to watch over me, when you need them, Stephen. I won't have it. I *won't*."

Stephen had sensed the unbreachable wall of her determination, she knew it. She had known he knew he would be forced to compromise.

"Very well." He had sighed. "I will not, however, leave you without adequate protection. There is always the possibility that Baldwin intends to distract me in one place merely to strike in another."

"This castle is impregnable. Very few are needed to keep it, or me, safe."

Stephen had smiled grimly. "Alfred," he'd said without taking his eyes from Mara. "You'll remain here with the baroness. Pick two other men to stay with you, and use the servants to help keep vigil on the walls."

Though his disappointment was evident, the older knight nodded. "Yes, my lord."

And so it had been settled. Stephen would ride to meet Baldwin. He had no choice. Mara knew it. She knew she could not stop him. And now he was about to leave.

Her heart was breaking, but Mara gave not the slightest sign. Stephen finally tore his eyes from hers.

"Walter, go ahead and ready the men and horses. I'll join you shortly."

Walter left without a word, all but Jack following him. At a glance from his master, however, the small man hurried out behind the others. Stephen returned his gaze to his wife.

"I know, Mara, that telling you not to worry is a waste of breath."

"Indeed it is."

"But I'm going to be very, very careful. Baldwin is baiting me, I know that. Yet I have no choice but to go. I must do what I can to save Gregory."

Mara lowered her gaze. "Yes," she murmured at last. "I know you must do whatever lies within your power to aid him."

Stephen raised Mara's chin with a fingertip. "I must also go now, my dearest."

Mara gave a barely perceptible nod.

"I love you."

"As I love you, husband."

There was no more to say. The most important words had already been said, murmured with lips against flesh during the too short hours of the night that had been shared by them. One long, last look—eye to eye, heart to heart—and Stephen turned, strode the length of the hall, bootheels clicking, and vanished into the predawn darkness.

Morning light had barely penetrated the dense gloom of the forest. The boles of the trees were but deeper shadows against the inky darkness of lingering night. Maggie huddled in her cape, chilled by the cool, damp air, and waited anxiously for the light. But when, at last, the world around her began to take on definition, she was not comforted.

The air was heavy with mist. It drifted through the trees, twined its tendrils about their trunks, reached up to tangle in the branches. It deadened sound, blanketed the earth in the soft and eerie down of its being. No birds sang; no creatures rustled in the undergrowth. Somewhere a horse impatiently stamped its foot, but the sound was muffled, unreal. Maggie shivered. She jumped when a twig snapped to her left.

"Startled you, did I?" A smile graced Baldwin's lips, though not his eyes. "You must be apprehensive."

"Don't . . . I don't like the dark much," Maggie stammered. "Or the mist."

"It'll soon burn away. Though I rather like it, myself. And it helps to conceal my men among the trees."

"You'll be . . . you'll be plannin' an ambush then?"

"How crass. Not to mention obvious." Baldwin chuckled mirthlessly. "No, nothing like that. Come. Come, and I'll show you."

The earl extended his arm to Maggie, but she hesitated. Nothing was the same anymore, not since she had watched her lord sever the priest's finger. Murder the king's men.

"Maggie?"

There was a sinister tone to the way he said her name. As much as she feared what lay ahead, whatever bloody and unpleasant surprise he had in store for the baron, she was more frightened of the earl himself. Maggie took her lord's arm.

"There. That's better." Baldwin patted the girl's hand. "Isn't it, Maggie? Now, come and see what I have planned."

Stephen, with Walter at one side, Thomas at the other, and Jack directly to their rear, rode at the head of his force until

273

they reached the forest. Over Walter's protestations, he took the lead alone as they moved onto the narrow trail. The weak dawn light and hovering mist made it impossible to see through the trees, but Stephen did not fear ambush. The forest was far too dense to allow any kind of surprise attack in force, and though a few well-placed archers might do some damage, visibility was too poor as yet to give them any serious thought.

The muffled *clomp* of the horses' hooves on the damp ground was the only sound to be heard in the close and misty wood. Stephen thought he might almost be able to hear his own heartbeat if he tried hard enough.

Then the air around him subtly changed. It seemed less dense and oppressive. A breath of breeze touched his cheek.

His column of men stopped when Stephen lifted his hand. Thomas edged his horse alongside his lord's chestnut stallion.

"The clearing is just ahead," Stephen said quietly. He squinted, as if he might see through the dim light and drifting mist to what lay ahead. "Have the men dismount and spread out among the trees on either side of the trail. It's my guess Baldwin has his own men arrayed in similar fashion on the opposite side of the glade. But keep the horses ready just in case. I doubt he wants any part of a hand-to-hand confrontation, but I'm not taking any chances. Let me know when the men are in place."

"Yes, m'lord."

Stephen clasped his charger's reins loosely and listened to the small noises his men made as they dismounted and moved into position among the trees. In a matter of minutes Thomas had returned to his side.

"All is ready, m'lord."

"Thank you, Thomas. If anything happens to me, guard the baroness with your life—you and Walter. He must not get his hands on her. No matter the cost." Stephen turned in his saddle. "Jack, you'll ride into the clearing with me. Are you ready?"

"As I'll ever be," Jack replied in an unusually subdued voice.

"Then we'll go. Walter, Thomas—don't make a move without a signal from me."

Then his great chestnut stallion moved forward through the clinging mist into the lighter, clearer air of the open glade.

Baldwin heard them coming before he was able to see them. Then they were visible before him, just the two of them, as he had expected. As he had known. The noble and handsome baron was so predictable. This was going to be ever so much easier than he had anticipated.

"Welcome, Baron."

"Baldwin," Stephen replied shortly.

"Thank you for coming. Or, I should say, the good father thanks you for coming."

"Where is he?"

"Now, now, now. Have patience."

"I have all the patience I need. I simply don't have time for you, Baldwin. Where is he?"

"All in good time. How is your lovely wife?"

The message from Baldwin, relayed through Brother Theobald, had been to come unarmed. It was as well. Had he a dagger, he would have thrown it directly into the man's heart.

"Where is Father Gregory?" Stephen repeated instead. His voice was flat, hard.

Baldwin shrugged with elaborate nonchalance. "As you wish. Have it your way. Follow me."

The sun crested the horizon and swiftly burned away the mist. Stephen was able to see the monk almost at once. His hands clenched into fists.

Father Gregory stood in front of his modest chapel. He

was bound from head to foot, tied so tightly his face had gone ashen from pain and shock.

"Untie him," Stephen commanded.

"Oh, but of course," Baldwin said lightly. "After you've done all I ask."

"What is it you want, Baldwin?"

"Why—I want you, naturally."

Stephen smiled grimly. "Naturally."

"You think I can't have you?"

"I think it will be a grand battle."

"Between your men and mine, you mean?"

Stephen remained silent.

"No, I don't think so," Baldwin continued. "Get off your horse, Baron."

"And if I don't?"

"It's extremely simple." Baldwin withdrew the dagger from the sheath at his side and moved close to Father Gregory. He held the blade against the monk's throat. "If you don't get off the horse, I shall slit your friend's throat."

"Then you will have nothing to bargain with."

"And you will have a dead friend." A smile twitched at the corner of the earl's lips. He had not expected Stephen to call his bluff. The man had some iron in him after all. Holding the baron's gaze, he twitched his blade lightly upon the monk's throat.

As a thin trickle of blood began to dampen the front of the father's habit, Stephen knew he had lost. Once again he had underestimated the depths of evil into which a man could sink. He could not let his friend die, and he had no doubt Baldwin would kill Gregory if he did not give himself up. He would have to give himself to Baldwin and trust to escape later, or to rescue later.

Silently cursing himself, his naïveté and stupidity, Stephen slowly lowered his reins to his stallion's neck. How could he have allowed this to happen? How had he so easily fallen into Baldwin's trap?

"Do I have to invite you again, Baron, to dismount?"

The blade of the earl's knife once again pressed to the father's throat. Fresh blood appeared and slid down Gregory's neck.

The thought of summoning his men briefly crossed Stephen's mind. But he knew they could not possibly come to his aid before the earl had opened Gregory's throat.

"Send your man away," Baldwin said when he saw that he had won.

"Go on, Jack," Stephen ordered.

"No, my lord! I—"

"Do it!"

Slowly, reluctantly, Jack turned his horse and rode into the disappearing mist.

Baldwin felt his chest swell with elation as Stephen climbed from his charger. "Seize him," he commanded evenly. Wulfric and one other burly knight came forward and took the young baron firmly in their grasp.

Stephen did not bother to struggle. "Now, release him, Baldwin," he said with equal, icy calm. "Release Father Gregory."

"Or what? What, Stephen of Bellingham?" The earl touched the point of the blade to the tip of his finger. "What will you do?"

Stephen remained stonily silent and glared at the man who regarded him so casually, idly touching the knife to one finger, then another.

"Will you call your men? Do you love the father so much, Stephen? Do you?" Baldwin strolled behind the cleric's back. "Will you attempt to save him even now? Is there that much love between you?"

"No!"

Baldwin's grin split his face. He lifted Gregory's chin and slowly, deliberately, with great relish, slit the man's throat from ear to ear.

Chapter Forty-one

The morning breeze moved tendrils of loosened hair against Mara's cheek and fluttered the hem of the dark blue tunic she had pulled over her soft leather breeches. She stood in the courtyard, facing the gate. She did not take her eyes from Jack as she watched him ride toward her. Walter and Thomas flanked him. But it was Jack she watched. She did not blink. She just watched.

The men rode at a jog. Their faces were stern.

Stern, Mara told herself firmly. Stern, not shocked and grieving.

They were in front of her at last. All dismounted. Jack removed his hat and held it to his chest. Mara still had not taken her gaze from him.

"He's alive," she said, no trace of question in her voice.

Jack nodded. "Aye. Alive. But . . ."

"Come to the hall," Mara ordered tersely. She marched across the courtyard. Unseen servants opened the doors as she approached, and she strode through without pause. In the center of the hall she halted and turned to

278

the men who followed her. "Bring these men ale," she ordered. "And something to eat."

Servants scurried to obey.

"Now speak to me, Jack. Tell me exactly what happened."

Jack bowed his head briefly, then raised his eyes to his baroness. "My lord is Baldwin's prisoner," he began simply, the only way he knew how.

Something seemed to break inside Mara's breast, but she did not betray a flicker of emotion. "Go on, Jack. Tell me all of it. Spare me nothing."

Jack did as he was bid, leaving out no detail. Mara's expression remained fixed until the small man had reached the conclusion of his grisly tale—Father Gregory's perfidious murder. Her hands flew to her face. Her eyes shut against the threatened flood of tears. But she controlled herself instantly, dropped her hands, and straightened her shoulders.

"In truth, Jack,"—Mara's tone was subdued, but her voice even—"I am not surprised by what transpired. Stephen was forced to rise to Baldwin's bait. It was, I have to admit, a brilliant stroke on the earl's part." She smiled without joy or mirth. "If I had ridden with Stephen, and the earl had asked for me in exchange for the father, Stephen never would have done it. He would have attacked, retreated, parlayed, anything—even knowing it might lead to the father's death. But he never, never would have given me up for Gregory." Mara took a deep breath, let it out in a sigh, and turned from the men.

"He, himself, however," she continued softly, "is another story. His own life for another's. That would be acceptable."

The food arrived, and Mara was grateful. Tears she could no longer deny scalded her eyelids, and she did not wish her husband's knights to see. She paced the room until she had her emotions under control once more.

279

She had to be calm, to think straight. The knights awaited her word, her order, the command that would set them into action.

But what action would it be? What course should she take?

Baldwin had grabbed Stephen, knowing full well she would come after her husband. He had even sent her word, as Jack had reluctantly related, to meet him in the glade.

As he had done with Stephen. So they might meet and talk.

Talk.

Mara rested her chin on her chest and pressed her fingers to her eyes. What was there to talk about? Of course she would trade her life for her husband's, as Baldwin had known she would. As he had planned so cleverly.

Or would he do as he had done with Father Gregory and kill Stephen anyway? How was she to know, and what was she to do?

"Lady, excuse me, please. But if I might speak . . . ?"

Mara turned her weary gaze to Jack and nodded.

"Why don't you let me try to sneak into the chapel?" the little man asked quickly. "I'm good at that sort o' thing, you know. I could get in, find Stephen, and—"

"No." Mara shook her head adamantly. "No, I'm sorry. If you failed, it would just get you both killed. And it would take too long. We have to move now."

"A direct attack, m'lady?" Thomas asked hopefully.

"As you yourselves told me, the earl said he would kill Stephen if we tried that, and I believe him. No, there is only one thing to do, I fear."

Walter's lips tightened into a thin white line. "I can't let you, my lady. The baron's last words to Thomas and me were an order to protect you with our lives. To keep you safe from the earl."

"Then I am overriding that order," Mara snapped. She

gazed levelly at the older knight. "Just as my husband felt he had no choice but to do what he could to try and save Father Gregory, I feel I have no choice but to try and save my husband. I must at least face the earl and see what he has to say."

"But, lady, we all know—"

"Yes, we *do* all know the depths of Baldwin's treacherous soul. Yet I'll not hear another word against it, Walter. I'll meet with Baldwin. And you will be waiting at the edge of the forest, as close as Baldwin will allow. You will be waiting. And you will watch for an opening, the slightest opportunity to put an arrow in the man. Failing that, watch for my signal. But above all, obey me. Is that understood?"

Walter nodded reluctantly. Thomas and Jack exchanged glances but remained silent.

"Good. We are agreed. And we will ride at once."

Mara turned to a knight standing in a corner and formerly unnoticed by the other three men. "Thank you for coming so swiftly," she said to him now. "I apologize for not acknowledging you earlier. But I needed to know what had happened to my husband. Jack, Walter, Thomas—this is Harold, head of the Earl of Northumberland's forces that he has sent to aid us. You and your men are a most welcome addition to our strength," she told the other knight. "If nothing else, perhaps it will make Baldwin think twice about the course of action he chooses."

The man briefly inclined his head in acknowledgment. Not only to make plain his consent, but to conceal the sudden and unaccustomed emotion manifesting in his eyes. Never had he met a more noble, courageous, or magnificent woman. He had thought at first he could not possibly follow a female. But he would follow this one into hell, if that was where she led him.

At Mara's instruction, a female servant appeared and assisted her mistress into one of the baron's hauberks, a mail shirt with a skirt to the knees, and a mail hood. She fastened her sword belt unaided and sheathed both broad- and short-sword. At her nod, the knights fell in behind her as she strode from the hall.

Hero awaited her in the courtyard, saddled with the trappings of war. As a groom held the horse's head, Mara fitted her booted foot to his stirrup. Seeing his mistress overloaded in armor, Jack hurried to assist her to mount. She thanked him tersely. Trey looked up at his mistress and whined.

"Don't worry, old friend. I wouldn't go anywhere without you."

Without another word, merely a glance at the similarly armed and mounted knights, she kicked Hero into a lope and passed beneath the castle gate. She did not look back once, only forward, as if her gaze might pierce the distance and spy her love . . . Whose life now lay in the palm of Baldwin's hand.

The fair breeze of morning had blown away the last of the clinging mist. The sun rose above the treetops, but the glade remained cool. In an hour or two the air would truly warm. Stephen could not help but wonder if he would be alive to see this day's noontime sun.

In spite of the cooling breeze, a trickle of sweat ran into Stephen's left eye and he tried to blink it away. Failing that, he tried to shake his head, but he was too tightly bound. Baldwin had even ordered a stake erected to tie him to. He couldn't move a muscle.

Yet he could speak. And when Mara arrived, as he knew she would, in spite of his most fervent prayers and final orders to Walter, he was going to beg her to leave him. It was the one and only way to foil Baldwin's diabolically clever scheme. He saw it all now, understood how it could not fail. Unless Mara refused to bargain. But would she?

No matter how hard Stephen tried to believe Mara

would not play into Baldwin's hands, he knew he was fooling himself. She would sacrifice herself for him in an instant, just as he would for her. Then his only hope would be to win her back in battle—if she survived.

He had witnessed the appalling depths of the earl's blood lust and cruelty, however, and the thought of Mara in Baldwin's hands frightened him to the very marrow of his bones. No, he could not count on getting Mara back alive should Baldwin take her. He was not even sure *he* would survive the day.

Stephen closed his eyes against the next trickle of moisture that coursed from his sweating brow, but he opened them again almost immediately. Like an animal sensing danger, he was able to feel the aura of evil that preceded the loathsome earl.

"Hello," Baldwin purred. He chucked his prisoner under the chin and laughed when Stephen tried unsuccessfully to pull away. "Feeling a bit testy, are we? Well, don't worry. I don't think you'll have too much longer to wait. I'm fairly certain your bride will absolutely fly to your side. Aren't you?"

Stephen's cold, dark gaze bored into the earl, and in spite of the fact the bound man was totally helpless, Baldwin experienced a prickle of uneasiness. He moved to Stephen's side where the disconcerting stare could not follow.

"I certainly hope your anticipation is as keen as mine," the earl continued, feeling safer. "It's been quite a while since I've had the pleasure of seeing the lovely Amarantha. She is a prize, isn't she? One well worth waiting for. Scheming for. And this is a brilliant scheme, isn't it . . . Baron?"

Baldwin giggled, and Stephen winced.

"Well, I shall leave you for now. Give you time to dwell on your thoughts. Most pleasant thoughts, I am assured." He strolled a few steps away, then returned his attention to his prisoner. "I'll be back shortly. I really don't think your bride will be too much longer."

Baldwin left then, crossing the dusty yard, anxious to get into the shade of the buildings. He glanced around him at the quiet and empty fields, and wondered idly how the monks were faring. Still mumbling prayers for their dear, departed Father Gregory, no doubt, under the watchful eyes of a few of his men-at-arms. The remainder of his knights were deployed throughout the surrounding forest, keeping watch on the baron's men, making sure no one made a false or foolish move. Mara would certainly arrive with a force of her own, but it was nothing he couldn't handle. He didn't plan on engaging in combat anyway. His forces had been diminished more than he liked, first by the attack on Ranulf's castle, then in the attack against the king's men. No, he wanted only revenge. And soon it would be sweetly, sweetly his.

As Baldwin moved into the cool, dim interior of the wooden hall, Maggie's huddled figure caught his attention. He experienced a surge of annoyance. "What are you all bundled up for?" he inquired irritably.

Maggie did not reply, but pulled the cloak a little tighter about her thin shoulders.

"What's wrong, I asked you?"

"No-nothin', m'lord," she answered. But there was a great deal wrong. Since she had watched her master and lover cut the monk's throat, she could not seem to get warm. She was barely able to repress a shudder when he walked over to her and tilted her face up to his.

"Don't tell me you're getting squeamish on me."

Maggie forced herself to hold the earl's gaze and gave him a smile.

"There, that's better," he said, suddenly jovial again. "Come with me, why don't you? We'll take a little stroll. Keep an eye out for the baroness. You'd like that, wouldn't you? I know how jealous you've been of the lady, but you have nothing to worry about anymore. Really. I think you're actually going to enjoy what I have planned for your rival."

It was true, Maggie thought. She had hated Mara once. Or thought she had. Certainly she had envied the lady, and feared losing the earl to her.

But now she felt only pity for the baroness, as she followed Baldwin out into the bright sunlight. Pity. And cold, dark, bottomless fear.

Chapter Forty-two

Stephen drew himself from the trance by sheer force of will. His face was awash in tears. The front of his shirt was damp. He licked his lips and tasted salt.

Amarantha. How ironic. Her name meant "immortal." Yet the only thing that was immortal was their love. And the agony of her loss. Mara was going to die, and there was nothing he could do to prevent it. That, too, was ironic. A dry, humorless chuckle erupted from his throat.

As the baron, he had been ready to sacrifice his life for Mara. She would willingly die for him. They would each sacrifice anything for the other. He still felt that way. Even now, in an instant, he would die for her. Even now, he would sacrifice his own life to save her. If only there was a way. If only.

Stephen buried his face in his hands. He had tried to pierce the veil, but he couldn't. He was unable to return to the past with his knowledge of the present. There was no way he could warn Baron Stephen of what was going to happen to his wife. There was no way to save her, no way to put himself in the way of the arrow that would kill her, because he did not, and would never, know. If only . . .

He had had so much hope in the beginning. Another irony. He had thought reliving the past would help him. He would find out what had been hanging him up, resolve it, and move on with his life. Instead, it was going to completely, totally destroy him once and for all. Mara was going to die again, and his soul was going to die with her.

If only he could have died in her place. If only there was something, anything he could do—someone to ask.

Stephen froze, almost afraid to move, the hope was so fragile.

Millie might know. He had wanted to call her before but had stopped himself because his number might be traced. And he had still had hope then, hope that he might be able to get through to the baron he had been.

There was no hope now. Mara was going to die. What difference did it make if they found him and put him away? If they strapped him to a bed and pumped him full of drugs, at least he would be out of his agony. So go ahead and let them trace his number and come and get him. But he had to ask Millie first. If there was any chance at all she might know something, at least he had to ask.

Millie Thurman clutched the phone receiver so tightly her knuckles were white. Her first impulse was to ask Steve where he was, but she had his number on her call monitor and the police would be able to find his location quickly enough. She also didn't want to put him off, scare him away, and have him hang up on her. She felt guilty enough as it was, responsible almost, for his condition. If she had realized how fragile his mental health really was, she never would have agreed to regress him. She spoke to him carefully now, softly.

"How are you, Steve?"

"It doesn't matter how I am," he replied bluntly. "I need your help. Please, Millie."

"How can I help you, Stephen?"

He had so little time. He knew he had to hurry, and in his anxiety the words tangled together in his brain. Forcing himself to take a deep breath, he swiftly ordered his thoughts. "You know a great deal about this . . . this reincarnation business," he began finally.

"I've . . . studied in depth. Yes," Millie replied cautiously.

"Have you ever . . . Have you ever heard of anyone, well, changing the past?"

"I'm not sure I know what you mean, Steve."

Stephen sighed in frustration. "Someone who goes back—you know, regresses. Have you ever heard that anyone was able to go back and . . . and maybe change what happened in that life?"

She wasn't sure where he was going with his question. He hadn't stayed with her long enough for her to know what was going on with him. But she was sure of her answer. "Absolutely not. The past is the past. We are only able to relive it. We are not able to revise it."

"You're certain there couldn't be the slightest chance."

She was about to reply that she was, indeed, certain. But Millie was an unfailingly honest person. She had not read everything. She did not know everything. "Let me put it this way, Stephen," she answered at length. "I've not ever heard of such a thing happening. I would be very, very surprised if I did."

"But you're not ruling it out. I mean, it's not totally impossible."

"I stand on what I said, Stephen. Perhaps if you gave me more information—"

"Like Mandy explained to me once," he said impatiently. "Sometimes someone dies by accident in a lifetime. Before it's actually their time, I mean. Would it be possible, somehow, to go back and change something like that? Is there some way to take present knowledge back to the past and somehow change things?"

Millie found herself shaking her head even before she replied. "I don't see how. I just don't see how. I've never heard of anyone regressing and reporting knowledge of the present during the regression. So, no. It wouldn't be possible to change things that way. If that's what you mean."

Yes, it was what he meant. But it wasn't what he wanted to hear. "Not even if someone wanted to save someone they loved—loved so much they'd die for them? Couldn't they go back and sacrifice themselves, maybe? Or even give up their life in the present somehow?"

"You're not . . . you're not talking about suicide, are you, Stephen? Suicide is never an answer. You know that, don't you? Stephen? Hello?"

No, he wasn't thinking about suicide. Had *never* thought about it. But he didn't answer Millie. He simply hung up.

It wouldn't be long now. Especially since Millie thought he might take his life. Exhausted and beyond caring, Stephen stretched out on the bed.

He didn't want to go back. Didn't want to go through it again. But he knew he wouldn't be able to stop it. He could only delay it while he whispered a short prayer. *Take me, God. Please take me instead and spare Mara's life. I know it wasn't her time. It should have been me. I know it should have been me. I broke my promise to her. I didn't keep her safe. I would have died to keep her safe. I'd give anything.* Stephen's lips moved faintly along to the words of his silent prayer. *I would have died for her then. I would die for her now.*

It was the only thing left he could say or do.

Chapter Forty-three

Somewhere off in the treetops two jays scolded, perhaps each other. A squirrel scurried along a branch while dusty sunlight filtered lazily downward through the leafy canopy. It was all so normal. So peaceful. How could her world have gone so terribly, frighteningly awry?

Baldwin. His sickness infected them all. The poison within him spewed forth and burned all it touched.

She would kill him if she could.

Only the servants had been left behind at Bellingham Castle. Thomas and Walter sat astride their chargers side by side behind Mara. Jack was off to her left, his horse's head even with her stirrup. She turned her attention from the open glade before her, to her husband's servant.

"This is where you stood with him only a little while ago, isn't it?" she asked softly. When Jack nodded, she said, "I'm sorry."

"No need, lady. My only sorrow is that I could do nothing t' help him. Mebbe this time."

"Maybe. I'm glad you're with me, Jack."

The man tried to speak but found the lump in his throat forbade it. Instead, he nodded a second time and thought that never again in his life would he see anything as grand and glorious as his master's lady.

There she sat, larger than life atop her huge, gray war stallion, incredible body sheathed in the silver of her husband's mail, broadsword to one side, short-sword to the other, prepared to die for her husband. He loved her. He was not alone.

At Jack's nod, Mara straightened in the saddle, gathered her reins, and put her heels to Hero's sides. The big horse lumbered forward, stepping into sunlight from the shadows of the trees. His dappled coat shone and he chewed impatiently at his bit, rolling one large eye toward the lean gray hound that trotted at his side.

It seemed to take an eternity to reach the buildings clustered on the opposite side of the glade. From the time she was halfway across, however, Mara was able to see her husband.

She suffered a small death when she first realized what she was seeing. Something within her simply passed away. But she gave not the slightest outward sign of emotion. Her hand on Hero's reins remained steady, her back rigid. Not the faintest twitch betrayed her when Baldwin's lean and stoop-shouldered figure appeared, moving lazily to Stephen's side. A heavily cloaked woman trailed in his wake.

"Halt!" Baldwin called when Mara was close enough to see his protuberant and watery blue eyes. "Have your man throw down his quiver."

Mara looked at Jack, who fumbled with the strap over his shoulder. He dropped the arrows to the ground, but he smiled at his mistress as he did so.

"Don't worry, m'lady," Jack said under his breath. "Go on."

Mara urged Hero forward again, but only a few more

steps. She halted him directly in front of Baldwin and her tightly bound husband. For the briefest moment the pair's eyes locked and a volume of silent words passed between them. Then Mara returned her attention to the earl.

"How pleasant to see you again, lady," he drawled.

"You may dispense with the niceties, Baldwin. Just tell me what you want."

"Oh, my, my." The earl steepled his fingers and rested his chin on them. "Aren't we anxious, though? You're spoiling my fun."

"I'll spoil more than your fun," Mara replied. "What do you want?"

"Well, let's play a little game, shall we? Let's guess what I want."

"I'll not play your games, Baldwin."

"You're no fun at all." The earl pouted. "Very well. I'll help you. All right? I'll bet you think I want you."

Mara remained silent, her stony, unblinking stare fixed on the repugnant figure who stood before her.

"Let's think about that for a moment, shall we?" Baldwin continued. "What would I do with you if I had you, if I traded you for your husband? Which you obviously think I wish to do. Would I have a loving and attentive wife? Would I have a gracious hostess to sit at my side in my hall? Would I have a willing partner in my bed? Oh, no, I don't think so." The earl shook his head. "I think you would fight me tooth and nail—with your last breath, if need be.

"And there would be the matter of the pesky husband you already have. I doubt he would leave us alone, do you? Furthermore, I don't think the king is going to leave me alone much longer either. I, uh, I had an unpleasant surprise for the deputation he sent."

Baldwin clasped his arms across his narrow chest, paced a few steps, then turned once more to Mara. "No, I think what I have planned today—my little revenge—

will be my farewell performance. I have no illusions. There is very little left ahead for me. But there is *one* thing."

An involuntary shudder coursed down Mara's spine as the earl's mad and evil gaze bored into her. She was vaguely aware of Trey growling, but even Baldwin paid the dog no heed.

"I want to see you bleed, Mara," the earl went on at last. His was a chillingly even tone. "Oh, not literally, but figuratively. Your pain will be so much more excruciating than mere death could afford. I want you to suffer as you made me suffer. I cannot possibly inflict upon you the humiliation you heaped upon me. But I can wound you. Deeply. Just watch."

Baldwin flashed a pale smile and withdrew his dagger from its sheath. Again he approached his prisoner.

A cry escaped Mara's lips when she realized what final evil the earl planned to execute. She couldn't help herself. Her hand went to her own dagger, but she was powerless and she knew it. There was only one thing left to do, one slim chance to take. She must ride Baldwin down, crush him beneath Hero's hooves before he could put his blade to Stephen's throat.

Yet Mara knew she wouldn't be able to make it, even as she put her heels to the great stallion and felt him surge forward beneath her. She saw the first drop of blood appear where the point of Baldwin's blade touched Stephen's neck.

Please, God, Mara found herself silently praying as Hero thundered beneath her. *Don't let him die.*

Then something amazing happened.

Maggie would never know what moved her. Perhaps the last, faint glimmer of love she bore for the man who was her master. For she knew that the act he was about to commit would condemn him to hell more certainly than any that had come before. He would suffer long in Purgatory, surely, for what he had already done. But she did not wish him to burn in the fires of hell for eternity.

Forgotten, swathed in her dark cloak, Maggie darted forward as the blade pressed against the prisoner's throat. She did not know what she was going to do, but she had to try and stop the awful deed. Instinctively, she grabbed at the arm that lifted Baldwin's blade.

It was the opportunity Jack had waited for, prayed for. Almost quicker than the eye could comprehend, as the upward motion of Baldwin's arm was momentarily stalled, he grasped the arrow he had concealed inside his sleeve, nocked, and loosed it. It flew true, pierced the earl's shoulder. But it did not kill him.

An expression of stunned horror painted Baldwin's features. He looked down at the arrow protruding from his shoulder. Then he turned his gaze to Maggie.

"You . . . you betrayed me."

"I *saved* you," Maggie whispered.

"I am your earl. Your *lord.*"

"You are my love."

Mara knew it was over for Baldwin. Jack had already nocked another arrow. There was no need to run the earl down. She hauled on Hero's reins.

Maggie saw the warhorse veer away from them. And when she looked again at her earl, she saw the madness in his eyes that had doomed them. She watched him, painfully, raise the blade once more to the baron's throat. From the corner of her eye, as if in a dream, she saw the second arrow flying for her lover's heart. She would not let him go alone.

Horrified, Mara saw Maggie fling her arms about the earl and throw him off balance. The pair fell directly into the path of Hero's hooves. She tried to stop, but it was too late. Tellingly, sadly, she saw Maggie look up at her . . . and smile?

Then the girl was gone, trampled, crushed, and bleeding along with her lover, beneath the flying hooves.

There was not time to mourn the brave, one-eyed

woman who had saved their lives once before, for Jack's arrow had not only signaled the earl's destruction, but was a signal to Baldwin's men. They poured forth now, issuing from the monks' wooden buildings and the surrounding forest like ants from their hill.

Mara saw them and realized her own men-at-arms could not cross the glade quickly enough to come to her aid. There was barely time enough to free Stephen and fight at his side.

She finally brought Hero to a skidding halt. She threw herself from the saddle and ran to her husband, short-sword in hand. She sawed desperately at the ropes that bound him, but a huge knight was nearly upon them.

Jack had retrieved his quiver, but now he was too far away for an accurate shot. Mara drew her broadsword and turned to face the knight.

Trey gave her the extra moments she needed. With a ferocious snarl, the hound launched himself at the approaching enemy and knocked him off balance. With a startled cry, the knight went down. Trey was at his throat.

Mara's blade did her bidding. Stephen's ropes loosened. Her husband shook himself free.

Untied at last, Stephen resisted the almost overpowering urge to take his wife in his arms. He cast a single glance her way instead, and went to the fallen knight. The dog had torn out his throat.

Stephen relieved the corpse of its sword and, almost at once, began laying about him. Several of Baldwin's knights surrounded them. Mara was pressed to his back, short-sword weaving its own pattern of death. Together, with Trey leaping and snarling around them, they held the earl's men at bay until they heard the pounding hooves of their own forces' approach.

Stephen's knights swept around them. Mounted, they easily laid into the earl's men-at-arms, whose horses were still hidden in the trees behind the abbey. Stephen's knights simply rode the men down. Powerful sword arms hacked, cleaving even helmeted skulls, severing mail-clad limbs.

The hooves of their chargers were as deadly. The magnificently trained animals wrought havoc among the Cumbrian earl's demoralized knights. One mighty stallion reared, taking his rider safely away from a previously well-aimed swordstroke. Still on his hind legs, he pivoted and pawed the air. His left front hoof, heavily shod, caught the knight on the temple and the man went down, dead before he hit the ground. Still another stallion, already grievously wounded by a blade that had struck his neck, wheeled and kicked at his tormentor. Chest crushed, that knight went down.

The earl's knights fell back. A few men turned and broke for the trees. Stephen's men followed and cut them down before they reached the safety of their mounts.

Alone, near the still and lifeless bodies of Baldwin and Maggie, Mara and Stephen still fought back to back.

Though Wulfric knew his earl was dead, the day lost, a red rage filled his heart. Before him, ably parrying each of his blows, stood the man who had humiliated and defeated him once before in the earl's own courtyard. He would not be so shamed again.

At Stephen's back, Mara parried the thrusts of still another knight, who was seemingly unaware of his comrades' retreat. Though not as tall as Mara, he was heavily built and powerful.

But he made one fatal error. He thought he might easily take a woman.

He was surprised, therefore, when she quickly, strongly, gracefully, countered each of his blows. There even appeared to be a smile on her lips. Enraged, he took the hilt of his sword in both hands and drew it over his shoulder, prepared to make one last, overpowering slice. It would cleave the head from her shoulders.

It was the opening Mara had awaited. She raised the

short-sword to block her opponent's next obvious move. With her left hand, quick as the dart of a sparrow, she unsheathed the broadsword she had heretofore been unable to take the time to reach. As the knight's blade clanged against her own, driving her arm back, she thrust the broadsword upward and embedded the point of the steel in the man's exposed throat. Spewing forth a great font of blood, he tumbled backward.

There were none left before her. Mara whirled to fight at her husband's side.

Wulfric never had a chance. He parried another of Stephen's blows, then one from the woman's broadsword. He did not have time to counter Stephen again.

Both hands on the hilt of his sword, Stephen raised the weapon over his head and brought it squarely down upon Wulfric's head. The force of the blow was so great Wulfric's helmet was driven into his skull. His eyes rolled up in his head and he went down, never to rise again.

The earth ran red with blood. The cries of the dying shattered the hush of the green and fragrant glade. The battle was over.

Stephen's knights, victorious, drifted back toward their baron, cleaning blades and patting the necks of faithful mounts. Stephen ignored them.

A moment ago Mara had been fighting at his side. Where had she gone? His eyes searched desperately for her. Sunlight glinting from bright armor made him squint. He turned and looked in the other direction. Saw her. She'd gone to help the others.

The form was unmistakable. Even among his knights, she was tall. Their gazes met.

Mara smiled. Her prayer had been answered. Stephen lived. She murmured a prayer of thanksgiving, pulled the mail hood from her head, and shook loose her magnificent hair. It tumbled in silvery waves across her shoulders and down her back, and Stephen knew there was not a more beautiful, desirable woman in the world. He started toward her.

There was blood on her hauberk, but he knew instinctively it was not hers. Thank God. *Thank God.* She had made it through the battle unscathed. He could tell by the way she moved, walked slowly toward him. The tip of her sword dragged on the ground. Hero plodded along behind her, head low. He, too, appeared uninjured.

Stephen let his blade fall to the ground. He opened his arms to receive her, and she stepped into the circle of his embrace.

There were no words; they were too exhausted. Yet none were needed. They were husband and wife, companions of both heart and soul, lovers. They were also victors. At long, long last, the terrible struggle was over. Many deaths were avenged. They were finally free to be together without fear. It was over.

For a long moment they simply leaned against one another, arms loosely clasped. Then Mara looked up at her husband.

Her eyes were the color of a deep, deep lake. The lake beside which they had first made love.

He did not see—*no one* saw—the hidden archer: one of the earl's men, hidden in the tree at the edge of the glade.

Stephen smiled into Mara's eyes. The blood, death, and destruction all around them disappeared. Trey whined and pushed at their legs, but they barely noticed. They could not tear their gazes from each other.

Then Stephen felt, or thought he felt, someone tap him on the shoulder. As the arrow sped toward them, he turned.

Chapter Forty-four

"Can't you just break down the door?" Amanda begged the police officer who stood nearest to her.

"That's exactly what we're going to do, ma'am," he assured her. "No answer on the phone either?" he asked a fellow officer who strode toward them.

The man shook his head. "I had the manager try three times."

"That's a charm, then. Let's go for it."

The cheap, hollow-core motel room door shattered on the first heavy-shouldered thrust. The police took a defensive stance, guns drawn, until they ascertained there was no threat; then they filed rapidly into the room. Amanda tried to follow them. Her husband held her back, hands on her shoulders.

"Let the officers go in first, Mandy," he said gently. He heard her snuffle as she tried to restrain a sob. Then he felt her tense as one of the officers came back out the door.

"Is he all right? Can I go in?"

299

John didn't like the look on the officer's face. He held on to his wife.

"I'm sorry, ma'am."

"What do you mean you're sorry?" Amanda twisted in her husband's grip, but he held on to her. "What do you mean?"

The officer looked perplexed. "I mean, I'm sorry, but your brother's not here."

"Not here? What do you mean?" Without waiting for a reply, Amanda pushed past the blue-clad officer.

At first she thought the officer had been mistaken. She saw something on the bed, recognized Steve's clothing.

But that's all it was. Clothing. Arrayed upon the bed as if had simply vanished while wearing it. T-shirt, jeans, shoes, and socks. Nothing else.

"Gone," Amanda whispered, her heart acknowledging a truth it would take her mind a great deal longer to grasp. "*Gone.*"

Chapter Forty-five

The arrow passed so close to him he felt the breeze of its flight. Thank God he had turned, Stephen thought, Mara still held tightly in his arms. Otherwise it might have struck one of them.

If ever there's a choice, God, he prayed silently, *take me.* He raised his hand to give the order to find and destroy the sniper, but it was already done.

A body dropped from a nearby tree. An arrow protruded from the man's eye socket.

"Good shot, Jack," Stephen called over his shoulder. He returned his attention to his wife. "That was close. Too close. And I promised I'd always keep you safe."

"You will. I have absolutely no doubt about it," Mara murmured, lips nearly touching the stubble on her husband's chin.

It was over. The long horror was finally over. The suffocating pall of premonition had finally been lifted from her shoulders. She was free. And in spite of the death all around her, she felt elation swell her heart to bursting.

"I love you, Stephen."

"I love you back, Amarantha. My immortal, precious love. My life."

"Take me home?"

"Yes. I'll take you home."

Jack watched them go, arm in arm, side by side. But for the warhorses that trailed in the dust behind them, it put him in mind of the first time he had seen them together like that. They had been in the courtyard at Ullswater. They had only just met. He looked down at Trey, who sat beside him as he had that first day as well.

"I almost feel like I've lived this moment before, old friend," he said to the dog. Trey whined in response. Jack patted him on the head. "It's been a good day's work. A good day's work, all in all. Things turned out, in the end, just like they should've."

He gave the hound another affectionate pat. Then, side by side, they followed in the footsteps of the baron and his lady.

DOMINION
MELANIE JACKSON

When the Great One gifts Domitien with love, it is not simply for a lifetime. Yet in his first incarnation, his wife and unborn child are murdered, and Dom swears never again to feel such pain. When Death comes, he goes willingly. The Creator sends him back to Earth, to learn love in another body. Yet life after life, Dom refuses. Whatever body she wears, he vows to have his true love back. He will explain why her dreams are haunted by glimpses of his face, aching remembrances of his lips. He will protect her from the enemy he failed to destroy so many years before. And he will chase her through the ages to do so. This time, their love will rule.

NIGHT VISITOR

MELANIE JACKSON

All self-respecting Scots know of the massacre and of the brave piper who gave his life so that some of its defenders might live. But few see his face in their sleep, his sad gray eyes touching their souls, his warm hands caressing them like a lover's. And Tafaline is willing to wager that none have heard his sweet voice. But he was slain so long ago. How is it possible that he now haunts her dreams? Are they true, those fairy tales that claim a woman of MacLeod blood can save a man from even death? Is it true that when she touched his bones, she bound herself to his soul? Yes, it is Malcolm "the piper" who calls to her insistently, across the winds of night and time ... and looking into her heart, Taffy knows there is naught to do but go to him.

___52423-6 $5.50 US/$6.50 CAN

SHOCKING BEHAVIOR
JENNIFER ARCHER

J.T. Drake has always felt he pales in comparison to his father's outrageous inventions. But with the push of a button, one of the professor's madcap gadgets actually renders him *invisible*.

Roselyn Peabody's electrifying caress arouses him from his stupor. The beautiful scientist claims his tingling nerve endings are a result of his unique state, but J. T. knows sparks of attraction when he feels them. And while Rosy promises to help him regain his image, J.T. plots to dazzle her with his sex appeal. Only one question remains: When J.T. finally materializes, will their sizzling chemistry disappear or reveal itself as true love?

FRANKLY, MY DEAR...

SANDRA HILL

Selene has three great passions: men, food, and *Gone With The Wind*. But the glamorous model always finds herself starving—for both nourishment and affection. Weary of the petty world of high fashion, she heads to New Orleans. Then a voodoo spell sends her back to the days of opulent balls and vixenish belles like Scarlett O'Hara. Charmed by the Old South, Selene can't get her fill of gumbo, crayfish, beignets—or an alarmingly handsome planter. Dark and brooding, James Baptiste does not share Rhett Butler's cavalier spirit, and his bayou plantation is no Tara. But fiddle-dee-dee, Selene doesn't need her mammy to tell her the virile Creole is the only lover she gives a damn about. And with God as her witness, she vows never to go hungry or without the man she desires again.

___4617-2 $5.50 US/$6.50 CAN

Dorchester Publishing Co., Inc.
P.O. Box 6640
Wayne, PA 19087-8640

Please add $1.75 for shipping and handling for the first book and $.50 for each book thereafter. NY, NYC, and PA residents, please add appropriate sales tax. No cash, stamps, or C.O.D.s. All orders shipped within 6 weeks via postal service book rate. Canadian orders require $2.00 extra postage and must be paid in U.S. dollars through a U.S. banking facility.

Name_____
Address_____
City_____State_____Zip_____
I have enclosed $_____ in payment for the checked book(s).
Payment <u>must</u> accompany all orders. ☐ Please send a free catalog.
CHECK OUT OUR WEBSITE! www.dorchesterpub.com

THE STAR KING

SUSAN GRANT

Careening out of control in her fighter jet is only the start of the wildest ride of Jasmine's life; spinning wildly in an airplane is nothing like the loss of equilibrium she feels when she lands. There, in a half-dream, Jas sees a man more powerfully compelling than any she's ever encountered. Though his words are foreign, his touch is familiar, baffling her mind even as he touches her soul. But who is he? Is he, too, a downed pilot? Is that why he lies in the desert sand beneath a starry Arabian sky? The answers burn in his mysterious golden eyes, in his thoughts that become hers as he holds out his hand and requests her aid. This man has crossed many miles to find her, to offer her a heaven that she might otherwise never know, and love is only one of the many gifts of . . . the Star King.

___52413-9 $5.50 US/$6.50 CAN

Dorchester Publishing Co., Inc.
P.O. Box 6640
Wayne, PA 19087-8640

Please add $2.50 for shipping and handling for the first book and $.75 for each book thereafter. NY, NYC, and PA residents, please add appropriate sales tax. No cash, stamps, or C.O.D.s. All orders shipped within 6 weeks via postal service book rate. Canadian orders require $2.00 extra postage and must be paid in U.S. dollars through a U.S. banking facility.

Name_____
Address_____
City_____ State_____ Zip_____
I have enclosed $_____ in payment for the checked book(s).
Payment <u>must</u> accompany all orders.☐Please send a free catalog.
CHECK OUT OUR WEBSITE! www.dorchesterpub.com

CONTACT
SUSAN GRANT

A BEAUTIFUL CO-PILOT WITH A TERRIBLE CHOICE.

"After only three novels, Susan Grant has proven herself
to be the best hope for the survival of the futuristic/
fantasy romance genre." —*The Romance Reader*

A DARK STRANGER WHO HAS KNOWN NOTHING BUT DUTY.

"I am in awe of Susan Grant. She's one
of the few authors who get it." —*Everything Romantic*

A LATE-NIGHT FLIGHT, HIJACKED OVER THE PACIFIC.

The
Very Virile Viking
Sandra Hill

Magnus Ericsson is a simple man. He loves the smell of fresh-turned dirt after springtime plowing. He loves the heft of a good sword in his fighting arm. But, Holy Thor, what he does not relish is the bothersome brood of children he's been saddled with. Or the mysterious happenstance that strands him and his longship full of maddening offspring in a strange new land—the kingdom of *Holly Wood*. Here is a place where the blazing sun seems to bake his already befuddled brain, where the folks think he is an act-whore (whatever that is), and the woman of his dreams fails to accept that he is her soul mate . . . a man of exceptional talents, not to mention a very virile Viking.